D0050142

PRIME SUSPECT

Nikki burst through the open gate into the alley, where there was a long row of multicolored garbage receptacles and recycling bins against the fence.

Nikki stopped short in front of the bins. Unfortunately, this was the third time she had come in direct contact with a dead body. It wasn't Jorge, though.

"Amondo, please," she said, sounding amazingly calm. She couldn't take her eyes off the blue receptacle directly in front of her. "Go back to the house and call nine-one-one. Give them our address, but tell them they need to come to the rear alley."

Amondo tried to block Victoria's view of the body, but she was not a woman to be kept from anything.

"Oh, heavens," Victoria sighed. "I was afraid something like this was going to happen." She gestured toward the body. "Didn't I tell you, Amondo, that it was only a matter of time before this happened?"

A pair of pruning shears protruded from Eddie's chest.

From where Nikki was standing, she could clearly read the name etched on the wooden handle: *J. Delgado.*

They were Jorge's pruning shears. The same shears she had seen him using on Victoria's azaleas the previous night, just before his argument with Eddie. The argument where he threatened to kill Eddie . . .

Books by Cheryl Crane

The Bad Always Die Twice

Imitation of Death

The Dead and the Beautiful

Published by Kensington Publishing Corporation

IMITATION OF DEATH

CHERYL CRANE

KENSINGTON BOOKS
http://www.kensingtonbooks.com

KENSINGTON BOOKS are published by

Kensington Publishing Corp.
119 West 40th Street
New York, NY 10018

Copyright © 2012 by Cheryl Crane

All rights reserved. No part of this book may be reproduced in any form or by any means without the prior written consent of the Publisher, excepting brief quotes used in reviews.

If you purchased this book without a cover you should be aware that this book is stolen property. It was reported as "unsold and destroyed" to the Publisher and neither the Author nor the Publisher has received any payment for this "stripped book."

All Kensington titles, imprints and distributed lines are available at special quantity discounts for bulk purchases for sales promotion, premiums, fund-raising, educational or institutional use.

Special book excerpts or customized printings can also be created to fit specific needs. For details, write or phone the office of the Kensington Special Sales Manager. Attn.: Special Sales Department. Kensington Publishing Corp., 119 West 40th Street, New York, NY 10018. Phone: 1-800-221-2647.

Kensington and the K logo Reg. U.S. Pat. & TM Off.

ISBN-13: 978-0-7582-5889-2
ISBN-10: 0-7582-5889-5
First Kensington Books Mass-Market Paperback Printing: August 2013
First Kensington Books Hardcover Printing: September 2012

eISBN-13: 978-0-7582-8906-3
eISBN-10: 0-7582-8906-5

10 9 8 7 6 5 4 3 2 1

Printed in the United States of America

TO JLR . . . We've been so many places
in our life and time . . .

Chapter 1

Nikki walked into her mother's kitchen, flip-flops slapping on the Italian tile floor, and opened the huge, commercial, stainless-steel refrigerator.

"If the bomb detonates, we don't have a chance," came a deep, sexy male voice from the terrace.

The sun was just beginning to set over the stone and wrought-iron privacy fence that framed the property and the sweet smell of bougainvillea drifted into the kitchen through the French doors. Her Cavalier King Charles spaniels spotted the open doors and shot through them, out into the backyard.

Nikki frowned, glancing in the direction of the escapees, then peered into the fridge: foie gras, hummus, star fruit, duck eggs. No plain old peanut butter and jelly here. She sighed. She wasn't really hungry, just bored. Friday night, all dressed up in sweatpants and a ratty tee, and nowhere to go.

"A hundred thousand American lives?" cried the

voice of Victoria Bordeaux, silver screen goddess of the fifties and sixties.

"Gone." There was a snap of a thumb and an index finger. "In a fiery explosion that'll be felt for a thousand miles in every direction."

"Please tell me you're not getting on that train, Dirk. You'll die!"

Cocking her head to hear better, Nikki let the refrigerator door close. *I should write a book,* she thought. *Because no one could make this crap up.*

"Probably, but I have to try. Otherwise, I couldn't live with myself," came the dramatic male voice.

"Let me go, too!" cried Victoria. "Maybe I could disarm the bomb myself!"

"And risk our unborn child's life? Out of the question."

Nikki stepped out onto the stone terrace and heard the sound of Lynyrd Skynyrd wafting in the air . . . which made for an interesting musical score for the scene unfolding in her mother's Beverly Hills backyard. "Marshall?"

"Shht!" Victoria warned, bringing a manicured finger to her pale peach lips. She was dressed in a white Michael Kors jogging suit, her platinum hair tied up in a cute silk scarf, and her trademark pearls on her slender throat. This was *her* Friday night staying-in attire, versus Nikki's. Victoria Bordeaux was one classy lady.

Victoria sat on a chaise longue, her legs stretched out, with pink foam spacers between her bare toes. She held a script in her hand, reading glasses perched on her nose. "A kiss! One more kiss before you go. Oh, Dirk, I can't believe you're going to get on that train."

"What the heck are you two *doing*?" Nikki asked, glancing at Marshall, her dearest, nearest friend.

Marshall Thunder, recently voted Sexiest Man Alive by *People* magazine, and box office boy wonder, drew a brush over Victoria's delicate toenail. The nail polish was pink. "Just one kiss." He pursed his lips. At six foot two, the forty-two-year-old Native American had one of those hard bodies that could have launched a thousand ships. A thousand ships of screaming, fainting, female fans. And his face . . . a chiseled masterpiece with dark eyes and high cheek-bones.

Victoria, probably thirty years Marshall's senior—Nikki didn't know exactly how old her mother was, and Victoria wasn't telling; her birth records were *allegedly* lost in a hospital fire in Idaho—pursed her lips and kissed the air.

"Tell our son I loved him." Marshall spoke the words poignantly as he grabbed an orange stick from the basket at his feet and touched up the polish on one of Victoria's toenails. "Good-bye, my love."

Victoria drew her hand over her forehead, fluttered her eyelids, and lay back in the chair in what would have been a swoon in her early days in cinema. "No, noooo."

"Mother! Marshall!" Nikki looked at one and then the other. "What are you *doing*?" She glanced around as the seventies Southern rock song got louder. "And where is that music coming from?"

Victoria opened her eyes and sat up, pulling off

her reading glasses. "What does it look like we're doing, Nicolette? My pedicurist cancelled my appointment and one can't very well go the entire weekend with chipped polish. Marshall kindly offered to do my pedicure and manicure for me." She smiled her perfect smile, flashing the Bordeaux blue eyes she was still famous for, even after years in retirement. Then she scowled. "The music is coming from next door. The Bernards'. Where else?"

"She's going over my script with me," Marshall explained. He glanced at Nikki's bare toes in her worn flip-flops. "I could do yours, too, sweetie." He lifted a dark eyebrow. "Your feet look awful. When was the last time you had a pedicure?"

Nikki dropped into one of the chairs and tried to nonchalantly hide the foot from which she'd scraped the polish off her toenail with a fingernail while on the phone. "I've been busy."

Her mother lifted her eyebrows.

Victoria was never seen in public without her hair done and makeup on her face. She didn't own a single ratty T-shirt or, God forbid, a pair of baggy sweatpants. It just wasn't in her genetic composition.

"Don't tell me you're doing this movie, Marshall." Nikki motioned to the script, trying to shift their attention to anything or anyone but her toes. She loved her mother, sometimes even adored her, but Nikki didn't find it easy to be Victoria Bordeaux's daughter. While gracious to her fans, Victoria could be critical of those closest to her, particularly Nikki. And Nikki, admittedly, could get defensive. The friction between them seemed worse since she'd been forced to move back in with her mother after a major water main break in her own home, followed by a painting disaster. Marshall had come for the evening, at Nikki's request, to serve as a buffer. He and Victoria *always* got along; he never took offense at anything she said. "That script's awful," Nikki observed.

"It's not so bad. I'm going to do it if Zoe what's-her-name does. It's going to be the hit of next summer, with or without me." Marshall screwed the cap back on the pink nail polish. "Let's let that dry a few minutes, and then we'll add a clear coat." He sat back and relaxed, returning his attention to Nikki. He was wearing a pair of corduroy shorts, a tight surfer tee, and Gucci sunglasses, making him look even hunkier than usual. (Of course, it was sunset. Only stars wore sunglasses in the dark.) "It might as well be me."

"I thought you were going to take a break." She found herself mouthing the words to "Freebird" as the song continued to blast from next door. "You said you and Rob talked it over and agreed you were working too hard. That when you finished the film you're shooting, you were taking a year off."

"Year off, shmear off." He waved his hand dismissively. "But don't tell Rob I said that," he warned, pointing his finger at her. "It's a delicate subject. I feel like I need to work while I can. You know how fickle fans can be. A year from now the only offers I might be getting could be made-for-TV movies and OxiClean commercials."

"I'll drink to that." Victoria raised a margarita glass and sipped from it.

Victoria liked her evening cocktails and Marshall liked making them for her. They were best buddies, these two. An interesting combination: the retired screen goddess and the still-in-the-closet blockbuster action star.

"What's going on next door?" Nikki asked, glancing around to see what mischief her *boys* were getting into. Stanley, a black, white, and tan tri, was on the trail of some bug or rodent, his nose to the ground. Oliver, a Blenheim, had parked himself under a hydrangea bush and was busying himself grooming his tail. "Has it been going on for long? I didn't hear the music from inside."

"We already worked our way through the *Nuthin' Fancy* album. We've moved on to their (pronounced 'L h-'nérd 'Skin-'nérd) album. It was their first."

Nikki looked to Marshall, duly impressed. "Hey, you know your Skynyrd."

He grinned. "Rob has all their albums, on vinyl."

Victoria cocked her ear in the direction of the Bernard mansion next door, then shook her head in irritation. "I told Abe that he'd better get control of his worthless son. I warned him, next time Eddie threw one of his parties and disturbed my peace and quiet, I was calling the cops. It's only a matter of time before his guests start climbing over the wall and crushing my begonias."

Their neighbor, Abe Bernard, was probably the best television writer and producer in Hollywood, certainly the most successful. His company, Bernard Television, reported higher earnings the previous year than the late Aaron Spelling's company. His current law drama had hit number one in the Nielsen ratings, two years running. While Abe was one of the most respected, most revered names in Hollywood, his thirty-five-year-old son was a loser. Eddie Bernard had tried his hand at being a model, an actor, and a businessman, all unsuccessfully. Eddie drank too much, had a drug problem, and was constantly in trouble with the law: drunk driving, possession of illegal substances, assault. So far, his father's money had been able to keep him out of a lengthy jail sentence, but the guy was bad news. He had none of the integrity or work ethic of his father.

"You're not going to call the cops, Mother," Nikki said dryly. "You always threaten, but you'd never do it."

"True. I don't have much use for the police." She waved a delicate hand. "No offense meant toward Rob," she told Marshall.

"No offense taken." He smiled sweetly.

Nikki noticed her mother was wearing the Howard Hughes sapphire ring: platinum, 3 carats, art deco, studded with very high-clarity diamonds. Hughes had given her several nice pieces of jewelry back in the day when he'd been trying to woo her to RKO Studios. Nikki had the feeling there had been more than business wooing going on there, but for decades, Victoria had remained calmly but firmly silent on the matter.

"I've never forgiven them," Victoria continued, "for the way you were treated that time you were picked up for—"

"Mother," Nikki interrupted. "Could we not talk about that?"

Victoria crossed her legs at the ankles and took another drink of her margarita. "You're certainly touchy this evening. Where's Jeremy? You should be out dining and dancing with your beau, not sitting around the pool with an old lady and her favorite bear."

Nikki and Marshall made eye contact. Nikki lifted an eyebrow.

"Oh, for heaven's sake," Victoria said, which was as close to swearing as she ever came. "I know what a *bear* is: a big, burly, man." She waved in Marshall's direction, frowning. "Although, I suppose they're supposed to be hairy, too."

"Weren't Eddie and Lindsay Lohan in rehab together?" Marshall artfully started a new topic of conversation and ran with it. "I thought I read that somewhere."

"In one of your tabloids?" Nikki asked. "You, of all people, know you can't believe a word they print."

"I read regular newspapers, too," he defended. "Just not about this," he added in a very small voice. "But this was his third or fourth stint in rehab in the last five years."

"Conniving, worthless little punk," Victoria muttered. "He's like the nephew in *Fifteen Green Street*. Remember that film I did with Willi Wyler?"

"The one set in New Orleans?" Marshall clutched his hands over his heart. "I adored you in that film. You were *so* beautiful. So strong-willed, right to the end. Do you remember that green gown you wore in the dinner scene, you know, when you discovered that your nephew had had your sister committed so he could take over the family business?"

Victoria smiled at the memory. "It was Persian silk. And that emerald necklace I wore—"

"Exquisite," Marshall finished for her, both of them lost in the moment.

"Were you nominated for an Oscar that year, Mother?"

Victoria's smile tightened. "No. And Julie Andrews ended up winning for *Mary Poppins*, of all things. But Audrey Hepburn wasn't nominated for *My Fair Lady*, either. I don't know what the Academy was thinking."

Nikki smiled. "You always said—"

The sound of an explosion next door cut Nikki off. She shot out of her chair, looking at Marshall. "Was that—"

"A gunshot!"

Chapter 2

Nikki sprinted in the direction of the sound of the gunshot. Marshall was right behind her.

"Nicolette!" Victoria warned. But she was already out of the chaise, too. For a woman in her seventies, in sandals, with a fresh pedicure, she was surprisingly agile.

Nikki ran across the side lawn toward the gate between Victoria's property and the Bernards'. Years ago, when Abe had demolished his quaint two-story colonial, bought the property on the other side of him, and built the French Regency mansion they lived in now, he had put up an eight-foot-high wrought-iron fence and had large hedges planted on his side. Because his longtime neighbor was *the* Victoria Bordeaux, he'd added a gate between the two properties that could be latched from either side. Nikki pushed through the gate. Lynyrd Skynyrd was even louder on the other side of the fence.

"Mother, stay here," Nikki huffed. "Stay with the dogs. Latch the gate, Marshall."

"I'm not *staying with the dogs*," Victoria intoned, barely out of breath. (Beyond amazing, considering her age and the fact that she'd been smoking for more than fifty years.)

Marshall closed the gate behind them as Nikki ran in the direction from which she'd heard the shot. The backyard was crowded; there were easily more than a hundred people in and gathered around the pool. More *guests* lounged on chairs in front of the guesthouse where Abe's ex-wife lived. There were glasses everywhere, a bar set up on the patio near the house. The smell of cannabis was thick in the evening air.

"Did you hear that?" a platinum and silicone blonde in a string bikini asked Nikki as she ran in the same direction. "Was it a bomb?"

"The driveway. It came from the driveway," her companion, who looked like she was wearing three cocktail napkins, insisted excitedly.

Nikki glanced over her shoulder. The minute they came through the gate, Victoria had slowed to a respectable trot. In her mind, once she passed through the gate, she was in public and became the iconic Victoria Bordeaux.

Someone pointed at her; someone else whipped out a cell phone to take a picture. Victoria would, no doubt, be on Facebook within seconds. Though most of the partiers appeared to be under forty (some looked like they were under fourteen) everyone seemed to recognize Victoria Bordeaux, even in a jogging suit. Must have been the Mikimoto Akoya pearls.

A female squealed and Nikki realized Marshall had been recognized. How could anyone miss a six-foot-two, Native American movie star, even in dark sunglasses and a ball cap?

As Nikki came around the front corner of the three-story French Regency mansion, she stopped short. She spotted Eddie Bernard, a young Hispanic woman, her mother's gardener, Jorge, and Jorge's brother-in-law, Hector, standing between a Mercedes and an Aston Martin in the middle of the motor court. Eddie and Jorge were slowly circling each other as if in a boxing ring. Eddie had some sort of automatic pistol in his hand. *Not* generally seen in a boxing ring. But Eddie was a known gun aficionado. In Eddie's circles, a party just wasn't a party if *someone* wasn't brandishing a gun.

"You going to shoot me in front of all these witnesses, Eddie?" Jorge taunted. "Are you?" Jorge was a nice-looking man with dark, lush hair, medium-toned skin, and a well-toned body. He was only Nikki's height, five ten, but muscular. He waved his fingertips toward his own chest and tilted his head back, the unmistakable gesture for *bring it on.*

Lynyrd Skynyrd's "Simple Man" wailed in the background: *Mama told me when I was young . . .*

"Jorge!" Nikki called as she pushed her way to the front of the crowd. Jorge wasn't *just* Victoria's gardener. He was her housekeeper Ina's son, and one of Nikki's best friends from childhood. She and Jorge had grown up together; they'd practiced kissing on each other, in preparation for the real thing.

"*Hermano*," Hector said quietly. He was a short man, no more than five foot five, but thick and brawny with a face badly scarred from acne he'd had as a teenager. "He ain't worth it, man." He cut his eyes at the young Hispanic woman. "Get out of here, Ree."

"Nikki, stay out of this," Jorge warned, barely glancing in her direction.

He'd been working in the front lawn clipping azalea bushes with a big pair of pruning shears when Nikki had glanced out her upstairs window half an hour ago. Hector, who worked for Jorge, had been raking.

"Eddie, sweetie, put away the gun." Eddie's mother, Melinda, Abe's ex-wife, stood opposite Nikki. At sixty, she was attractive for her age: slightly plump, with white-blond hair below her shoulders and only minimal plastic surgery. She was wearing denim capris and a cute age-appropriate blouse. "Please, Eddie. Your parole," she whispered under her breath, softly enough so that only those closest could hear.

And listen closely to what I say . . .

The Skynyrd lyrics, Melinda's plea . . . it would have been funny had there not been a loaded gun and male tempers involved.

"Mind your own business, Jorge," the drop-dead gorgeous young Hispanic woman spat. "Go back to your lawn mower." She was wearing cheap platform sandals and something that could only be described as *hot pants*. Unlike Jorge, she had a heavy Mexican accent.

. . . some sunny day . . .

Nikki saw blood on the young woman's split lip

and realized someone had hit her. Recently. As in, the last few minutes.

Nikki's quick assessment of the situation told her it was Eddie. He was known to be *heavy-handed* in a relationship; he'd been arrested the previous year for assault against a girlfriend. That happened with Eddie a lot. He was charged with a criminal offense, but there never seemed to be serious consequences for his behavior; Nikki had always suspected it had something to do with his father's net worth.

And Jorge didn't hit women; Ina had raised him better.

"Jorge, what's going on?" Nikki demanded.

Jorge held up his hand. His suntanned face was bright red with anger. His green T-shirt with the JORGE & SON logo on it was ripped at the neckline. It hadn't been ripped when Nikki waved to him through the window a short time ago.

"Hector's right. You don't want to do this with him," Nikki warned, taking a step closer, trying to get Jorge to look at her. "Not with him, like this," she murmured, noting Eddie seemed twitchy, his pupils too big.

"And him having a *gun*," Marshall said under his breath from behind her.

Nikki glanced over her shoulder, and was relieved to see that Marshall was holding Victoria back by the hood of her Michael Kors, which was good, because knowing her mother, the woman might have gone into the middle of the fighting ring. Both Victoria and Marshall were now attracting plenty of attention. The partiers didn't know in which direction to gawk—at the gunfight or the honest-to-goodness stars. More people whipped out their cell phones to get candid pictures of Victoria and Marshall.

The crowd seemed to press against Nikki as she moved closer to Jorge. She had to get him out of here before something bad happened to one or both of them.

Fact one, Jorge was a hothead. Fact two, Eddie was obviously high. (So much for Dr. Drew and rehab in Pasadena.) Fact three, and perhaps the biggest mitigating factor, was that the two had hated each other since they were all kids. Jorge had always been jealous of the rich, white boy who had everything and was always willing to throw it away. Eddie . . . he just liked picking on sons of Mexican immigrant housekeepers. Self-esteem issues out the yin-yang.

"Eddie, please," Melinda begged. She rested her hand on her son's arm, her fingernails, always filed too pointy for Nikki's liking, sinking into his flesh a little. "Don't do this. This is all behind you now."

Eddie pushed his mother away, none too gently. He was of average height, average looks, with a three-hundred-dollar Daddy's-money haircut and muscles that came and went depending on how much time he spent at the gym. It looked like they *went* this time in rehab; he looked pudgy and bloated. What he really looked like was a punk headed for jail and the tabloids again.

"Hey!" Jorge growled, flexing his hands into fists at his sides. "Didn't I just tell you to keep your hands off women?"

"This is none of your business, Jorge," Ree shouted, playing the tough girl.

"You ought to be ashamed of yourself, Ree," Jorge

growled. "Letting him treat you this way. Shaming our family. And you, Eddie,"—he thrust out his chest like a rooster—"how can you do this? After everything your parents have done for you. How long have you been out of rehab? A week? Less than a week, and you're already drunk and coked up?"

Eddie sniffed and ran the back of his hand over his mouth. He quickly looked left, then right, as if paranoid. Unfortunately, Jorge's observation was accurate. Nikki could practically *see* the white powder under his nose.

"Just put the gun away," Nikki said evenly, trying to sound calm, even if she was shaking inside. Guns did that to her; she didn't like guns. She raised both hands. "You don't want to hurt Jorge, Eddie. You don't want to hurt anyone."

Eddie's hand holding the pistol fell slack to his side. "You can't tell me what to do," he told Jorge, his words sharply punctuated. "She's my girlfriend. This is none of your business."

"I'm not your girlfriend, Eddie, you stupid fu—"

"I don't care what she is to you," Jorge erupted, pointing accusingly, "but if I ever see you hit a woman again, I swear to God, Eddie, I'll kill you." He raised his fist. "Maybe I ought to kill you anyway."

A hush fell over the crowd as everyone waited to see who would do what, next.

"Give that to me." Melinda put out her hand. "Eddie, give me that thing before you hurt yourself or one of your friends."

Nikki was surprised by Melinda's backbone. She hadn't known Melinda had it in her. Watching her now, Nikki felt sorry for her. Melinda had spent the last thirty-some years of her life running after Eddie, trying to keep him from harming himself or others.

Melinda took the pistol from her son's hand and held it by the handle, between two fingers, as if it were something infectious.

"What the hell is going on here?" shouted a woman from the street end of the motor court as she marched through the open gates. Nikki looked up to see Ginny Bernard, Eddie's stepmother, barreling up the front driveway in Jimmy Choo heels and a short skirt. Gucci and Prada shopping bags hung off her arms.

"I couldn't even pull in to park in my own driveway! I thought I told you no more parties," Ginny screeched, pointing. She was attractive with below-the-shoulders blond hair precisely the same color as Melinda's, and a knockout body. Nikki had always thought it interesting that when Abe replaced his wife after more than thirty years of marriage, he had done so with a younger version of Melinda. Ten years younger.

"Melinda! How did you let this happen?" Ginny demanded. "He just got out of rehab!"

"How did *I* let it happen?" Melinda, who had passed the pistol to someone else, pressed her hand to her chest. "You think I wanted this?"

Ginny took one look at her stepson's face and shook her head. "You're high. One week out of rehab, and you're partying? At my house? I swear to God, Eddie, if your father doesn't kill you this time, I will."

Eddie spit something under his breath and twitched again. Melinda grabbed her son's arm.

"Where is he?" Ginny gave Melinda a sour look and pranced away, her Jimmy Choos clicking on the pavement. "Abe! Abraham! Do you have any idea what's going on out here?" She slammed her fist down on the Aston Martin as she went by it.

"Jorge," Nikki said quietly, leaning toward him. "It's over. Walk away." With Ginny here now, the circus could definitely go three-ring. The police would be at the gates next.

"I won't stand by and see my cousin get hit by this worthless *bastardo*." Jorge made a sound and spat on the driveway as if disgusted by Eddie's very presence.

Eddie rose to the bait. "Come on, *chico*, you wanna try to take me?" He began posturing, and sneering, his shoulders thrown back, making him look like the complete ass that he was.

Of course, Jorge wasn't looking all that rational right now, either.

Nikki linked her arm through Jorge's. He smelled of freshly cut grass and aftershave.

Jorge resisted for a second, then let Nikki pull him away. Hector moved in to walk on Jorge's other side.

Jorge whipped back around. "Go home, Ree! And don't come back. I don't want to see you here. You're not to ever see Eddie Bernard again!"

"Who do you think you are, Mr. High and Mighty?" the young woman shouted after him, the disdain thick in her accented voice. "You're not my father—"

"What *would* your father think?" Jorge snapped back, his anger seeming to rise and bubble over again. "God rest his soul." He crossed himself.

"Get off my property, Jorge. Mind your own business," Eddie shouted. "No *spics* allowed."

Jorge jerked free of Nikki's grip and lunged toward Eddie. Luckily, whoever Melinda had passed the gun to had carried it into the house.

"Whoa, easy there."

Nikki saw a big, tanned hand shoot out and grab Jorge by the arm, stopping him short. She looked up gratefully to see Marshall, calmly reeling Jorge in. Though muscular, Jorge wasn't a big man; Marshall towered over him.

"Come on, Jorge," Marshall intoned. "Let's go back to the house."

Hector grabbed Jorge's other arm.

Nikki met Melinda's gaze across the driveway. Melinda had her twitchy son by the arm, trying to tug him in the opposite direction. Nikki gave her a quick smile of understanding—maybe a little pity—and turned away, following Marshall, who had released Jorge, but was only two feet behind him.

"He's *loco*," Victoria whispered to Nikki, her Spanish accent pretty darned good. She fell into step beside her daughter. "I don't know why Melinda didn't drown him at birth."

"Mother!" Nikki cut her eyes at her.

"I'm just saying he was always a worthless punk," Victoria said under her breath. "Even when he was a child."

Marshall gave Jorge a gentle push through the gate and Hector followed his brother-in-law. Marshall waited on the Bernard side of the fence for Nikki and Victoria.

"Miss Bordeaux? I don't want to bother you, but . . ."

Nikki and Victoria both stopped and turned to see a young man in shorts and bare feet. He had a golden tan and a serious gym membership. He was holding out a black Sharpie marker.

"I can't believe it's you," he babbled. "I've seen all your movies like a million times. *Sister, Sister* makes me cry every time." He offered her the Sharpie. "Would you mind?"

Victoria hesitated, then smiled that gorgeous smile of hers and accepted the marker. "What would you like me to sign, dear?"

"My name's Astro, Astro Wharton."

Nikki raised her eyebrows, and then raised them even farther when he stepped toward Victoria and pulled his ripped muscle shirt to the side, flexing his massive pec.

"My left side; it's my best."

Victoria arched a brow, popping the cap off the marker. Mouth pursed, she signed her name with great flourish across his bare skin. Left pec. *The smile.*

Astro Wharton looked down at her signature as he accepted the marker back. "Oh my God, my friends at the gym aren't going to believe this. Thanks."

"You're welcome." She flashed *the smile* one last time and walked away.

Nikki stood staring at the eye candy for a second. Had this guy really just asked a seventy-year-old woman to autograph his *pec*?

"Nicolette?" Victoria sang, curling a finger to beckon her.

Nikki flashed her best imitation of the smile her mother had made her practice in the mirror as a teenager. This smile was required in any public situation. "Have a good day."

With Nikki, Victoria, Jorge, and Hector safely on

the other side of the fence, Marshall swung the gate shut. "What the hell do you think you're doing, Jorge?" Marshall demanded. "You're lucky he didn't blow your brains out. You know better than to mess with Crazy Eddie."

Jorge threw back his shoulders. "He's lucky I didn't—"

"Gentlemen, gentlemen." Nikki stepped between the two, afraid Jorge was going to get into it with Marshall next.

They'd attended the same elementary school, Nikki and Jorge; Victoria had thought it important that her daughter see how *regular folks* lived. Even in those days, Jorge had been a hothead, getting into fights, defending honor and pride. Nikki had ended up having to stick up for Jorge against teachers and the principal. In middle school, Nikki had joined the ranks of the privileged children and gone to private school and Jorge had been left to fight his own battles.

"I think I'm going to finish my cocktail." Victoria halted in front of Jorge. "Are you all right?" she asked in a motherly tone Nikki didn't hear often. "Not hurt, are you?"

Jorge shook his head, and lowered his gaze. He'd always been in awe of Victoria, maybe a little scared of her. Which was smart. She certainly scared the bejeezus out of Nikki.

"Good." Victoria gave a regal nod, back in movie goddess mode. "Join me, Marshall?"

"By all means." Marshall offered his arm and the two strolled across the side lawn toward the back.

Nikki heard her dogs barking and saw them appear in the yard, then take off after Victoria and Marshall. Nikki turned her attention to Jorge. "What happened? How did you end up in Eddie's yard?"

"I was trimming," Jorge explained, motioning to the azaleas. "I heard Ree's voice. Like she was in trouble."

"And she's your cousin?"

He nodded. "My uncle's daughter, Maria Gaza," he said stiffly. "We never had much to do with them. Mom thought they were . . . low class. They haven't been in the States long."

Nikki nodded. She felt guilty that she knew so little of Jorge's life now. They had never had a disagreement; they had just sort of drifted apart. "So you heard your cousin," she encouraged.

"I told him to stay out of it," Hector put in. "Ree can take care of herself."

Jorge glanced at his brother-in-law and then continued. "I saw them through the fence. She and Eddie were arguing." He shrugged. "He hit her, so I went out the gate."

"And onto the Bernard property."

"Gates were open. He can't hit Ree," Jorge insisted. "He can't hit women."

Nikki glanced away, her gaze settling on the still-flowering azaleas. He'd been trimming off the old blooms. "You have to stay out of this, Jorge. As Hector said, let Ree handle it. She should call the police."

"Call the police? Really, Nikki?" He laughed, but without humor. "*She's not legal.*"

Nikki looked at him again. "Then she needs to stay away from him."

"Or I could just kill him," Jorge said.

"I'd do it for you, *hermano*," Hector put in quietly. "You know I would."

Nikki frowned, looking from one man to the other. "You're not killing anyone. Either of you. It's a Friday night. Both of you go home, take a shower. Hector, play with your kids. Have dinner with your wife. Jorge, go out on a date. Have a beer with your friends." She gave Jorge a gentle push on the arm. He had dark, expressive eyes. Ina's eyes. "Have some fun, Jorge. You never look like you're having any fun."

He met her gaze and his features softened. "Haven't seen you in awhile. You look good, Nikki. I like your hair longer, like this." He motioned to her hair, which fell past her shoulders. "It's pretty."

Feeling weirdly embarrassed by his compliment, more so because he said it in front of Hector, she took a step back. She tucked a lock of strawberry blond hair behind her ear.

"I hope Jeremy realizes how lucky he is to have you," Jorge said, his tone slightly teasing. Jeremy had grown up down the street; the three of them had been pals when they were kids.

She smiled. "Go home, guys. Workday's over."

Nikki walked away. In the days to come, she'd wish she hadn't.

Chapter 3

No one expects to wake up to a bloodcurdling scream. Certainly not in Beverly Hills. Nikki sat straight up in her bed, her legs tangled up in Sferra Italian bed linens, disoriented. The dogs leapt down, barking wildly, and ran for the closed door.

Nikki blinked, trying to chase the cobwebs from her mind. Had she been dreaming?

No, that was definitely a scream. The second one left no doubt in her mind of the existence of the first. It took only another second to figure out that it was her mother's housekeeper, Ina, screaming.

Nikki flew across the room and slipped out the door, pulling it closed behind her. Whatever was going on downstairs, Ina didn't need two nosy Cavies in the middle of it. Behind the closed door, her dogs continued to bark. Still in her preferred pj's—a T-shirt and sweats—she ran barefoot down the upstairs hall toward the open, winding staircase to the foyer.

Victoria's door banged open and she emerged,

tying a pink silk sash around her robe. She looked up at Nikki, her still-gorgeous face devoid of makeup and the goddess persona. She wore a white silk turban over her platinum hair, and even though half asleep, she appeared much younger than her true age. "What is wrong with Ina?"

"I don't know." Nikki ran past her. "You should wait here."

"Ina!" Victoria called in an authoritative voice, hurrying after Nikki. "We're coming."

"What's wrong?" Amondo ran down the stairs behind Nikki and Victoria. He too was tying on his robe.

Had Nikki had the time to think about it, she would have wondered where Amondo had come from. Her mother's bedroom? He had been Victoria's assistant, her bodyguard, her chauffeur, for more than thirty years. She received him in her suite all the time; her pink boudoir was her command center. But this early?

Ina screamed again from the back of the house. She was talking half in English, half in Spanish. Nikki rushed into the kitchen to find the housekeeper fumbling with the cordless phone.

"Ina! What's wrong?"

"The . . . ga . . . garbage!" Ina was hyperventilating. She was a tall, thin, regal woman with golden-brown skin and the same expressive eyes as her son, Jorge. But right now she looked as if she had seen a ghost.

"*Nueve, uno, uno.*" She tried to punch the numbers into the phone, made an error, punched the OFF button, and tried again.

"Ina, I'll call for you." Nikki gently took the phone from her, but didn't dial. "What's going on? What's happened?"

"Calm down, Ina." Victoria took her house-keeper's hand and rubbed it between hers, peering up into her face.

"What's happened?" Amondo, not usually excitable, was still fumbling to get his robe closed.

"*Muerto.*"

"Who's dead?" Nikki murmured.

"*Lo han puesto en la basura!*"

"Slowly," Victoria insisted, lifting up on her tiptoes to look eye to eye with Ina. "*En Inglés, por favor.* You know my Spanish is atrocious."

Ina pressed her free hand to her chest. "In the garbage. They . . . they put him . . . out in the trash!"

"*Who* is in the trash?" Nikki asked, still not following.

All Ina could do was point to the back door, left standing open.

"The garbage? In the back?"

"I . . . I was . . . carrying out . . . the trash," Ina managed. Her English was perfect. It was just that after all these years, she probably still thought in her native language. "I took . . . the trash . . . to . . . to the receptacle in the alley. And there he was. Dead." She pulled her hand from Victoria's, clutching her head and rocking back and forth. "My *hijo*! My poor *hijo!*"

Her *hijo? Jorge?* Suddenly, Nikki couldn't breathe. She dropped the phone on the counter and raced out the open back door. Her heart was pounding. *Please, please no,* she prayed silently. She ran down the sidewalk that led to the back gate to the alley behind

Victoria's house, and ran past Ina's little Honda. Ahead, the small back service gate was still open.

Ina, Victoria, and Amondo hurried after her.

"Amondo, take her back!" Nikki called over her shoulder. "Take them both back."

"*You* stay with them. Let me go," Amondo insisted. He, too, was spry for his age; he had to be somewhere in his sixties.

Amondo and Victoria both wore slippers. His were blue corduroy. Hers were pink silk mules, which didn't seem to slow her down.

Nikki burst through the open gate into the alley, where there was a long row of multicolored garbage receptacles and recycling bins against the fence. The alley ran the entire length of the 1000 block of Roxbury Drive.

Nikki stopped short in front of the bins. For a moment, she thought she might be sick. But only a moment. Unfortunately, this was the third time she had come in direct contact with a dead body. It wasn't Jorge, though.

"Amondo, please," she said, sounding amazingly calm. She couldn't take her eyes off the blue receptacle directly in front of her. "Go back to the house and call nine-one-one. Give them our address, but tell them they need to come to the rear alley."

Amondo tried to block Victoria's view of the body, but she was not a woman to be kept from anything.

"Oh, heavens," Victoria sighed, sounding more sad than horrified. The body was posed like a wax figure, eyes open wide. "I was afraid something like this was going to happen." She gestured toward the body, propped up against the trash barrel. "Didn't I tell you, Amondo, that it was only a matter of time before this happened?"

Ina cried quietly, her hands covering her mouth.

A pair of pruning shears protruded from Eddie's chest.

From where Nikki was standing, she could clearly read the name etched on the wooden handle. *J. Delgado.*

They were Jorge's pruning shears. The same shears she had seen him using on Victoria's azaleas the previous night, just before his argument with Eddie. The argument where he threatened to kill Eddie.

"*Dios a mio,*" Ina mumbled. She and Amondo crossed themselves simultaneously.

The shock of the moment passed. Nikki turned to the others. "Everyone, go back to the house. Amondo, call nine-one-one. I'll stay here." She swallowed hard. "With the body."

"Nicolette."

Nikki met her mother's gaze, Bordeaux blues to Bordeaux blues. Nikki knew what Victoria was thinking. This was Nikki's third dead body, but it was the second time she and her mother had been together in the presence of one. A tumble of memories filled Nikki's eyes with tears.

"Nicolette, I'll stay. You go back to the house." In a rare demonstration of affection, Victoria rested her hand on Nikki's forearm. Her eyes were dry. The woman was honed of steel and, at this moment, Nikki realized how thankful she was for that. Victoria's strength gave *her* strength. It had always been that way between them.

"No," Nikki said. "You're not dressed. I'm sure the police will want to speak with you. You need to be ready."

Amondo had his arm around Ina. Her chest was heaving with each sob and she laid her head on his shoulder. He offered his free hand to Victoria.

Victoria lifted her chin a notch, refusing his assistance. "I suppose there's no rush, at this point, but the call has to be made. It's my garbage can. I'll make the call." She brushed past Amondo and Ina, her pink silk gown fluttering in the morning breeze like a queen's robe. As she made her dramatic exit from the alley, she glanced over her shoulder. "I'll send Amondo back with a pair of shoes for you, Nicolette."

And then Nikki was alone. Sort of.

Her gaze settled on Eddie again. It was truly a horrific scene. His pudgy body was propped up, elbows back as if he were casually leaning on one of the rolling blue garbage bins. His bare feet were crossed, his vacant eyes wide, his skin tone ashy. He was wearing the same pair of pink hibiscus-flowered swim shorts and red Ralph Lauren polo that he'd been wearing the evening before. The shirt looked stained beneath the trademark polo horse appliqué, around the blades of the pruning shears, but Nikki didn't want to get close enough to see if it was blood.

Did it matter?

Jorge's name was practically flashing at her in neon lights.

But surely Jorge couldn't have done this. He wouldn't.

Nikki looked up and down the alley. It was only eight A.M. None of the neighbors were up and about on a Saturday morning. The only movement she saw was the flutter of several Burger King hamburger wrappers caught around a spike in the wrought-iron fence. She wondered which of Victoria Bordeaux's ritzy neighbors was a closet Burger King addict.

She glanced at Eddie again.

He was looking at her. Sort of.

She took a step closer. Should she close his eyes? They did that on TV. But that would be tampering with a dead body at the scene of a homicide. Probably not a good idea.

She exhaled, feeling shaky. By now her mother would have made the emergency phone call. She'd soon hear sirens.

She waited.

Eddie seemed to be waiting, too.

She caught a whiff of blooming roses and sour milk on the cool morning breeze. Someone had had fish for dinner the night before. She took a step back from the garbage bins, now acutely aware that she was barefoot and that she may have spilled raspberry sorbet on her T-shirt last night.

She scratched at the spot over her breasts; she was braless, but she doubted anyone would notice. Victoria had been referred to as *stacked* once upon a time; she had been the decisive sweater girl of the silver screen. Nikki had inherited her father's mammaries, apparently.

She glanced at Eddie again. She really wanted to

close his eyes. She wanted to pull the shears out of his chest and . . . dump them elsewhere. The Pacific Ocean came to mind.

"I'm sorry," she said softly under her breath. She made herself look into Eddie's eyes. Victoria had always insisted that was important, no matter who you were addressing—Robert De Niro or the girl who worked the grill at the studio commissary. "I'm really sorry this happened to you, Eddie. Even if I didn't like you," she added, not wanting to seem two-faced. Eddie had always known she didn't like him. She just didn't want him to think—

Realizing how crazy her thoughts were, she walked to the other side of the alley, crossing her arms over her chest. (If she kept them like this, maybe the police wouldn't see the sorbet.) She looked in both directions of the alley again, wondering from which way the cops would approach. The Beverly Hills Police Department was on Rexford, but—

Nikki heard the wail of a police car, then a second, and she shivered. She glanced at the bloody shears. Ina had good reason to cry. The police would waste no time in arresting a first-generation American gardener from Mexico if he was a suspect in the killing of famous producer Abraham Bernard's only son.

The question was, what was Nikki going to do about it?

Chapter 4

By the time Amondo returned with a pair of shoes for Nikki (Bruno Magli vintage black flats, which went *fabulously* with her sweats and tee) the police had arrived in full force. The alley was full: black-and-white Beverly Hills precinct cars, two ambulances, and several unmarked police cars. Nikki sent Amondo back to the house to retrieve her cell phone and take her dogs out while she remained to answer the police officers' questions ... without giving up any information on Jorge. She needed to talk to him. Better yet, she needed to see him. But first, she had to deal with this mess.

The first officers on the scene were a Mutt and Jeff pair, one tall, one short, only the tall one had the gut and the short one looked like he needed a sandwich. They both wore black uniforms with shiny oval badges and shinier shoes. Once Nikki identified herself and the victim, it only took the tall cop, Officer Mendez, three questions to get to the owner of the

gardening shears, information Jorge had conveniently etched in the handle for him.

"This J. Delgado, you know him?" Officer Mendez
(Mutt) asked, pen poised over a little notepad. So
far, he'd been very professional about Eddie's
celebrity status and hers; maybe it just went with working Beverly Hills. Drew Barrymore, Johnny Depp, An-
nette Bening, Ron Howard—Nikki never knew who
she'd run into at the post office or the market.
Mendez had recognized her immediately as Victoria
Bordeaux's daughter, but had been polite enough to
pretend not to notice that she was wearing the odd
combination of sweats and designer shoes, no
makeup, and had a zit coming up in the middle of
her forehead. Not exactly the way celebrities liked to
be seen in public.

"We have a friend of the family, his company does
our gardening," Nikki explained. "His name is Jorge
Delgado. I . . . I don't know if those are his, though."

"Right." The officer scribbled something down.
He was standing close enough that she could smell
garlic on his breath. Everything bagel?

Down the alley a little ways, behind the Bernards'
portion of the fence, a nice-looking plainclothes cop
in khakis and a white polo was talking with a guy in
bare feet and wrinkled shorts and T-shirt. He looked
pretty hungover. A by-product of Eddie's party?

"Ms. Harper?"

There were so many people in the alley by now,
cops and bystanders, making so much noise, that
Nikki had to concentrate to hear what the uniformed cop was asking about Eddie's next of kin.

"His parents. That's their house. Someone should

go over and tell them what's happened," she said, glancing at their portion of the fence. "There's no way someone at the house hasn't heard the sirens." All she could think of was poor Melinda. No mother should have to see her child this way.

Nikki glanced at Eddie. He still hadn't been moved. His eyes still stared, sightless, at the fence across the alley. The cops were still taking photos. "Or at least call them. Someone should call the Bernards."

"I need you to answer my questions, Ms. Harper, and let us do our jobs."

He seemed to be taking a lot of notes. What could he be writing?

"We're going to have to talk to everyone who was in your house. And the housekeeper who found the body. Her name, please?"

"Ina . . . Delgado."

He didn't look up. "Illegal?"

She frowned, and tried not to sound as irritated as she felt. The police weren't supposed to be biased, and certainly not one with the surname Mendez. But when did mankind ever live up to Nikki's expectations?

"*No.* She's a U.S. citizen, same as you and me." It was on the tip of her tongue to ask him if *he* was a U.S. citizen. She left it there.

He flipped back a page in his notebook and looked down at her. "Delgado? Maid's name is Delgado? You sure the pruning shears aren't hers?"

"Ina Delgado is my mother's *housekeeper*, not a maid." She paused, giving him time to think on that for a moment. "As I said, Officer Mendez, I don't know who the gardening shears belong to." *A white lie, really. Jorge had a pair that looked like those, exactly like those, but who could say for sure if they were his?*

"Jorge. That's spelled with a J. Probably his."

"Even if they are his, how do we know he had them? This is too easy. It's obviously a setup," she argued. "For heaven's sake, my mother was pruning roses yesterday morning. *She* could have used them, for all we know."

"Victoria Bordeaux?" He looked up from his notes. "She have a beef with the deceased?" *Scribble. Scribble.*

He was serious. It was all she could do not to laugh. The answer was yes, of course. She had a *beef* with him. So did half of L.A. "No," she answered.

"But these are her garbage cans?" More scribbling.

The guy's questioning seemed random. Was that his technique? To rattle a witness so badly that they accidently confessed?

"I guess, technically, yes, these are my mother's bins, but *she* didn't kill him. Neither did Ina Delgado or Jorge Delgado."

"You know who *did* kill him?" *Scribble. Scribble. Scribble.*

Was he taking down recipes or something? Maybe he was actually a writer for the *National Enquirer.* With a badge, a gun, and a cop car.

Nikki massaged her temples with her thumb and forefinger. She was beginning to develop a headache. She needed a latte. A venti. Possibly splurging on 2 percent milk instead of the usual skim. It was looking like a 2 percent–milk kind of day. "I don't know who killed Eddie. But as you can see, the entire block leaves their cans here. And it's an alley. Anyone could come back here."

"*Sister, Sister,* it's one of our favorite movies. The wife and me. Some of the best work Victoria Bordeaux ever did. I don't know why she didn't win an Oscar for that one."

It took Nikki a beat to catch up. "A lot of people say that."

He looked up from his notepad, glanced in the direction of Eddie's body, then back at her. He lowered his voice. "I'd ask for an autograph, if it was . . . you know . . . appropriate. For the wife. Her being a big fan and all. She collects autographs. She's got sixty-some. Brad Pitt, that's her newest." He shook his head. "But . . . I'm on duty. I'd never ask."

She smiled distractedly. Who had gone to the Bernards' house? She couldn't see that any of the first cops on the scene were missing. "Right." She glanced up at him. "Officer Mendez, are you sure someone's gone to tell the Bernards? I would hate to have Eddie's mother or father . . . see him this way."

"Taken care of, ma'am."

"Good." She folded her arms over her chest. "Then . . . do you think I could go back to my house and take a shower? Get dressed?"

"We'll have more questions for you later." He nodded in the direction of the cutie in the polo shirt who had a *The Way We Were*–era Robert Redford look. "Lieutenant Detective Dombrowski will need to speak with you."

Mendez's garlic breath was mixing with the aroma of sour milk in the alley and Nikki was beginning to feel a little nauseous. Maybe she'd just go for black coffee. Amondo made decent coffee, better than Ina, who always skimped on the coffee beans. "I'll be happy to answer as many questions as you want, but I'm in my pj's here." She opened her arms wide. "No woman likes to be seen in her pj's, Officer Mendez. It's only a matter of time before the paparazzi show up."

He looked at her and seemed to notice, for the first time, that she was, indeed, dressed . . . casually. Even for an early morning homicide in the alley. "My wife would never be seen in her pj's," he told her. "Fire alarm goes off in our apartment building, she has to get completely dressed. Lipstick, too. She doesn't have a lot of pigmentation in her lips." He motioned to his lips with his pen.

Nikki didn't know what it was about her that made people tell such personal things about themselves. It happened to her all the time.

She offered a quick smile, giving him a flash of the Bordeaux blues. "So it's okay. If I grab that shower?"

"This is your house?" He pointed to the open pedestrian gate leading to Victoria's property. He didn't seem to be taking in the Bordeaux blues . . .

"My mother's house. I was staying the night . . . actually, staying a few days. I had a water leak and my house is being painted." *And repainted*, she thought. She'd apparently hired the paint contractors from hell. Three days ago she'd walked into her carefully restored 1940s bungalow to find that her kitchen had been painted Pepto-Bismol pink. Somehow, her color swatches had gotten mixed up with another client's.

Officer Mendez hesitated. "Hang on a second." He turned to the guy in the white polo. "Hey, Dom."

The cop walked over to them and waved, indicating the barefoot stranger should approach them. "Yeah?"

"Okay if Ms. Harper here goes to her mother's home and gets dressed? Lieutenant Detective Dombrowski," Mendez introduced.

Nikki nodded, glancing at the guy standing behind Dombrowski. He looked like he wanted to be anywhere but here. Who didn't?

"Sure," Dombrowski said. "I need you to get this guy's information and let him go. He doesn't need to be seen, either," he said.

Nikki gave the guy a little nod. She didn't know who he was, but apparently he was someone. "Nikki Harper," she said.

The guy nodded but didn't offer his name.

"No problem, Lieutenant." Mendez turned to Nikki. "You can go back to your mother's house, but you need to stay there. Everyone who was there at the time of the discovery of the body needs to remain in the house for questioning."

"Right. Sure. No problem." Nikki took one last look at Eddie and headed for the back gate to her mother's property. She wanted to go straight to Jorge's house, but it didn't seem like that was going to be possible. This wasn't the kind of news you wanted to break over the phone, but she was afraid she might have to.

She wanted to get to Jorge before the cops did.

*　　*　　*

Nikki grabbed her cell phone off her nightstand and hurried for the *en suite* bathroom. Stanley and Oliver beat her to it. "Out," she ordered, pointing with one hand as she hit SEND on the phone with the other. "No dogs in the shower."

Stan darted out. Ollie lowered his head, looking pitiful, but did as he was told. Nikki turned the lock on the bathroom door; Victoria was as bad about respecting the privacy of others as the dogs.

Jorge's line rang.

She had no idea what she was going to say when he picked up. How would she say it? She stepped out of her sweatpants; she'd left her Bruno Magli shoes at the end of her bed. Sending them had to be Victoria's work. Amondo would never have gone into her closet and chosen a pair of shoes; he'd have grabbed the flip-flops.

Nikki turned on the shower in the Italian marble stall. Her mother had had Nikki's bathroom remodeled a couple of years ago while remodeling her own. Victoria didn't seem to care that Nikki hadn't lived at home since she was sixteen. "Just in case," her mother had insisted.

In case what? In case Nikki lost her mind?

Which, apparently, she had, since she'd been here more than a week, with no escape imminent.

Jorge's line continued to ring in Nikki's ear. She pulled her T-shirt over her head. "Come on . . . come on," she muttered. "Answer your phone."

It rang until it went to voice mail. This wasn't the kind of thing you left a message about. One of the dogs scratched at the bathroom door.

"Go lay down, Stanley," Nikki ordered, knowing

very well it was him. He was the more outgoing of the two. The one more willing to dare scratch the paint on one of Victoria's white doors. The other day he'd pulled a silk pillow off a couch in the living room and dragged it halfway across the room before taking a nap on it.

Nikki dialed Jorge's phone again. "Come on, pick up." It was still early. He was probably asleep. Probably hungover. She didn't think Jorge had a drinking problem, but he occasionally *tied one on* on a Friday or Saturday night, especially if there was *fútbol* on Telemundo.

The call went to voice mail again. "Damn it, Jorge."

There was a knock on the bathroom door. "Nicolette? Are you in there?"

Who else would be in here?

"I'm in the shower, Mother," Nikki called, hanging up, and dialing again. She glanced at herself, naked, in the mirror. Not bad for forty-one years old. Not curvy like her mother, but tall and slender. Nikki had always envied Victoria's gorgeous platinum-blond hair, but she'd come to accept and actually *like* her own red hair. Victoria referred to it as *strawberry blonde*. The Bordeaux blue eyes made her face. She turned away from the mirror; it was beginning to steam over. "Go away, Mother."

Victoria knocked again. Then turned the locked knob. Then knocked again. "The police are here," she announced. "They want to speak to us."

"I'll be down in a few minutes. I have to shower and dress. They said I could shower." Jorge's line was ringing again.

Nikki heard her mother sigh with irritation. "Well,

don't take long. I'm trying to keep Ina busy. She wanted to call Jorge, but I told her not to. That it would look bad. You're going to call him, aren't you?" It was quiet long enough for Nikki to think she might be gone.

Then . . . "Nicolette?"

"I'm trying, now, Mother."

"You think I should call my attorneys?"

"Why would you call your attorneys?"

"I don't know, Nicolette. It's the kind of thing one does in this sort of situation."

"I'll be down in a few minutes. We'll talk about it then."

The dogs barked. Nikki heard Victoria say something to them and then the bedroom door closed.

By some sort of miracle, Nikki's BlackBerry clicked in her ear.

"Nikki?" It was Jorge. He sounded half asleep.

"Jorge . . ." She didn't know how to break this kind of news, so she just blurted it out. "Eddie's dead and I'm pretty sure the police think you did it."

"*Eddie?*"

"Eddie Bernard." She stuck her hand in the shower to test the temperature. "Someone murdered Eddie Bernard last night, or early this morning . . . I don't know when. I just know he's dead. I saw him, Jorge. Dead."

"*Oh, God*, Nikki," Jorge whispered.

It was a strange *Oh, God*. One she couldn't quite interpret. Was he saying *Oh, God* because he felt badly that Nikki had had to see another dead man? Was it *Oh, God*, poor Eddie? Or something else, entirely?

"Your mother found him."

"My mother?"

"She's okay. She's worried about you, is all." She took a deep breath. "You may have to turn yourself in."

"What are you *talking* about? Turn myself in *for what*?"

That was better. He was angry now. Anger was a good response.

"He was killed with your pruning shears, the ones with your name on them."

"Oh, God," he repeated. Now he sounded scared. Even more appropriate.

"The police are here. Asking questions. I'm guessing they're at the Bernards' by now, too."

"And someone is going to tell them about our fight," he said in a small voice. "Where was he killed?"

"I don't know, but he ended up in the alley behind Mother's house. He was posed, Jorge, as if whoever did it meant for him to be taken away with the trash." She then filled him in on the more mundane facts, as if anything about finding a man's body by her mother's trash was mundane.

He said almost nothing.

When she finished, she said, "I have to go, Jorge. But I'll be there as quickly as I can. If the police come for you, *don't say anything.* Okay?"

There was silence before he answered. "Okay."

Jorge hung up and Nikki jumped in the shower. Twenty minutes later, she walked down the stairs, dressed in slacks, the Bruno Magli flats, and a short-sleeve sweater she'd picked up at a vintage shop on Santa Monica. Her hair was still damp, but she'd taken three minutes to throw on some cover-up (the pimple), lipstick, and mascara. She was preceded by a double-dog entourage. From the black-and-white tiled front foyer, she heard male voices and followed the sounds to the dining room.

There must have been a dozen police officers, uniformed and plainclothed, milling around the tasteful dining room, carrying luncheon plates and teacups from Victoria's art deco 1920s Noritake china. Victoria stood in the doorway, dressed in a cute blue skirt, white top, and Chanel kitten heels. Every hair was in place, her makeup was perfect, and she was wearing *the smile.*

"A *buffet*, Mother? You've got to be kidding me."

Stanley and Oliver barreled into the dining room, scampered under Victoria's dining table (seating for twelve, with Chinese Chippendale chairs), and flew down the hallway toward the kitchen. Amondo, dressed in black slacks and a white Armani shirt, stood near the white sideboard and added coffee to a silver urn.

"It's *not* a buffet," Victoria corrected. "I simply offered our guests coffee and danish. Amondo had the danishes delivered from that little bakery I like on that corner." She lowered her voice. "I told Ina it was all right if she threw a fruit salad together, but that was all I wanted her to do."

"Mother," Nikki whispered.

"What? The fruit was going to go bad in the refrigerator, anyway."

Nikki shook her head.

"You speak to him?" Victoria whispered through her smile. "Jorge."

"Yes. I'm going over as soon as I can get away from here."

The Robert Redford–looking detective Nikki met in the alley approached, carrying a delicate teacup of coffee. Nikki matched her mother's smile.

"This was very kind of you, Ms. Bordeaux." He glanced at Nikki with . . . interest. "Certainly not necessary."

"Lieutenant Detective Dombrowski." Nikki offered her hand. "Nikki Harper. But you know that."

"I imagine it will be a long day, Lieutenant Detective. I just thought some coffee might be in order." Victoria leaned around him. "Amondo, could you check with Ina to see if we have any disposable cups? In case any of these gentlemen would like to take their coffee to go." She looked up at the detective, who towered over her. "Shall we get to your questions?" She folded her hands neatly. "So you can get on with your day, and I can get on with mine."

Chapter 5

Nikki eased her Prius to the curb in front of the tiny bungalow where Jorge, his sister Rosalia, and her husband, Hector, lived. Two of Jorge's JORGE & SON pickup trucks were parked in the driveway. Jorge had no sons, no daughters. He was divorced, but he had liked the name when he went into business seven years ago. Maybe it had been wishful thinking.

The house was old, built in the fifties, but well maintained. The yard was lush and, of course, immaculate. Nikki left her bag in the car and took her key. She hurried up the cement sidewalk, through a trellis gate framed with fragrant yellow roses. A black wrought-iron security door, which stood slightly ajar, covered the front door.

A dog barked from the backyard next door and Nikki hustled up the steps. She didn't really feel unsafe, just out of her element in the working-class neighborhood of El Sereno. There was no doorbell.

She raised her hand to slip it between the two doors and knock.

The inside door opened before Nikki had the chance. It was Hector. She wasn't sure who was more startled, her or him. He looked as if he was on his way out.

Nikki took a step back, dropping her hand. "Hector."

"Nikki." He rested his hand on the security door and pulled it toward him. This morning he sported a ball cap advertising Bohemia beer, bottled in Mexico. He glanced over his shoulder. He looked . . . nervous.

"Is Jorge here?" Nikki asked, unsure how much Hector knew.

Jorge appeared behind Hector. He was taller, broader-shouldered, and better-looking than his brother-in-law. Nikki didn't know Hector well, and couldn't say whether or not she liked the guy. Like Jorge, he had a short fuse, only his, according to stories she'd heard from Jorge and Ina, was shorter.

"Oh, good, Jorge," Nikki said with genuine relief. "You're still here." She looked at both men through the wrought-iron bars, thinking it was a little weird that Jorge hadn't asked her in. But who thought of manners when they were about to be arrested for murder, right?

"Can I come in?" she asked.

Hector looked back at Jorge.

"Let her in," Jorge said.

Nikki looked at Hector, then Jorge. She still couldn't tell how much Hector knew about what was going on. "Everything okay here, Jorge?"

"What do you think?" Jorge reached around his brother-in-law and pushed open the door.

Nikki walked into the house. Hector walked out. She glanced over her shoulder, wanting to ask Jorge where the heck Hector was going, but she held her tongue. Maybe Hector didn't know about Eddie.

Jorge's sister, Rosalia, was sitting on a couch on the opposite side of the living room. Like the outside of the bungalow, the inside was immaculate, with plain, simple furniture: a couch, a chair, a couple of end tables, and a small, flat-screen TV. The walls were a cheery yellow, hung with original paintings of flowers: white daisies, red poppies, white lilies. Jorge's hobby. Behind the couch, over Rosalia's head, was a large oil painting of sunflowers, à la van Gogh; there was something special about it. Something very . . . Jorge. The colors were brilliant, the textures so lifelike that Nikki felt as if she might be able to reach out and pluck one of the flowers from the painting. He was quite good, Nikki realized. She had known for years that he painted. *Why hadn't she known how good he was?*

"Rosalia." Nikki smiled kindly. Rosalia's eyes were red, her cheeks blotchy; she looked as if she had been crying for a while. Did that mean she knew what was going on with her brother? Which would mean Hector would have had to know, too.

Rosalia was seven years younger than Nikki and Jorge, so she and Nikki had never been close. But Nikki had always liked the shy girl. And Jorge had always been there to protect his little sister. When Rosalia had gotten pregnant with their first child, Jorge had been the one who insisted that she and Hector get married; he had also been the one to hire Hector, who had a criminal record from his days of gang involvement as a teen. Jorge had welcomed them into his home, and still paid the lion's share of the mortgage, Nikki suspected.

"Nikki. Thank you for coming." Enormously pregnant with her third child, Rosalia rose slowly from the couch, her small hand supporting her back.

Nikki turned to Jorge. "She knows?"

He nodded.

Nikki crossed the room to give Rosalia a hug. "Your mother wanted to come, but Mother thought it better if she stayed put. We were afraid it might look . . . incriminating, if she ran to her son. And the police are still everywhere on Roxbury Drive. At our house and the Bernards'. I told them I was leaving to run to the office to get some information for a client." She looked down at Rosalia. "I didn't want Jorge to have to go to the police station alone."

Jorge stood at the door. A loud engine started outside and then a car squealed down the street. Hector. There had been a red 80s Mustang parked out front. Nikki wondered why he was leaving at a time like this. Leaving his pregnant wife. Leaving his brother-in-law, who was in trouble. She didn't ask.

"You don't have to take me to the police station, Nikki." Jorge was dressed in khaki shorts and a pale green plaid shirt; he looked neat and well groomed, as always. "I'll drive myself."

"You sure?" She felt so helpless. She wanted to help him, she just didn't know how. "At least let me go in with you."

"Absolutely not." Jorge turned his back on her, then faced her again. "They really think I did this?" he asked, passionately. "That I would kill a man? Even a worthless piece of crap like Eddie?"

"Jorge," Rosalia admonished softly. "Don't say things like that."

Nikki turned to him. "All the police have to go on right now is whatever was said at the Bernards' . . . and they have the pruning shears." Her gaze strayed to a duffel bag sitting next to the door. Like someone was about to take off. "You know where you left the shears last night, Jorge?"

"No . . . I don't know. The whole . . . thing with Eddie and Ree. I was upset. Hector and I, we packed up and . . ." He let his voice trail into silence. "I don't know." He looked up suddenly. "If I did it, would I really have left the weapon there? With my name on it?"

"I know it sounds crazy . . . but you *did* threaten him," Nikki said softly.

"I did," Jorge agreed.

Nikki was quiet for a minute. Then, "Well, I think it's best if you go to the Beverly Hills police station sooner rather than later. Amondo overheard some uniformed cops talking before I left. Someone's definitely going to be headed here. I was afraid I wouldn't make it here before they did."

Rosalia began to cry and Jorge closed the front door, went to his sister, and put his arm around her. "Go lay down for a little while. I'm sure Hector will be back soon."

"No, Jorge. I don't want you to go." She threw her

arms around him and Nikki glanced away, feeling awkward at such an intimate moment between brother and sister.

"I'll be fine. I didn't do this, Rosalia."

"I know you didn't," she sobbed. She whispered something in his ear.

He hugged her. "You have to stop crying." He smoothed her shiny dark hair, cut in a bob that framed her pretty, heart-shaped face. "You have to think of the baby. Now, go on. Go lay down. Rest while you have the chance."

Rosalia's lower lip trembled. "Hector?"

"He'll be back," Jorge reassured her. "You know he will."

"You're sure?" Another stream of tears ran down her cheeks. "Because I can't do this alone, Jorge. Not with two little ones and another on the way—"

"He'll be back," Jorge repeated. His tone was sharp this time.

Nikki watched her waddle slowly down the hall. "The children?" she asked Jorge, referring to his niece and nephew.

"With our next-door neighbor. She's promised to keep them all afternoon. I didn't want them to see me taken away in handcuffs if—"

"I understand," she said quickly. "And now Rosalia can rest." She stood there for a minute looking at Jorge, remembering him at age fourteen, and how understanding he had been when Nikki had been struggling with her relationship with her mother, with her own identity. They'd known each other so well then, but she felt as if she didn't know him at all anymore. It made her sad. "You should get an attorney."

"I don't need a lawyer. I didn't do anything wrong." He looked at her. "We live in America, Nikki. Here, we're innocent until proven guilty."

She glanced away, thinking how naïve he sounded. And wishing she was a little more like him. The justice system's complete failure in the handling of her father's murder in New York City had left her . . . jaded. Because of police errors in the investigation, the judge had set the killer free. Three months later, the killer struck again only a block from her father's penthouse apartment. The second time, the psychopath murdered a financier, his wife, and his ten-year-old daughter. So, Nikkie didn't have the confidence in the legal system that Jorge had. "If it's the money you're worried about, Mother—"

"It's not about the money," he said firmly. "It's about what's right. I don't want a lawyer. I don't *need* a lawyer."

She considered bringing up the fact that he was Hispanic and that Eddie was Caucasian . . . and filthy rich. But Jorge wasn't stupid. He had to know the chance he was taking. He didn't like to be told what to do. Never had. "You should go," she said quietly.

Jorge nodded and, always the gentleman, opened the front door for her.

Nikki stopped just as she was about to walk out onto the stoop "Is that yours?" she asked, glancing down at the bag.

"No." He gave the duffel bag a push with the toe of his sneaker. There was something he wasn't saying.

"Let's go. Let's do this. I want to be home by dinner."

* * *

Jorge was not home by dinner.

That evening, Nikki sat on the floor in her mother's bedroom suite and nibbled on Uruguayan Osetra caviar, toast points, and fresh fruit. Victoria's idea of a TV dinner. After the police had finally left, Victoria had insisted that Ina take the remainder of the day off. She'd even offered to drive her home or to Jorge's to be with her daughter and grandchildren and to wait for her son, if Ina wasn't up to driving herself. Which was interesting because Victoria didn't drive; she was *driven*. She didn't even have a driver's license. Ina, touchy about her independence from her employer, had driven away in her Honda.

Nikki sat on the floor in front of the large—but not obnoxiously so—flat-screen TV and scooped caviar from a small dish on the Parisian coffee table with a toast point and added a little dollop of crème fraîche. Ollie sat on one side of her, Stan on the other. Both dogs stretched out their necks and sniffed the delicate aroma of the caviar.

"Watch it there, buddy," Nikki warned, tapping Stanley on the nose with her elbow. "You're about to cross the line."

Stanley dropped obediently to the pale blue and pink Persian carpet, but Oliver crept closer. Nikki used her fingertip to push a bit of the grayish caviar more squarely on her toast, then offered her finger to Oliver.

"Are you feeding those dogs Uruguayan caviar?" Victoria wiped the corner of her mouth with a white linen napkin.

"Feeding the dogs caviar? Of course not." Feeling

sorry for Stanley, Nikki pushed her finger into the dish and gave the dog a lick before popping the whole caviar-covered toast point into her mouth.

Victoria changed the channel on the TV with the remote. "It certainly *looks* like you're feeding them caviar."

"Mother."

Victoria glanced at the dogs. "They can have the dish when we're finished. That will have to suffice."

Nikki turned her attention to the TV, taking a swig of Perrier. Ordinarily, Victoria would have had Amondo open a bottle of champagne, but neither was in the mood for bubbly. It seemed ridiculous to her to be sitting here, eating caviar, when Jorge was still at the police station being questioned. But as Victoria had pragmatically pointed out, there was nothing anyone could do right now. And Nikki hadn't eaten all day. She'd been too upset. Too worried.

Victoria halted the channel-changing on an entertainment news program. The story was about a rap artist Nikki didn't recognize, but the news ticker that ran along the bottom of the screen, offering the latest news from Hollywood, caught her eye.

Edward Bernard, son of TV producer Abraham Bernard, brutally murdered in screen actress Victoria Bordeaux's backyard. Bordeaux's gardener arrested.

"That isn't music," Victoria said, watching the clip of the artist as he bounced across a stage, singsonging a rhyme, so many words bleeped out that it was hard to follow the lyrics. She changed the channel.

"No, no, go back." Nikki sat up on her knees. Both dogs looked at the TV screen with interest. "Turn it back."

"Really, Nicolette. If people would stop listening to rubbish like that, there would be no record deals and no gold records for songs featuring copulation."

Nikki's BlackBerry on the coffee table vibrated.

"I'm not interested in the rapper, Mother. The bulletin on the bottom."

Victoria changed the station back. The ticker now read something about the surrogate birth of some TV celebrity's daughter.

Nikki picked up her phone, saw who was calling, and answered.

"You just see that? On *Entertainment Tonight?* O-M-G, Nikki."

"Marshall, I thought you had that fund-raiser to go to."

"I'm going," he groaned. "My *date* is running late. Some French supermodel. My agent made the arrangements. Did they really arrest Jorge? Nikki, what's going on over there? Eddie was killed in your mother's backyard? That's not possible. I was just there last night."

"Eddie wasn't killed in Mother's yard." She exhaled. "He was found dead in the alley."

"And I have to hear about this on TV? And they've got it wrong, as usual?"

"I'm sorry. I didn't have time to call you." Nikki got up to pace. So they'd done it. The police had arrested Jorge. She had to do something. But what could she do? "Things have been crazy here."

"Is that Jeremy?" Victoria asked. "It's about time. I left him two messages today."

Nikki glanced at her mother. "You called Jeremy?"

"No, I didn't call Jeremy," Marshall said. "I'm supposed to be your best friend. Your next-door neighbor is murdered by your gardener and you can't bother to ring me?"

"Jorge didn't do it," she insisted.

"Tell him I think he should come over." Victoria pointed at Nikki with a toast point.

"Mother, it's *not* Jeremy. It's Marshall."

"Victoria called Jeremy and not me?" Marshall sounded hurt.

Nikki rubbed her forehead. She could smell the caviar on her fingertips and she wished she hadn't eaten it. "I'm not sure what to do," she said into the phone, closing her eyes.

"You should stay out of it, this time." Victoria flipped through channels. "*Diners, Drive-ins and Dives* is coming on. Shall we?"

Nikki walked to the far side of the luxurious bedroom suite that, despite all the pink, was decorated in good taste. "Mother offered to pay for an attorney. Jorge said no. I shouldn't have left him there alone at the police station," she fretted. "I should be there."

"You were right to go home," Marshall insisted. All the silliness was gone from his tone; he was someone Nikki could always count on when she really needed him.

"That would have made him look guilty, being there with him," Marshall continued.

"How would my being at the police station make Jorge look guilty?" Nikki asked, exasperated, not so much with him, but with the situation.

"It just does," Victoria said.

Nikki almost tripped over Ollie as she turned to pace in the other direction. "I can't just sit here and let this happen."

"Stay out of it!" Marshall and Victoria spoke simultaneously.

"Marshall, go to your fund-raiser," Nikki said into the phone.

"What are you going to do? Ah, hell's bells," Marshall muttered. "She's here."

"Who's there?"

"Who's where?" Victoria asked. "Lobster rolls." She pointed to the TV with the remote. "You see this, Nicolette? It's a little place in Massachusetts. I do enjoy a good lobster roll."

Nikki felt as if she were going to explode. She couldn't imagine what Jorge was going through right now, and her mother was talking about lobster rolls. "Please go to your dinner, Marshall. Go looking handsome and straight with your supermodel date on your arm and I'll talk with you tomorrow."

"Nikki, I know that tone," Marshall said. "What are you going to do?"

"Good night." Nikki hung up and marched over to the coffee table. She swept up an unopened jar of caviar. She grabbed the delft china plate of toast points. "I'll be back."

"Where are you going with the caviar?"

Nikki headed for the door. "To offer my condolences."

"To the Bernards? Nikki, I'm not sure that's a—"

"I won't be long, Mother. I just have to see what's going on over there. I have to try and find out what they know about Eddie's murder. What's being said about Jorge."

Victoria came up off the couch. "You're not going to the—"

"Yes, I am. Stay," she ordered the dogs as she opened the door.

Stanley and Oliver dropped their bottoms to the floor.

"You most certainly are not." Victoria tossed the remote on the couch as she followed Nikki. "Not without me, you're not."

Chapter 6

Victoria and Nikki walked out the French doors from the kitchen, across the well-lit side lawn, toward the side gate between their house and the Bernards'. They didn't dare go in through the front gates. When Nikki had returned from the police station, Roxbury Drive had been mobbed with news vans and paparazzi.

"I think you need to consider adding video cameras around the property, Mother," Nikki said at the gate.

Victoria sighed. "I hate the cameras. We've already got them at the front gate, at the front door. It's not the way we did things in the old days."

"In the old days, your neighbors weren't being murdered and left in the alley. Didn't your friend Lola just have to take some nut to court because he was stalking her?"

"He wanted to marry her and live in Cuba in a commune." As Victoria opened the wrought-iron gate, she lifted her nose into the air. "Ridiculous. She claims to be seventy-five, but she's eighty if she's a day . . . and she's a Republican! What on earth would that young man have thought they would have in common?"

Nikki smiled to herself. She loved the way her mother looked at the world. "I think we'll go around to the front door," she said over her shoulder.

"Mourning is not for a kitchen entrance. I'm glad I taught you good manners. Even if you don't always choose to exercise them," Victoria added. She just couldn't resist.

Nikki didn't take the bait.

As they walked past the pool, Nikki noticed that nothing had been cleaned up in the aftermath of Eddie's party . . . his last party, it turned out. There were still paper cups and napkins and trash everywhere, but there were bud vases on the tables with a pink rose in each. They looked sadly out of place. She felt badly for the Bernards, for all of them. They were nice people, too nice to be going through a tragedy like this.

As they walked along the fence, a security light with a motion detector on the rear of the house came on. Nikki saw a young man wearing black pants and a white shirt slip out the rear door of the breakfast room and pull a pack of cigarettes from his pocket.

From the side yard, Nikki and Victoria entered the motor court where there were several parked cars. Beyond the double gates, Nikki saw the bright lights of news vans and assorted media campers parked on Roxbury Drive. She and her mother walked between

the house and the fountain at the center of the
motor court, which featured a six-foot-high sculpture
of a dolphin with a girl on its back. Lit with bright
white lights, water cascaded out of the dolphin's mouth
and into the massive marble bowl below.

Victoria always liked to say that having money didn't
guarantee having good taste. Nikki had thought that
Abe Bernard's taste was proof of where he had been
and where he was now: an eclectic mix of Hollywood
multimillionaire and the boy who had lived in a
Brooklyn flat with his grandmother in the forties.
The dolphin fountain definitely belonged to the boy.

The three-story, white stone, French Regency Abe
had built, however, was the epitome of good taste,
with elegant arched windows and doors and a scale
that was breathtaking. Nikki, real estate agent to the
stars, thought it was one of the finest examples of
French Regency architecture in L.A.

"Let me do the talking," Victoria instructed, cutting in front of Nikki as they approached the front
door.

Somewhere between her boudoir and the gate,
Victoria had located a tube of pink lipstick and managed to apply it perfectly. Nikki considered asking to
borrow it, but her mother wasn't in the mood to ac-
quiesce, even an inch.

"We're just going to offer our condolences," Nikki
explained. "And see if there's anything we can do."
She hurried to catch up as her mother reached the
glass-and-iron door. "We'll only stay twenty minutes."

"Right." Victoria rang the doorbell, which played
Mozart's *Eine kleine Nachtmusik.* "I'll make nice, you
snoop around."

"*Mother*," Nikki warned as the video monitor mounted to the right of the door blinked on.

A young blond woman's face appeared on the screen. Her eyes were red from crying. "May I help you?"

"Hi," Nikki said, feeling awkward. She leaned closer to the camera and monitor, balancing the plate and jar of caviar. "I'm Nikki—"

"Nikki Harper," the woman said. "From next door."

Victoria shouldered her way in front of her daughter. "We've come to offer our condolences to the family and bring a little something." She smiled into the camera.

"Ms. Bordeaux!" The young woman's face lit up. "Oh my God, I can't believe you're here. Can you hang on just a minute? I'll be right there."

It wasn't more than a minute before the door opened and the young woman appeared in person. She was tall and skinny and looked like every other young woman in L.A.—bleached blond, flat-ironed hair, and double-D enhancement.

"Thank you so much for coming," the woman gushed. "I know they'll be glad to see you." She moved a crumpled tissue from one hand to the other and offered her hand. "I'm Ashley Carter, Ms. Bernard's assistant. *Ginny's*," she qualified. Melinda had kept her last name after Abe had divorced her, Marshall had once told Nikki, which annoyed the hell out of Ginny.

With the caviar in one hand and the plate of toast points in the other, Nikki had no free hand to shake with the assistant.

Victoria thrust out her hand; she was wearing a ring with an emerald the size of a robin's egg. It had been a gift from husband number three . . . or perhaps four. Nikki couldn't recall.

"A real pleasure to meet you," Victoria said. Without waiting to be asked in, she entered the foyer, which was tiled in limestone with slate insets. "How are they doing?" she asked quietly.

"As well as can be expected." The assistant patted her eyes with the tissue, obviously impressed by Victoria Bordeaux's presence, but trying not to appear so. "It's such a shock to Mr. Bernard, his only son. . . . And Mrs. Bernard, of course. Both Ms. Bernards, of course," she added awkwardly.

"Of course." Victoria offered her million-dollar smile. It was that smile that had taken her from an ordinary teenager on a stool in a soda shop on Sunset, to an Oscar-nominated actress living in Beverly Hills. The smile, and the curvaceous figure, which was still pretty darned curvaceous, considering her age. "We brought a little something to nibble on."

Ashley accepted the plate and jar of caviar from Nikki. "They're right this way. We've been fielding phone calls all day, Mr. Bernard's assistant, Jason, and I, but he went home with a migraine. I'm supposed to be turning everyone away. Just family and friends allowed tonight. I know Mr. Bernard will want to see you." She halted in front of closed French doors that led to one of the two formal rooms built off the grand, paneled hallway. "Could you?" she asked, realizing she couldn't hold on to the snack and open the door.

"Thank you, dear," Victoria said kindly, patting

the assistant on the arm. "Why don't you find a nice little silver bowl for that caviar and we'll show ourselves in?"

The assistant beamed at the attention and stepped back.

Victoria met Nikki's gaze as she opened the doors. *I'll chat, you snoop,* she mouthed.

Nikki rolled her eyes.

"Abe, oh dear heavens," Victoria cried, sweeping into the French-paneled room with its patterned wood floors and twelve-foot ceilings.

The room was smartly decorated with French antique furniture, Turkish carpets, and modern artwork. A large, gold-gilded mirror on the wall, which Nikki had always admired, was draped in black fabric, a sign of mourning.

Abe Bernard and his ex-wife, Melinda, rose from a settee where they had been sitting, heads together in a private conversation. Abe extended his hands as he crossed the room. "Victoria, how kind of you to come." He was a short man, with a paunch, white hair, and heavy, black-framed glasses. A Martin Scorsese look-alike. Unlike most in Hollywood, he looked his age: seventy. His eyes were a pale blue, almost gray . . . and red from tears.

Nikki's chest felt tight at the thought of Abe crying for the son he had just lost. Even if Eddie was a jerk, he was still Abe's child.

Victoria ignored the hand Abe offered and lifted up on her kitten heels and hugged him, her emotion genuine. "I'm so sorry," she said, looking up at him. "Let's face it, we all feared something like this might happen to Eddie, but—"

"Mother," Nikki intoned.

"What?" Victoria glanced over her shoulder at Nikki, then back at Abe. "Abe and I have been friends too long and we're too old for dancing around issues, any issue, no matter how touchy it might be." She grasped both his hands in her tiny ones, looking up into his eyes. "I'm sorry about Eddie and I'm sorry that our gardener is a suspect. He didn't do it, but that's neither here nor there right now, is it?" She gave his hands a squeeze before releasing them.

Abe bowed his head. "This is my fault. It's my fault. If only I'd dealt with Eddie differently. If only I'd—"

"Now, now," Victoria interrupted. "You mustn't do this to yourself."

"Abe." Nikki gave him a quick hug. He smelled of Old Spice cologne and cigars. She looked into his kind eyes. "I'm so sorry."

"So are we, for all of us," he agreed. "Your mother's right. Such a tragedy. And such a mess. I know Ina must be beside herself." That was Abe. He probably knew the names of all the housekeepers on the street. The gardeners, too.

Victoria was hugging Melinda, the two speaking quietly. Victoria asked her if her daughter would be arriving soon. Emily, Eddie's younger sister, was traveling out of the country, with her rock star boyfriend. Apparently, Emily was trying to make arrangements to return to the States.

Next, Nikki hugged Melinda, whose appearance reflected that her only son had just been murdered. Her clothes were uncharacteristically rumpled, her face red, and there was mascara smudged beneath her eyes.

Ginny stood, dry-eyed, on the far side of the room, near the fireplace with the white marble mantel, nursing a drink. She seemed to be hanging back, which Nikki thought was appropriate, in this situation. After all, Eddie had been Abe and Melinda's son, not hers. Nikki nodded in her direction. Ginny nodded back, lifted her glass, and took a sip.

Ginny's twenty-year-old daughter, Lissa, dressed in a short, red knit skirt, body-skimming tank, and spike heels, stood behind her mother, texting on her cell phone.

Abe introduced Nikki and Victoria to several people in the room: two male friends from the studios and their wives, a producer Nikki knew, a female cousin of Ginny's, and a few others. A writer immediately started talking to Victoria about a guest spot on a new series he was developing.

Nikki made her way across the room, feeling totally awkward. The mourners had broken up into groups, the largest one now gathering around Victoria. Lissa was still in her own little world, texting. Nikki walked over to near where Ginny stood; Ginny didn't say anything.

Ginny seemed to be standing on the outside looking in, as if she was somewhat a part of the family, but not completely. Which was sort of true. She was married to Abe, the wife of the famous writer/producer and got invitations to all the movie premières and awards shows, but she was a second wife and, therefore, very possibly a temporary entity, and everyone knew it. She lived in the big, new house, had an assistant, housekeeper, and maid at her beck and call, but first wife, Melinda, who lived in the guesthouse, was still very much in charge. And, tonight, Abe was at Melinda's side and there seemed to be no room in their place of grief for Ginny. Maybe Ginny didn't want to be there.

"You never think something like this will happen to you," Nikki said, trying to make conversation with Ginny since she was the only one in the room not engaged in conversation. Nikki was actually thinking about her father's death and how numb she had felt in the days following his murder. The Bernards had to be feeling the same way.

"And then it does." Ginny frowned. She was wearing slacks, high heels, and a silk blouse, all freshly pressed. Her makeup, hair, and nails were perfect. It didn't appear as if she'd cried anytime lately.

Of course, Eddie wasn't Ginny's son, Nikki reminded herself. And they had not been the best of friends. Eddie had not made Ginny's life, or her marriage to his father, easy. He had been very vocal against Abe divorcing his mother to marry Ginny, and he hadn't attended the Palm Springs wedding three years ago. Eddie had embarrassed the family, including Ginny, time and time again, being in and out of jail, in and out of rehab. He'd appeared on the cover of the gossip magazines regularly, never in a good light.

"I'd offer you a drink," Ginny said to Nikki, raising her empty glass.

Nikki glanced at her. "Oh, no thank you. I don't need a drink."

Ginny turned to look her over. "You in AA, too? I swear, half of L.A. is a member."

Nikki chuckled. "No. I just . . . I don't need a drink. We don't expect you to entertain us. Mother wanted to offer her condolences." (It was only a tiny lie, barely more than a fib.)

"Well, I can tell you, I could use another gin and tonic. It's been a hell of a day."

Nikki couldn't resist a little smile. She hadn't wanted to like Ginny. She had always liked Melinda and Ginny had usurped Melinda's position. Nikki had tried hard in the beginning to *not* like her, but she just couldn't help herself. Nikki might not have liked her fashion choices, but Ginny was sharp and she said what was on her mind, even if it was unpopular. You definitely didn't see much of that in Tinseltown.

Ginny tipped her glass and one tiny ice cube clinked. "My assistant took the ice bucket to refill it, but she never came back." She glanced over her shoulder at her daughter, who was still engrossed in her phone messaging.

"Ice? I can get you some ice." Nikki jumped at the opportunity to get out of the room. Seeing Abe and Melinda so broken was hard. So sad. Besides, the kitchen was always the pulse of a home, any home, whether it was a multimillion-dollar mansion in Beverly Hills or a rundown apartment in South L.A. If Nikki expected to hear anything about the circumstances of Eddie's death, she had a better chance of hearing it in the kitchen.

"You don't mind?" Ginny asked. She glanced at her daughter again and frowned. "I'd ask Lissa, but she's in *a mood*. She was supposed to go clubbing with her friends and Abe forbade it. With all the paparazzi crawling all over us, he was afraid it would be misconstrued as being insensitive to her stepbrother's passing."

"The ice bucket?" Nikki asked, already headed for the kitchen.

Ginny shrugged. "Ashley took it."

Back in the center hall, Nikki quietly pulled the doors closed behind her and went through the arches to a cross-hall. She passed the stunning great room, with its honey-glazed wood paneling and another marble-manteled fireplace lined with glazed herringbone brick. The mirror in that room was also draped in black. On the other side of the hall was a light-filled space that could have been used for a morning room or a music room. She walked past the wrought-iron black-and-gold staircase that was characteristic of the French Regency time period. Past the stairs was a handsome study with paneled walls and a floor of polished wood.

Up the stairs, Nikki knew, was a master bedroom with a balcony and his and hers dressing rooms and bathrooms. There was a "lady's office" on the same floor and two additional bedrooms. On the third floor were four more bedroom suites. Below the stairs, in the basement, was a media room, a wine cellar, an additional bedroom suite, and a large mancave, where Abe enjoyed spending time alone. It was a gorgeous house, one that maybe only a person like Nikki, who had seen a million gorgeous houses, could truly appreciate.

She followed the hall to the opposite wing, through

a breakfast room with a double-barreled vaulted ceiling, to the cook's kitchen, featuring a stone hood over a Lacanche range and a striking marble center island. Sure enough, there on the counter was a Tiffany & Co. sterling-and-crystal ice bucket. Ashley-the-assistant was MIA.

A tall woman with rich ebony skin, silky black hair, and the most amazing blue eyes, stood at the counter. She was wearing a white chef's coat and teasing Victoria's Uruguayan caviar into a tiny silver server.

The woman, who Nikki thought she recognized, looked up as Nikki entered the room. Nikki could tell that the woman recognized *her*. It was a familiar look. She got it a lot.

"Hi. I'm Nikki Harper, from next door."

This was Ellen Mar, who had won a competition on a food wars show on the Food Network, making her an instant celebrity. Nikki had read an article a few days earlier, touting the Baltimore native as the latest, greatest TV chef in America. She had won the competition by creating desserts that appeared to be main dishes from around the world: Nutella crepes that looked like Pad Thai noodles with peanut sauce, a lemon tart that looked like Bath Street sushi, and cupcakes that looked like spaghetti and meatballs. Her prize had been a hundred thousand dollars and her own TV show on the Food Network, featuring this new, bizarre form of cuisine.

"Ellen Mar. It's nice to meet you." The chef walked around the kitchen counter, which was the size of a small aircraft carrier, offering her hand.

"I'm a friend of Abe's." Her handshake was firm. Confident.

Nikki liked her at once. She didn't seem intimidated by Nikki, nor overly impressed. "It's so nice to meet you. My mother's a big fan. We watched you compete on the *What It Isn't* food challenge. I'm fascinated by the way you can take ground beef and make it look like a cupcake . . . or the other way around." Nikki chuckled. "Though I have to admit it weirds me out a little. I sort of like my Jell-O pudding to look like Jell-O pudding."

Ellen laughed; she had a musical voice. "That's okay. The whole idea weirds me out a little, too." She walked back around to where she'd been working at the counter. "That was definitely not my forte, originally." She shrugged. "But the opportunity presented itself."

"And now you've got your own show," Nikki said.

"Thanks mostly to Abe. He's got a small satellite company that's going to tape the show right here in L.A."

"Have you started taping?"

Ellen opened a drawer and produced a mother-of-pearl caviar spoon. "We start this week."

The sound of Ashley's voice caught Nikki's attention. She was in a room off the kitchen, talking on the phone. Nikki glanced in that direction, then back at Ellen. "Well, congratulations." She indicated the ice bucket. "I came for more ice."

"I can do that, if you want to join the others," Ellen offered.

"It's fine. Really." Nikki picked up the bucket.

Ashley's voice was getting louder. Nikki could pick

up a word here and there. She was talking about not being able to go somewhere tonight.

"Honestly," Nikki said to Ellen, trying to half listen in on Ashley's conversation. Apparently, Ashley had intended to go to a Jay-Z concert, but had had to cancel because of the death of her boss's stepson. "It gives me something to do." She walked to an icemaker installed in a drawer beside the commercial refrigerator. Like most million-dollar kitchens, if you didn't know what you were looking for on what appeared to be a solid paneled wall, you might be searching for twenty minutes. Fortunately, she'd been in the house often enough to know where the Bernards hid the icemaker. "I'm not good at this sort of thing."

Ellen glanced over her shoulder in Ashley's direction. She must have been catching part of the conversation, too. "I know. I feel that way, too. Which is why I'm in the kitchen, hiding in this chef's coat," she told Nikki. "But, honestly, who *is* good at a time like this?"

Nikki lifted her eyebrows. "My *mother.*"

Ellen's face lit up. "Oh, my gosh. Mine, too."

As Nikki used a plastic scoop to dump ice into the ice bucket, Ashley walked into the kitchen cradling a cell phone, her attention obviously on the call.

"I don't know. I haven't gotten to talk to her privately," Ashley said in a gossipy tone, "but I can tell you one thing, Ginny Bernard is not all that broken up that the prick is dead. I wouldn't be surprised if she's the one who did it."

Chapter 7

Nikki met Ellen's gaze.

Realizing for the first time that she was not alone, Ashley stopped short. "I'll have to call you back," she whispered, sounding scared out of her pants.

For a moment, all three of them were silent. Nikki and Ellen both looked at the assistant, who looked back at them. Nikki slid the icemaker drawer shut with her knee, which seemed to make an amazing racket.

"I'm so sorry," Ashley breathed. "I . . . I didn't mean that. I was just . . . I obviously didn't mean for anyone to hear that."

Ellen cut her eyes at Nikki as if to say, *No duh* . . .

Nikki pressed her lips together, amused by Ellen . . . intrigued by what she'd just heard. "It . . . it's okay, Ashley."

"Please don't tell her. Please, please, please don't tell Ginny I said that. I didn't mean it. I'm angry. It's just that I was supposed to go to this concert tonight with my boyfriend, and . . ." Ashley rushed toward Nikki, tucking her phone into her hip pocket. "I can't get fired. I . . . I've got rent and a car payment, and—"

"It's okay," Nikki repeated, setting the three-thousand-dollar ice bucket on the marble counter. "I'm not going to say anything." She glanced at Ellen.

"This is certainly none of my business," Ellen muttered, turning around to grab a silver tray off the counter behind her. "I'm just the kitchen help."

Nikki would have laughed in other circumstances. She liked this Ellen Mar. She liked her sassiness. "It's been a crazy, awful day, Ashley. A lot of emotion involved," she soothed, her thoughts going a thousand miles a minute. *What had Ashley meant? Was she really just running her mouth off because she was annoyed with her employer? Or was there more to the story?* "We all say things we rethink later. Things we wish we hadn't said. Things we wish we had said differently."

"I'm going to take this caviar in. I seem to have lost my help. He said he'd be right back. He was just going outside for a quick smoke. Anything I can get either of you?" Ellen asked.

"No, I should get the ice to Ginny." Nikki reached for the bucket.

"I'll do that." Ashley practically snatched the ice bucket out of Nikki's hands. "She asked me to get more ice forty-five minutes ago. It's just that the phone has been ringing off the hook and I'm trying to answer Ginny's phone and Mr. Bernard's phone, and . . ." Her sentence trailed off as she tucked her head down and headed out of the kitchen behind Ellen.

Ginny's assistant was getting away. Nikki had to think fast. "Ashley?"

Ellen kept going.

Ashley stopped and turned back, a look of dread on her pretty face.

"If you need anything." Nikki spotted a notepad and pen on the counter. "If Ginny or . . . anyone needs something, you could give me a call. This is my personal cell number." She jotted it down.

Ashley gave a quick smile, looking obviously relieved that Nikki wasn't going to squeal on her. "Thanks."

Nikki ripped off the corner of the paper. "And maybe I could get your number," she asked as she offered hers. "Just so I can check on Ginny and the family, through you."

"Oh, sure. Of course." Ashley gave Nikki her number.

Nikki tucked the slip of paper into the pocket of her slacks as she followed Ashley and the ice bucket out of the kitchen.

Ten minutes later, Nikki and her mother were on their way home, through the side gate, of course.

"You know anyone at the Staples Center?" Nikki asked, her thoughts still racing. "Or someone who has a connection to Jay-Z?"

"What's a *Jay-Z*?"

"Never mind, just a thought," Nikki said, as much to herself as to her mother.

"So," Victoria asked. "You hear anything good? I

thought maybe you'd run home for ice, you were gone so long."

"Um . . . I don't know." Nikki wasn't sure if she was ready to share with her mother. They walked across Victoria's yard, side by side. "But I met Ellen Mar, you know, from the Food Network."

"That nice girl who makes food look like other kinds of food? I met her, too. Pleasant young woman. You should have lunch. I think you two could be friends."

"I'm not calling her for lunch, Mother. We just met, in passing."

"Nonsense." Victoria started talking about Nikki needing to make female friends.

Nikki's thoughts drifted back to Jorge. She wondered if he'd been released from the police station; she suspected he hadn't. She'd give Ina a call when she got back to the house. "Oh, but I got Ginny's assistant's phone number."

"Excellent." Victoria strolled beside her daughter; it was a cool evening, with a slight breeze. "And I got Melinda an appointment with my new hairdresser tomorrow."

"Mother, tomorrow is Sunday."

"Melinda's son is dead. She wants to go to temple. She can't very well go with bad hair," Victoria reasoned. "So I called Fifi—I know, silly name, sounds like a poodle, but she's French, or at least wants to think she is—and she agreed to come to the house, so Melinda wouldn't have to drive to the salon."

"That was very nice of you." Nikki walked into the kitchen.

"Always willing to help a neighbor in need," Victoria explained, going to the refrigerator. "I'm still hungry. Are you?" She opened the refrigerator door and peered in. "The good thing about Fifi is that she's better than any psychiatrist. If Melinda knows anything about the case against Jorge, Fifi will find out."

"You asked your hairdresser to interrogate Melinda?" Nikki asked, incredulous.

"Of course not." Victoria frowned, still studying the contents of the refrigerator. "That would be inappropriate, Nicolette. I'm just saying, if Melinda feels like talking, she'll talk to Fifi. Then, naturally, Fifi will talk to me. We could have Brie and French bread."

"No thanks." Nikki sighed, suddenly feeling tired. "I'm going to call Ina and probably turn in."

"You're worried about Jorge."

Nikki stood in the doorway between the kitchen and the hall. "Of course, I am."

"So am I. I think I should call my attorneys in the morning, if Jorge hasn't been released."

"I told Jorge that." Nikki lifted her hand and let it fall. "He doesn't want a lawyer. He says he believes in the American justice system."

"Silly boy." Victoria sighed. "I don't suppose it will do any good for me to suggest you stay out of this?"

It was Nikki's turn to sigh as she rubbed her temples. "If Jorge's arrested, and he refuses to get a lawyer, do I have any choice?"

Victoria let the refrigerator door close. She met Nikki's gaze. Her tone was kind when she spoke again, bordering on motherly. "Just be sure, Nicolette, that this is about Jorge and not your father."

"It won't be about my father," she answered softly. "It'll be about making sure the justice system doesn't fail our family again."

Nikki was dressing the next morning to take the dogs for a walk when there was a knock on the bedroom door. More like a bang. Nikki knew that bang.

"Phone, Nicolette." Victoria knocked again, not giving Nikki time to answer. "Phone for you. Nicolette!" Her mother's pitch reached a high note on her name.

Nikki pulled a T-shirt over her head and opened the door. The dogs bounced up and down at her feet, excited to see Victoria. Of course, they greeted everyone that way. Oliver barked, but Nikki held up her finger to him and, for once, he obeyed and fell silent.

"It's Ina," Victoria said in a stage whisper. She was already dressed in her signature outfit: a jogging suit, this one pink, by Christian Dior. She wore a white silk turban that exposed only the front of her platinum hair, and a short string of pearls. "She wants to talk to you. Jorge's been arrested, but he doesn't want his mother to come to the jailhouse. He doesn't want her to see him like that. Ina wants you to go. Can you go?"

"Ina's still on the phone?" Nikki asked, pointing at the cordless house phone in Victoria's hand.

"Yes, she wants to talk to you. I just said that."

"Let me have the phone, then." Nikki put out her hand, wondering why her mother was telling her all of this if Ina could tell her.

Victoria handed over the phone, but stood there.

"Ina." Nikki turned around and walked away. "I'm so sorry. I know you're worried sick about Jorge."

"Thank you. I'm just sorry your mother's name has to be dragged into this."

"Is there anything I can do?" Victoria interrupted. "Maybe I should be the one to go to the jail to see him."

Nikki ignored her mother. "It's all right, Ina. Anyone can be *accused* of a crime. That doesn't mean he or she is guilty."

"He's a hothead. He's always been a hothead. I told him his temper would get him in trouble one day," Ina fretted. "He says he doesn't want me to come to the jail, to see him like that, but I'm worried about him."

"Ask her if he's been arraigned yet," Victoria instructed.

Nikki walked farther away from her mother. The dogs were now racing back and forth between the two of them. "So he was arrested last night, or this morning?"

"I don't know," Ina said. "Sometime last night, I think. They held him for hours. Questioned him. Then they arrested him. But I don't know—"

"Has bail been set?" Victoria asked. "Ask her if bail's been set."

Nikki couldn't hear Ina over Victoria's talking. "He hasn't been arraigned, right?" she said into the phone.

"Tomorrow, he thinks, but he doesn't know."

Nikki walked to her window and opened the heavy

draperies, letting the morning sunlight in. "He'll be arraigned tomorrow, Mother."

Oliver began to chase Stanley and bark.

"Well, bail can't be set," Victoria said with great authority, "until he's seen a judge at the arraignment. Bail is set by a judge, Nicolette."

Ina started talking again, but between the dogs barking and Victoria shooting questions at her, Nikki was only getting every other word.

"Ina, I'm sorry, could you hang on for a second?" Nikki covered the mouthpiece with her hand. "Mother, could you do me a big favor and run them downstairs? They're making so much noise I can't hear Ina. I'll be right down."

Victoria looked disappointed, but walked out of the room with a flourish of her hand. "Come along, gentlemen. We've been dismissed. I suppose we'll have to go to the kitchen for treats."

At the sound of the word *treats*, the dogs took off after Victoria.

"Sorry, Ina. I'm back," Nikki said into the phone. She gazed out the second-story window to see the pink and white azaleas Jorge had been pruning Friday afternoon when she had waved to him. She couldn't help but think of the pruning shears she had seen in his hand. The same shears protruding from Eddie's chest the next morning.

"Did Jorge seem to think he'd be allowed any visitors?" Nikki asked. "I'd be happy to go to the police station. He's still at the Beverly Hills police station, being held there, right?"

"He's still at Beverly Hills, yes," Ina said. "I don't know if he's allowed to have someone. He just said he didn't want me to come. Nikki, he says he doesn't want a lawyer. But I have money saved."

"I don't think it's about the money, Ina." Nikki's gaze drifted to the closed gate between their property and the Bernards'. She could see over a portion of the fence, between the hedges. There was someone on the pool deck in her bathrobe, fiddling with something on one of the tables. The area was still littered with glasses, napkins, towels, and other party remnants. "I think Jorge feels that he doesn't need a lawyer, that no one needs to spend money to prove their innocence in America."

"Well, that's ridiculous," Ina huffed. "I've never heard of anything so ridiculous."

Nikki smiled to herself, still looking down onto the Bernards' pool deck. She couldn't tell, from her vantage point, if the woman was Ginny or Melinda. Both had the same color blond hair and were approximately the same height.

"Do you think you can go talk some sense into him?" Ina asked. "He's always listened to you, Nikki. He loves you. He'll listen to you."

"I'll see what I can do, Ina. How about if I make a phone call, see if I can get in to see Jorge today, and then I call you back?" She turned away from the window. "How are *you*, Ina? Is there anything I can do for you?"

"I'm fine. I'm with Rosalia. I'll be fine. Just talk to Jorge. Talk some sense into my *hijo testarudo*."

Nikki smiled to herself. Ina always called Jorge that—her stubborn son. She looked out the window again. The woman poolside turned toward the Bordeaux property. It was Melinda. She was just standing there now. Nikki's heart ached for her. She didn't know what she could do for a mother who had lost her son, but maybe she could keep another mother from losing hers.

"I'll see what I can do," Nikki said. She hesitated. "You're with Rosalia, you say? Did . . . is Hector there, too?"

"Of course he is. Her brother's been arrested for murder," Ina said indignantly. "I know Hector has not always done things the way we'd like, but he loves my Rosalia. Of course he's here with her. He went to Mass with us this morning. Why do you ask?"

"No reason," Nikki said, thinking about the duffel bag that had been beside the door at Jorge's house. Maybe it belonged to one of the children? But that seemed doubtful. It was dark and worn, with streaks of dirt or grease. It wasn't a child's bag. "Let me make a call and see what I can do about getting in to see Jorge today."

"Thank you, my *hija*. I knew I could count on you. I can always count on you and your mother."

"I'll call you as soon as I know something."

Nikki made a phone call to Marshall, then talked to his partner, Rob, an L.A. police detective who worked in the gangs division. She wasn't really looking for any favors, just some guidance as to how to navigate the system and get in to see Jorge today. Preferably without alerting the press. Long-haired and tattooed, Rob looked like a motorcycle gang member off a movie set, but he was the sweetest, kindest guy. He called her back in half an hour. An hour later, Nikki was at the Beverly Hills Police Department.

Chapter 8

"Going to be a high-profile case," the police officer escorting Nikki down the narrow hall said. He was tall for an Asian. Six foot. Big.

"You think so?" she asked, not really wanting to chat with the cop.

"Oh, yeah. I bet it's already got the DA's office all hot and bothered." He glanced over a brawny shoulder, eyeing her. "I know you?"

She gave him *the smile*. "I don't think so."

"I think I do." He waggled a finger. "You on TV? One of those reality shows, *Dancing with the Stars* or something?"

"No. Sorry."

He looked at her again. "One of those singing shows, maybe? It's your hair. Nice color. Red. I have this thing for red hair. My wife watches all those reality shows: *American Idol*, *Dancing with the Stars*, all that *Housewives of Wherever* crap. I hate them, but she's always trying to get me to watch them with her. You know, after the kids go to bed."

Was there something written on her forehead that said *Tell me your personal business because I'm dying to hear it?*

"I *know* I know you," he muttered.

Nikki was beginning to feel as if the hall was a mile long.

He looked over his shoulder again. "In some movie?"

She forced the next smile. "Nope."

He took another step, then spun around, snapping a thumb and finger. "Some Hollywood news show. Last week. You were at some children's cancer benefit or something. On the red carpet. My wife watches those shows, too. Your mother's one of those famous old broads from the movies. Kim Novak? Jane Russell?"

He obviously wasn't going to move until she answered. "Victoria Bordeaux."

"That's right!" He snapped his finger and thumb again. "That's how I know you. Victoria Bordeaux's oldest child. Some fancy real estate agent. Nicole Harper, right?"

"Nicolette," she corrected. "Nikki."

"Man, my wife is going to be so excited when I tell her I saw you. I mean, I see celebrities all the time. Locked up a few." He chuckled as he started down the hall again. "But she *loves* Victoria Bordeaux. She watches all those old movies, you know, on Sunday afternoons on TV."

"I'll pass that on to my mother. Thank you."

"This isn't the way we usually do things, this kind of special treatment. We've got rules about visitation. I hate high-profile cases." He stopped at a closed door. "But the boss says this is the way we do it, so this is the way we do it."

She stopped and waited.

"This is how it goes. You go inside. I stay here in the hall." He pointed to her bag. "You don't have any contraband in there, right? You know, drugs, weapons . . . a lock pick?" He laughed at his joke.

This time all he got was a tight smile. "Someone checked my bag at security, but you're welcome to look again." She slung her vintage Prada bag off her shoulder.

"That's all right." He held up both hands. "But just so you know, even you being a celebrity and all, he'll still get searched before he's returned to his cell." The cop shrugged. "Just so you know."

Nikki looked through the window in the door and saw Jorge. She glanced at the cop. "Can I go in?"

"Oh . . . sure. Yeah." He opened the door for her. "Like, no more than ten minutes, okay? We're short-handed today. Coworker's wife's having a baby. Third."

Nikki walked in and closed the door behind her. "Jorge," she said.

He was seated at the small table in the cubicle-size room that had to be used for some sort of interrogations: gray walls, gray carpet. He was still wearing his own clothes from the day before. It hadn't occurred to her to bring him clean clothes. She'd just assumed he'd be in some sort of prison jumpsuit.

"You shouldn't have come, Nikki."

She walked around the table to give him a hug. He came half out of his chair, hugging her back.

There was a tap on the door window. "No physical contact, please. Have a seat, Ms. Harper."

Nikki gave Jorge another quick squeeze and went back around the table. She dropped her bag over the back of the chair and sat down across from him. "Your mother said you didn't want to see her. She's pretty worried about you."

He shook his head. He didn't look like he'd slept, but his hair was combed, his clothes amazingly presentable, considering. "Not in jail. No mother should have to see her child in jail," he insisted. He looked away, then back at her. "She okay?"

"You know your mother. She's a pretty strong woman."

"Rosalia?"

"I haven't seen her since yesterday, but your mother says she's okay. Your mother was at your house this morning."

"Hector there, too?"

She nodded, thinking that was a slightly odd question. But maybe not. Hector made routine trips back to Mexico to see friends and family. According to Ina, sometimes Rosalia knew about the trips ahead of time, sometimes she didn't. Jorge had never said so, but Nikki suspected that was one of the reasons he had never suggested Hector and Rosalia try to get their own place. It was important to Jorge that he be there for his sister and his niece and nephew.

Nikki and Jorge were both quiet for a minute.

She folded her hands and sat back in the uncomfortable plastic chair. "So they arrested you, *officially?*"

He nodded, not meeting her gaze.

"Based on?"

He exhaled, seeming to be concentrating on some invisible spot on the wall over her left shoulder. "He was a rich, white boy. I'm a Mexican gardener."

"I don't think they can arrest you based solely on those facts," she said evenly.

He ran his hand over his dark beard stubble; he'd apparently not had an opportunity to shave. "Everyone at that party heard me threaten to kill Eddie. Then the pruning shears, with my name on them, turn up in Eddie's chest. Why do you think they arrested me, Nikki?"

"Circumstantial evidence. Which is why you need an attorney."

"I'm not getting an attorney. I told you that. I didn't do this. I shouldn't need an attorney. If I do, I'll act as my own."

She wanted to tell him that was the dumbest idea she had ever heard, but she knew that would only make him dig his heels in even harder. She glanced over her shoulder. Through the window, she could see the officer. He was looking at his fingernails the way a man did, his palm up, his fingers curled. She looked back at Jorge. "I don't suppose you have any idea who did kill Eddie?"

Jorge cut his dark eyes at her.

"Okay. Okay." She folded her hands on the table. Someone had etched a perfect cube into the surface with something sharp. There were initials on one side. T.B. You wouldn't think there would be graffiti *inside* a police station. "Okay," she repeated, trying to think. "I need you to think hard. Do you know what you did with the pruning shears that night? You were pruning the azaleas in the yard—"

"How do you know I was using them to prune the azaleas?" he interrupted.

She looked at him for a second, trying to interpret his tone. Was he angry with her? "I saw you out my bedroom window. Remember?" she said slowly. "I waved to you. Those were the same pruning shears, right? The ones you've had for years, the ones with the green wooden handles?"

He was silent.

"So, the pruning shears? When you heard Eddie and your cousin fighting . . ." She waited for him to finish her sentence.

It took him several seconds to speak and she couldn't help wondering why he was so reluctant to tell her anything. "When I heard Eddie and Ree, I hung the shears on the edge of the bucket I was dropping the clippings into."

"And when we got back to Mother's yard and I told you and Hector to go home?"

"I don't know, Nikki!" He threw up his hands and then brought them down to hold his head as if it were about to burst.

There was a knock at the door. "Everything okay in there?"

Nikki spun in her seat. "Everything's fine," she called cheerfully. Victoria would be proud of her. *Never let them know how you're really feeling*, her mother always warned when Nikki was growing up, fighting the perils of being a movie star's child. *Feelings are for private situations, never public.* "Thank you, Officer." She turned back to face Jorge, lowering her voice. "What did you do once Mother and Marshall and I went into the house?"

"We loaded the equipment into my utility truck and then we went home."

"You put the pruning shears in your truck?"

"I don't know." Jorge placed his hands on the table again. "Yes. I think so." He frowned. "I think I did. I don't know." His hands went up in the air. "I can't remember, Nikki! I was still pretty pissed off."

"Maybe I should talk to Hector. Maybe he knows."

"No. No, I don't want you talking to Hector about this." He leaned across the table.

Nikki stared at him. "Why not?"

"I don't want him involved." He glanced at the door and lowered his voice. "Hector's got a record. You know that."

"I'm not talking about sending the police to question him, although you know very well they're going to," she put in. "Jorge, I'm talking about asking him if he remembers what happened the other night. I know you were upset. So you don't remember, exactly. Maybe Hector can jog your memory."

He looked as if he was thinking, his gaze unfocused. "I put them in the truck. In the white plastic bucket. I'm almost positive." He looked up at her. "I'm sure I did, Nikki."

"So how did whoever killed Eddie get his hands on your pruning shears?"

"I don't know." Jorge's voice trembled with emotion.

Nikki gave him a moment. How the hell did someone get his shears out of Jorge's utility truck? She
tried to keep her tone neutral when she spoke again.
She wasn't here to upset Jorge. She was here to help
him. "Did you stop anywhere on the way home?"

He nodded. "The market. The one down the
street from our house. Rosalia needed a few things."

"Both you and Hector went in?"

He sighed. Nodded. "I got the groceries. Hector
got the beer."

"But you both went in together and out together
and the truck was locked while you were inside?"

He shook his head slowly. "Honestly, I don't know.
I was pretty upset. I usually lock my truck. I've got a
lot of tools and sprays and stuff in there, but . . . I
can't say for sure that I locked it. I think I did."

She knew exactly what he meant. A few months
ago, she'd been on the phone with a client when she
parked her car to run in to get her dry cleaning. The
client had been unhappy about the way his escrow
account was being set up. She thought she'd locked
her door. Apparently, she hadn't. She was in the dry
cleaners less than five minutes. Long enough for
someone to steal a cute 1980s Marc Jacobs skirt in a
bag off the front seat of her car.

The cop knocked on the door again. "A couple
more minutes."

"Thank you," Nikki sang sweetly. She met Jorge's
gaze. "I want to help you, Jorge."

"I don't want your help," he said stiffly.

She tried not to feel hurt. She knew things had
changed between them over the years, that they'd
drifted apart, but she still felt like he was one of her

brothers. "I'm afraid you could get railroaded on these charges. Eddie being Abe's son, you being—"

"Non-Caucasian and a workingman," he put in, staring at that spot on the wall again.

"Exactly. And I'm not going to let that happen to you."

"Nikki, I need you to let this go." His eyes filled with tears and he glanced away, obviously embarrassed. "This isn't about you." His voice fell. "It's not even about me—"

"Jorge, how can you say that? You're talking about a *murder* charge. First degree murder could mean life in prison."

He stood up. "You need to go. Officer!" he called. The door opened.

She was afraid *she* was going to start to cry. She didn't understand what was going on. Why Jorge didn't seem to want to fight for his innocence . . . or let her fight for him.

"Take care of my mother and sister for me, will you?"

She nodded, afraid to speak. She got out of her chair and grabbed her bag. At the door, where the officer waited for her, she turned back. "Call me. Let me know when the arraignment is."

"Let it go, Nikki. If you love me, let it go."

When Nikki got back into her car, she did something she never did. A cry dial.

Her boyfriend, Jeremy, picked up on the first ring. "You okay, hon?" he said. He had a sexy, soothing dentist's voice . . . which was convenient since he *was* a dentist.

Their relationship was complicated. She had grown up with Jeremy; he had been a child star. As a teenager, she'd been half in love with him, but never did anything about it. After high school, while she was busy *sowing her wild oats*, as Victoria had once said—once a girl from Idaho, always a girl from Idaho—he'd left the business, gone to college out of state, gone to dental school, and married. He and his wife had returned to Beverly Hills, had children; he'd set up a practice, catering to the stars. They had the perfect family life, until his wife died of breast cancer.

That was when things got tricky between Nikki and Jeremy. They'd had a crazy, passionate affair right after Marissa's death. Then the guilt began to sink in and, fearing it was a rebound kind of thing, he broke it off. Then they got back together, minus the sex. They were just easing back into the sack recently, which was complicated further by his children, and by Nikki taking up residence in her mother's house.

"I got your mom's messages," Jeremy said, his voice filled with just the right amount of concern. "I tried to call you. It went straight to voice mail."

She sat in her Prius with both hands on the wheel. "I know Mother called you."

"She's worried about you."

She pressed her lips together, her urge to melt into a puddle of wet tears subsiding. "I was just in the Beverly Hills jailhouse, seeing Jorge."

"How is he?"

She was relieved that he didn't point out that they'd had a conversation similar to this only six months ago when her best friend had been arrested for killing a man who was already dead. At least this was the first go-round for Eddie. "It's Jorge. You know how he is. Pretty stoic."

"Victoria said he's refusing an attorney."

"That's what he says." She closed her eyes for a few seconds. Traffic whizzed by on Rexford Drive. "This is bad, Jeremy. He got into an argument with Eddie Friday night. Eddie was having a party, got drunk, high, whatever, and hit his girlfriend—"

"Wait. I thought Eddie just got out of rehab."

"It's *Eddie*, Jeremy."

"Right. Sorry. Go on."

She exhaled and opened her eyes. "Jorge hears the argument next door, goes over only to discover it's his cousin Ree that Eddie is arguing with. She's got a split lip. So the two of them, Eddie and Jorge, are dancing around like in a boxing ring like guys do and Eddie pulls a gun on him."

"Oh, jeez," Jeremy muttered. Then, "No, sweetie. Finger paints only on paper, not the chair."

"I'm sorry," Nikki said. "Is this a bad time?"

"It's fine. Jerry's playing at a friend's. Lani's upstairs playing with her Breyer horses and Katie and I are finger painting at the kitchen table. Which I covered with plastic. I did not, however, cover the white chairs with plastic."

Nikki rested her head on the window of the door for a moment and smiled. Jeremy was such a good dad. "I can talk to you later. It's Sunday afternoon. You should spend time with your kids."

"Nikki, we talked about this. It's nice that you've been trying to give me my space, but we have to figure out how to make this work. I need to spend time with my kids. But I need some adult contact, too, beyond my patients in the chair, who are not great conversationalists," he chuckled. Then his tone grew serious. "I need *you*, Nikki. And I need to be a part of your life if you're going to be a part of mine."

Tears stung her eyes again. She didn't know what was wrong with her. She wasn't a crier. You didn't survive in Victoria's household if you were a crier.

They were both quiet for a minute.

"Okay," Jeremy then said. "So, Eddie pulls a gun on Jorge."

"Right, apparently in front of like fifty people. Mother, Marshall, and I are out on the terrace, we hear the gunshot, and we run next door."

"He *shot* at Jorge?"

"No, not at him."

"But he was holding a gun on him?"

"Sort of," Nikki said. "So we break up the fight, but Jorge is still being all Latin male and he threatens Eddie, saying that if he ever hears of Eddie hitting a woman again—any woman—he's going to kill him."

"So he threatens him, but not directly. Yup. Right here on the page. Red, I love red." Then back to Nikki, "Go on."

"So we get Jorge and Hector back in our yard."

"Wait, Hector?"

"Jorge's brother-in-law. Lives with him. Works with him."

"Right."

"Okay," Nikki goes on. "So back in Mother's yard, I tell the guys to pack up and go home. He still had shrubs to trim, but I didn't think it was wise for Jorge to stick around. You know Eddie's parties, they go on all night."

"Right."

"So, Mother and Marshall and I all go in the house. Jorge and Hector clean up and go home. The next morning, Ina finds Eddie dead, propped up against Mother's trash can in the alley. With the pruning shears Jorge was using the day before, stuck in his chest."

"Oh, Nikki," Jeremy sighed.

"Yeah." Spotting a news van pulling up behind her on the street, Nikki started her engine. "Hang on, Jeremy. Let me switch your call over to my Bluetooth. I have to get out of here. Media invasion."

"Paparazzi?"

"Nope. Looks like evening news. I don't think they saw me, though. If I lose you, I'll call you right back."

Nikki was able to successfully switch the call and pull away from the curb and head for Santa Monica Boulevard. "Okay, I'm back. So, I tell Jorge he needs to go talk to the police, you know, be proactive. I take him to the police station and they end up arresting him."

"You can't blame them for that, Nikki. I mean, the evidence does point toward him. And knowing Jorge, I can imagine how cooperative he was." Jeremy had known Jorge well as a child; there had been a time, a very short time, when Nikki, Jeremy, and Jorge had called themselves The Three Musketeers. The funny thing was, Jeremy was the only one who had read the book. Nikki and Jorge had just seen the movie.

"I understand why they arrested him." She came to Santa Monica and signaled to make a left. "What I don't understand is why he doesn't want an attorney. Mother offered to pay. *His* mother offered to pay." She got a green left-turn arrow and turned onto Santa Monica.

"Why does Jorge say he doesn't want a lawyer?"

"Some nonsense about this being America, innocent until proven guilty, so on and so forth."

"Nope. I think we're all done here, sweetie."

"Jeremy, we can talk tonight."

"You think I can't multitask?"

She heard water running.

"Hands under the faucet. There you go," he said. "So what's Jorge's explanation? Where were these pruning shears that someone could get to them?"

She exhaled, not even wanting to say it out loud. "He's not sure."

"He's *not sure?*"

She heard the water turn off and Katie's voice.

"Okay, you're free. Go bug your sister." Then into the phone, "What does he mean he's not sure where they were?"

"He's pretty sure he put them in his utility truck, but he can't remember."

Jeremy was quiet for a second. "This is bad, Nik."

"I know."

"He doesn't want a lawyer. He doesn't know where the pruning shears were."

A black SUV with dark tinted windows cut in front of her. Nikki laid on the horn, afraid her little Prius was going to be absorbed by the rear bumper of the enormous vehicle. "I know," she repeated. "Which is why I have to help."

"Please tell me you're not going to get involved in another murder case, Nik. First Jessica, now—"

"Jeremy, we're talking about Jorge. Ina's Jorge. *Our* Jorge."

"Nikki."

"I can't just let the police, the DA, and the media railroad him because he's a laborer and Eddie's the son of a famous TV producer."

"Nikki."

"You know it's not supposed to work this way, but Jorge's Mexican. Eddie's a white guy. Without a lawyer—"

"Nikki," Jeremy said firmly. "Do you hear what you're saying? Did you add up the facts?"

She hit her brakes hard to prevent going through a red light on Santa Monica and Rodeo. Shoppers rushed across the crosswalk. "What do you mean? Yes, I know the facts," she said, suddenly annoyed. "That's why I have to help Jorge. That's why I need to figure out what happened."

"What if he's guilty?"

Chapter 9

"What did you say?" Nikki demanded.

"Don't get angry with *me*, Nik. I'm just playing devil's advocate."

A horn blared behind her, followed by several more. Green light. Her *bad*. She hit the gas. She hated L.A. traffic. She hated L.A. drivers. Right now, she was pretty sure she hated Jeremy. "What if he *did it?*" she repeated.

Jeremy's tone was somber. "What if Jorge's guilty? What if that's why he can't tell you what happened to the pruning shears? What if that's why he doesn't want an attorney? What if he couldn't get his temper in check and he went back later and killed Eddie? Who knows, maybe Eddie threatened him with the gun again."

"He didn't do it, Jeremy."

"You know that for sure?" He went on before she could respond. "You were there? You can account for the pruning shears' whereabouts? For every moment

of Jorge's time after the argument he had with
Eddie? Right up to the time he was murdered?"

A lump rose in her throat. "Jorge wouldn't kill
anyone. Not even Eddie."

"You and I both know what kind of temper Jorge
has. You and I also know that Eddie is an ass, and that
he's been an ass to Jorge, Jorge's entire life. Remember the time he accused Jorge of stealing his stereo
when he was twelve? He had his mother call the police on the son of the *Mexican who worked next door.* He
had the police outside your mother's gate, wanting
to question Jorge *and* Ina, only to find out later that
Eddie had sold the stereo to get money for pot."

"Jorge didn't kill Eddie," Nikki said in a small
voice.

"I'm not saying he did," Jeremy told her gently.
"I'm *saying* you need to consider the possibility, in
light of Jorge's behavior."

She cruised through another intersection. It was a
beautiful, sunny day in Southern California, but suddenly it seemed dark. Jeremy was right. She *did* need
to consider the possibility. She just didn't want to. "I
understand what you're saying."

"Aw, Nik." He was quiet for a second. "Why don't
you come over for a sleepover? We'll talk about it."

"I thought we weren't doing sleepovers. It'll just
confuse the kids."

"I think you're more worried about it confusing
you," he teased. "So come over after they go to bed.
Or . . . come now. Why don't you come now? I'm
making some kind of cheesy noodle-bake thing for
dinner. I got the recipe from a women's magazine in
my waiting room."

She didn't know how he did it, but she was smiling again. "The boys are at Mother's."

"Let Amondo take care of them. He loves those dogs as much as you do; he just won't admit it. Or go get them and bring them over for cheesy noodle-bake, too. They can play in the backyard with the kids. You know they've been begging me for a dog."

She hesitated. She felt as if she needed to go home. Maybe go home to Mother's and sit around in sweatpants and mope. There was probably Häagen-Dazs in the freezer.

"Come on, Nik. This is part of our *new relationship* plan. Remember? Us doing things together. With the kids and without."

"Mother's asked me twice if you're coming to movie night. It's Thursday night this week," she said, stalling.

Victoria Bordeaux had started her movie night back in the days when there were no media rooms in private homes in Beverly Hills. An invitation to Victoria's movie night was highly coveted in Hollywood. Everyone who was anyone was invited, at one time or another, to Roxbury on a Thursday night. Unless dead, or seriously maimed, Nikki was expected to be there.

"She's playing *A Man for All Seasons*. You know, Mother was supposed to play Alice More in the film. Then she had some sort of conflict and Wendy Hiller ended up playing the part."

"I love *A Man for All Seasons*."

"I think Mother said Will and Jada Pinkett Smith are coming."

"Will and Jada? You're kidding me!"

"I know, Mother's pretty hip." Nikki's phone beeped. She glanced at the dash. "Speak of the devil, she's calling in."

"Talk to her. Tell her I'll get a sitter and be there Thursday night. And you come over. We want Nikki to come for dinner, don't we?" Jeremy crooned to his daughter.

"Nikki! Nikki!" Katie hollered into the phone.

"Okay. Fine. I don't need the Häagen-Dazs anyway."

"What did you say, hon?"

"Never mind. See you in a little while." Nikki hit a button on the dash and successfully hung up with Jeremy, *without* hanging up on her mother. "Hello?"

"Nicolette?"

"This is she," Nikki said. Her mother always had to confirm it was Nikki, even though obviously it was.

"For heaven's sake." Victoria sounded perturbed. "This is your mother."

Nikki chuckled to herself. "I know, Mother."

"How was Jorge?" Before Nikki could answer, Victoria went on. "You've got me on that speakerphone thing in your car, don't you? You know how I dislike that contraption. Having what I say practically broadcast. Honestly. You can tell me everything when you get home."

Nikki chose to ignore the broadcast comment. Did her mother think there was a megaphone on the hood of her Prius? The windows were closed, for heaven's sake. "Actually," she said, "I was going to Jeremy's for dinner first."

"Good. You should sleep over."

Nikki didn't say anything.

"*Anyway.* That wasn't why I was calling you. Am I still on that speakerphone? I was calling to tell you I got those tickets. They'll be delivered here, by courier, first thing in the morning. I got backstage passes, too, though why anyone would want backstage passes to see a rapper person, I don't know."

"What tickets are you talking about?" Nikki moved to the right lane, without bothering to signal, to prevent being mowed down by another enormous SUV. Possibly the same one that had tried to swallow her up a couple of blocks ago.

"The tickets you asked me for," Victoria said impatiently. For the concert tomorrow night at the Staples Center. To see *Jay-D.*"

Nikki didn't like the term *lying in wait.* But for lack of a better phrase, that's exactly what she found herself doing the next morning. *Lying in wait* for Ginny Bernard's assistant.

Nikki had both Ollie and Stan on their leashes, an envelope with the tickets tucked into her bag, which she wore cross-body style. As she lingered outside the gates of Victoria's house, she kept an eye on the street while she checked e-mails on her Berry.

Nikki really didn't feel like working today, but there was no way she could cancel her appointments. First, she had her Monday Morning Meeting (her boss was into alliteration) with the other agents, then, in the afternoon, a pop-star client and her on-again-off-again boyfriend wanted to see a house in Malibu for the second walk-through. *Promising.* Nikki also had an appointment to have a look at a house in

Holmby Hills, down the street from the Playboy Mansion, possibly going on the market. Nikki was just meeting the possible client's two assistants today, but this was the kind of legwork that brought success, long-term. Celebrity clients liked working with Nikki because their celebrity didn't faze her; she'd grown up in the limelight of a celebrity among celebrities. She knew how to be discreet. Besides, they knew Nikki would work her tush off to sell their houses.

Stanley kept tugging on his leash and Nikki looked up. He was sniffing a pile of something she couldn't identify and suspected she didn't want to. "Leave it," she warned. Oliver immediately trotted over to join his friend and check out the *forbidden fruit*.

"I said *leave it*, guys." She gave both leashes a tug. It was hard to juggle her phone and both dogs at the same time. But they weren't getting walked enough, as it was, and there was no way she had time to take them out separately.

Jeremy's sister had just started a dog sitting/walking business in the area. Nikki was beginning to think she needed to hire her a couple of days a week. Amondo was always willing to check in on the spaniels at Nikki's house when Nikki was running late getting home in the evenings, but she didn't like having to ask him to walk them in the middle of the day. Nikki often ran home to let them out midday, or if Rob or Marshall were home, they did it for her, but she really needed to come up with a better plan.

A car approached on Roxbury and Nikki glanced up. She didn't know what kind of car she was looking for, but this was a white Porsche. Probably safe to assume it was *not* Ashley; assistants weren't paid particularly well. Three BMWs, two Land Rovers, and a maintenance truck later, a small blue Toyota slowed and signaled, either turning in Victoria's driveway or the Bernards'.

Nikki spotted blond, flat-ironed hair. It was Ashley. Nikki waved. Ashley waved and drove past Nikki, turning into the Bernards' drive and stopping at the closed gates.

"Come on, guys," Nikki whispered, tugging on their leashes. She dropped her cell into her bag and hurried across to the Bernard drive, behind Ashley's car. Fortunately, Nikki was wearing a short-sleeve vintage Calvin Klein skirt suit and black boots, which made it easier to hurry. A good argument against the four-inch stilettos so many women in Beverly Hills wore. When might a girl have to run down someone's assistant, dragging two Cavies along?

"Ashley."

The young woman put her window down, which took a moment because it kept sticking and she had to put it up, then try to put it down again. And again. It gave Nikki a second to collect herself.

"Ms. Harper." Ashley smiled as the window slowly chugged downward.

"Please. Call me Nikki." She leaned in toward the window. "I'm so glad I saw you, Ashley, because I was going to give you a call."

"You were?" She didn't seem to quite believe Nikki.

"Yeah. Crazy story, but I was telling my mom about how you'd had to miss the Jay-Z concert the other night." She softened her tone. "Because of Eddie's death. And, turns out, Mother had access to some tickets." Nikki pulled the envelope out of her bag as if pulling a rabbit out of a hat. Which was exactly what Victoria had done. "For tonight."

Ashley stared at the envelope Nikki offered through the window of the car, which she had still not quite managed to get all the way down.

"*Tickets?*" Ashley said.

"To the Jay-Z concert. Oh, and there are backstage passes, too."

Ashley slowly took the envelope. "For me?" The look on her face suggested she had been offered tickets to heaven.

Stanley plopped down on the toe of Nikki's right boot. Nikki looked down at the dog, then up at the assistant again. "Yup. They're for you. I thought you and your boyfriend might need a night out. After the *weekend* you've had."

"Oh my God!" Ashley's hands were practically shaking as she opened the envelope and pulled out the tickets and passes. She looked up at Nikki. "Victoria Bordeaux got these tickets . . . for me?"

Nikki nodded with a smile. "Honestly, she gets free tickets to things all the time." Nikki chuckled. "And *honestly*, between you and me, Mother's not a big Jay-Z fan. But if you meet him"—she wrinkled her nose—"don't tell him I said that."

Ashley laughed. "Right. Oh my God." She slid the tickets carefully back into the envelope. "I can't believe this. Victoria Bordeaux . . . *Victoria Bordeaux* got me tickets to see Jay-Z in concert! And backstage passes." She practically squealed with delight.

"So . . . Ginny still wanted you to come in today, huh?" Nikki glanced at the gate, which remained closed. Fortunately, she had caught Ashley before someone at the house buzzed her in.

"Yeah." Ashley looked up, then back at Nikki. "She's got some things for me to do this morning. Personal errands, I imagine. We don't even know when the funeral's going to be, yet. Mr. Bernard would have liked for Eddie to be buried today, you know, him being Jewish and all. Mr. Bernard, not Eddie. Something about their rules." She shook her blond head. "I didn't really understand."

"So . . ." Nikki tried to, nonchalantly, slide her foot out from under Stanley, but he wasn't budging. Oliver cooperated by walking around Nikki, wrapping his leash around her ankles. "Why *isn't* the funeral today?"

"Autopsy." Ashley said the word with an audible shiver.

"An autopsy's necessary?" Nikki asked, thinking back to what she had seen in the alley Saturday morning. The pruning shears in his heart had seemed like a pretty cut-and-dried case. "Don't they know . . . what killed him?"

"I guess any murder requires an autopsy. But Ginny said the same thing. That they were idiots if they couldn't tell what he'd died from. She was on the phone Saturday giving someone *hell* about respecting religious beliefs. It was really her more than Mr. Bernard who was angry, which is interesting, because *she's* not Jewish. Mrs. Bernard is . . . the *other* Mrs. Bernard," she corrected herself. "Melinda, she is."

"Did *she* want the funeral today? Melinda?" Nikki didn't know what she was going to do with that information right now, but she had learned from Rex's murder that you never knew what would later prove to be a vital detail in an investigation. Rex March had been one of Nikki's famous clients. He'd been killed in a plane crash, only to be found dead in Nikki's business partner's bed six months later. In trying to prove Jessica's innocence, Nikki had learned a few sleuthing techniques and one had been to pay attention to details, even when the details didn't seem, at the time, to be important.

"I don't know. I just heard Ginny on the phone with someone from the county, then she was talking to Melinda and Mr. Bernard in Mr. Bernard's study. Then I had to go over to the Wilshire to get her bags." The moment the last words came out of her mouth, Ashley had a look on her face that told it all. She'd slipped up.

Nikki wrinkled her forehead. She knew she wasn't supposed to. She knew she was probably Botox-bound, but she couldn't help herself. "You had to go to the Beverly Wilshire to pick up Melinda's bags?" she asked. "What bags?" Nikki leaned closer, taking the dog, still perched on her boot, with her.

After Abe had filed for divorce, Melinda had moved into the guesthouse, refusing to get her own place. According to what their housekeeper, Pete—weird name for a fifty-year-old Jewish woman—told Ina, Melinda insisted it was important that she be near Eddie during his outpatient rehab, following an inpatient stint. That had been two or three stints back. Once Abe and Ginny were married, everyone assumed Melinda would be on her merry way. Melinda hadn't left, and Abe had refused to make her go, even when Ginny demanded it. According to Pete, according to Ina. Had Ginny finally gotten her way? Had Melinda moved out? But Melinda had been there at the party that night. And so had Ginny . . .

"You had to get her luggage?" Nikki prodded when the young woman didn't respond right away. "So, Melinda had been staying at the Beverly Wilshire?"

"Yes." Ashley shook her head. "I mean, no. I *did* go for luggage, but it was Ginny's, not Mrs. Bernard's—Melinda's," she said, cringing. "I'm probably not supposed to be telling you this." She glanced at the gate. "I should go in." She looked back at Nikki. "Thanks a lot for the tickets. I can still keep them, right? If . . . I don't tell you about Ginny being at the Wilshire?"

"Of course!" Now Nikki felt guilty. Had she crossed the line? But she wasn't doing anyone any harm, gleaning information about the Bernard household. She had no intention of telling anyone anything she heard . . . as long as she didn't have to. This was about saving Jorge, not spreading gossip. "Enjoy the concert." Nikki tapped on the car door.

The assistant gripped the steering wheel, but she didn't pull forward. "I guess it wasn't a big secret. I mean, people saw her at the Wilshire, I'm sure."

Nikki waited: one dog on her foot, a leash tied around her ankles. She couldn't go anywhere easily, anyway.

"So Ginny was moving out?" Nikki asked. "I'm so sorry to hear that."

"Not . . . really . . . moving out." Ashley made a face. "Staying at the Beverly Wilshire doesn't really count as moving out, does it?" There was a hint of disdain in her voice when she said *Beverly Wilshire*.

Nikki gave a little, silent sigh of relief. She knew that tone. Ashley was annoyed with her boss about something and she had information, information she was pretty much dying to share.

"I mean, she has money to stay at the Beverly Wilshire, but I can't have a raise? I'd make better money selling shoes on Rodeo, and the hours would be better."

Nikki waited.

Ashley went on without further invitation. "Ginny and Mr. Bernard had a bad fight last week. Last Monday . . . no, it was Tuesday. She'd just had it with Eddie. You know, Melinda had made a big fuss over him getting out of rehab. Again. They had a big family dinner the Saturday night before Eddie died. Ellen Mar made this gourmet meal. They had family and friends over. There was no alcohol allowed, not even any wine."

"Mr. Bernard and Ginny fought about the dinner?" Nikki asked.

Ashley shook her head. "Over the fact that Melinda had made a big fuss and Eddie was already using again. I guess Ginny caught him and told Mr. Bernard, but Mr. Bernard didn't do anything. Ginny told me she knew it wasn't for real the day Eddie got out of rehab. She was just hoping it *was*, you know, for Mr. Bernard's sake."

"So the argument was about . . ."

"Eddie. Same thing it's always about. Ginny said she was tired of Eddie making a mess of their lives. She hated all the bad publicity. She and Melinda both did. She said Melinda just didn't have the guts to say so to Mr. Bernard. Mrs. Bernard always got really upset seeing Eddie on the covers of the tabloids. And I guess it was all Ginny ever heard about at her charity meetings and stuff. Mrs. Bernard said it was bad for Mr. Bernard's business, and Ginny agreed and thought it was time Mr. Bernard kicked him out."

Nikki's foot was beginning to fall asleep; she was getting pins and needles in her ankle, but she didn't want to distract Ashley by trying to move the dog or unwind the leash. "So Ginny left Mr. Bernard over this?"

Ashley shrugged her skinny shoulders. "I don't think she *really* left him. She was just trying to make a point. I heard her tell Mr. Bernard the night of the fight that either Eddie had to go, or she was going. I guess Mr. Bernard called her on it because he was the one who asked his assistant, Jason, to make the hotel reservation for Ginny."

"And she actually moved out?"

"Not really. I mean, she slept there a couple of nights, but she kept coming back to the house to get stuff, to put stuff back in her closet. That's how she ended up here Friday night and found out Eddie was having that party. She was *really* pissed. But . . . what you heard me say on the phone the other night. About Ginny not caring that Eddie was dead and her killing him. It wasn't true. She was *really* upset. She felt bad for Mr. Bernard. I know what people say about her being a trophy wife and all, but I really think she loves him."

A white van pulled in behind Ashley and Nikki glanced at the side of the panel van. "*Carrie's Cleaning?*" she read to Ashley.

"Oh, shoot. I need to get inside. We called them to clean up the mess in the backyard. Melinda said she'd do it, but Mr. Bernard said that was ridiculous, for her to be cleaning up, considering the circumstances. He's been really nice to Mrs. Bernard since it happened. Ginny's been going out of her way to be nice to her, too. She's the one who had me call this cleaning company and leave a message yesterday. Guess they got it."

Nikki grabbed Oliver's leash in her left hand and drew it over her head, unwinding herself. She unceremoniously dumped Stanley off her foot and took a step back. "You'll let us know as soon as you know about the funeral, right? I know Mother will want to attend." Victoria liked to attend all the important funerals in Hollywood.

"Sure." Ashley pulled her car up a little to reach the security camera and intercom. "I've got your number." She grinned, looking back. "Please thank Ms. Bordeaux for the tickets. I still can't believe she got them for me."

"Enjoy!" Nikki waved and took another step back, watching as Ashley pushed a button, waited, then spoke into the intercom. Nikki waited until the gate opened and Ashley and the cleaning van went in to the motor court. Only after the gate had closed again did she hurry across the drive toward the open gate to her mother's driveway.

She was going to have to hurry or she was going to be late to her Monday Morning Meeting with the other agents at Windsor Real Estate. And the sooner she got out of that meeting, the sooner she could start finding out what happened the night Eddie Bernard was murdered.

Chapter 10

The fifth time Nikki's cell phone vibrated and she checked it, Mr. Downy, her boss and one of the senior partners at Windsor Real Estate, turned to her mid-presentation. "Dear, do you desperately desire to take that?"

Did he realize how ridiculous he sounded with the whole alliteration thing? He reminded her of a caricature of Roger Sterling on the TV show *Mad Men*: tall, slender, white-haired. Always with a hint of male chauvinism in his tone. A Marlboro dangling from his lip would have made the look complete. Nikki wasn't a fan.

Nikki had let each of the previous calls go to voice mail and already left the room once to check them: Jeremy, just leaving a message between appointments, telling her how much he'd enjoyed the previous night, even without a sleepover. Her mother, who called twice and left no message, except to say she *didn't want to leave a message*. And Rosalia. Nikki had tried to call Ree twice since Saturday, getting no answer, just a full mailbox. Rosalia left a message saying she hadn't been able to get ahold of Ree, either, and she would have Hector stop by Ree's place after work to check on her. Apparently no one in their family had heard from Ree since the fight with Eddie Friday night.

Nikki looked down discreetly at the phone in her lap; this call was worth taking. It was Ginny's assistant. "I apologize, Paul. A new client. Possibly a big one," she said, using her mother's technique, the stage whisper.

Downy responded appropriately with a wolfish grin. "Always cleverly clambering for clients. That's our Nikki."

Afraid she'd lose the call, she hit the CALL button as she slid out of her chair at the conference table. She smiled, nodding to several of her coworkers as she made her escape. She could see the jealousy on their faces. Right now *they'd* have chatted with Ginny's assistant to get away from Paul Downy.

"Nikki Harper," she said into the phone.

"Hey . . . um. It's Ashley. Ginny Bernard's assistant."

Nikki made a beeline for the door. "You didn't catch me at a bad time. Not at all. How can I help you?"

"Um . . . I can call back if this is a bad time."

Nikki walked out of the conference room, closing the door behind her so that Downy and the other agents couldn't hear. "No, no, Ashley, you're fine. You got me out of a boring meeting."

She walked down the hall to a small break room, which was a misnomer. This wasn't a place where a girl could take a break; it was the place she could feed, which was why Nikki generally avoided it. Basically a galley kitchen with a table, the break room's counters were covered with boxes of snack crackers, bags of chips and pretzels, and plates of cookies and cake. Nikki wondered what happened to clients sending over a good old-fashioned fruit basket once in a while. The only fruit available today was an elaborate fruit bouquet with a note that read *Thanks a Million!* with a smiley face drawn inside the letter O; the fruit was covered in chocolate.

"So what's up?" Nikki asked Ashley. She grabbed a clean, white Windsor Real Estate/90210! coffee cup off an open shelf, ignoring the enormous chocolate chunk cookie at three o'clock calling her name.

"Um, sorry, I was expecting an assistant or an answering service. This is really *your* phone number?" she asked, sounding excited and incredulous at the same time.

"I don't have an assistant," Nikki said. "This *is* really my number."

"Wow . . . okay." Ashley seemed to be trying to wrap her head around that. "I was calling about Eddie's funeral. It's tomorrow. At Mr. Bernard's temple. On Burton Way. You know it? It's at two o'clock."

Nikki rifled through a couple of boxes searching for a respectable tea bag. She just wanted plain tea, not pomegranate, not chamomile, not green leaf tutti-frutti. Just tea. It didn't have to be organic. It didn't have to be gourmet. Lipton would be just fine. She nabbed one with the familiar yellow tag. "I know just where it is. Mother and I will be there." She hit a red button on the faucet and filled her mug with boiling water. "So . . . that means the autopsy was completed?"

"I guess so," Ashley said. "I have to take clothes to the funeral home later." She sounded less than enthusiastic.

"Ginny and the Bernards are lucky to have you, Ashley." Nikki meant that sincerely. She remembered how hard it had been to take a suit to the funeral home where her father's body had been. And because his apartment in New York City had still been considered a crime scene, even days after his murder, she couldn't even get in to get his own clothing. She'd bought a suit for him at Saks and taken it to the funeral home. Armani. Her dad had always liked Armani. It still had the tags on it. A suit that would only ever be seen on a dead man.

"Someone has to do it, Ashley." Nikki dipped the tea bag in and out of the water. "The Bernards are fortunate to have you to do it. Otherwise, who would? One of his parents? Ginny? They shouldn't have to do that today." *No one should ever have to take their child's clothing to a funeral home*, she thought.

"I guess you're right. I hadn't thought about it that way. I was thinking more like—you know—that I had to take clothes somewhere for a dead guy."

"I understand." She kept dunking the tea bag, her thoughts moving from dead Eddie to locked-up Jorge. "So the cleaning crew get the backyard in order? I know it was a mess."

"All cleaned up, but we had a little *incident*."

"Did you?" Nikki grabbed a spoon from a drawer, eyed it, dropped it in the sink, and tried for another, hoping this one would be cleaner. Windsor Realtors were known for their fashion sense and high-priced properties, not their ability to wash cutlery. "What happened?"

"There was some trash over by the guesthouse and I guess one of the crew stepped into some of Mrs. Bernard's rose bushes. Those pink ones. She about had a cow; started hollering and swearing at the guy and when she realized he didn't understand English, I guess she started cussing him in Spanish."

"You're kidding?" Nikki pulled the tea bag from the mug with the spoon and wrapped the string around it to get the last drop.

"That's not usually like her, to go off on someone like that. Now, Ginny, you know how she is, *she* can cuss you."

Nikki laughed as if she understood completely, though, in truth, she'd never been the victim of one of Ginny's attacks. But she'd heard, through Ina, who heard from the Bernards' housekeeper. "Oh, I know what you mean." She tossed the tea bag into the trash can and grabbed a packet of sugar, treating herself. She usually tried to use sugar substitutes, but she really liked sugar. "So what happened? To the poor clean-up guy?"

"Mr. Bernard came out and smoothed things over. He walked Mrs. Bernard into the guesthouse and stayed awhile with her. I think Ginny was glad he handled things, but she was a little peeved that he was in there that long with her."

"Huh." Nikki added a second packet to her tea. It could turn out to be a long day; she didn't want her blood sugar to run low.

"But you know Ginny. She's always been a little jealous of Mrs. Bernard. Which I always thought was kind of weird, you know, because Ginny's the one married to him now. Mrs. Bernard ought to be the one pissed at Ginny."

"Relationships are complicated." Nikki picked up the mug, blew on her tea, and watched the surface ripple.   *Relationships . . . relationships . . . Everything was always about relationships. Maybe even murder.* "Hey, Ashley," she said suddenly. "This is going to sound like a weird question, but do you know who was at the party Friday night?"

"No, not really. I wouldn't have been caught *dead* at one of Eddie's parties." She paused. "Sorry, that was inappropriate. No pun intended." She took a breath and went on. "Ginny had given me the whole day off, so I was in Monterey with friends."

"Right. And I don't suppose it was the kind of party with a guest list."

"Definitely not," Ashley agreed. "I imagine the usual losers were there, though, like with his other parties. The gym rats, the unemployed sons and daughters of other celebrities. Probably some hookers and drug dealers. You knew Eddie. You know what kind of people he hung out with."

"Right," Nikki said, trying to wrack her brain to recall who she had seen there that night who she knew, other than the Bernards. Then suddenly—just like in the cartoons—it was as if a lightbulb went on over her head. She hadn't *known* anyone at the party, but someone had introduced himself. Right before he had Victoria Bordeaux autograph his pectoral muscle. Astro. Astro Wharton. You couldn't forget a name like that. "Hey, Ashley, do you know what gym Eddie went to?"

"Um . . . it was on North Bedford. That big one with the red sign. B. H. Fitness, I think." She hesitated. "Why?"

Nikki exhaled. Why did she want to know? Because she wanted to talk to Astro. Because she wanted to know who had been at the party. Because she wanted to know who might have wanted Eddie dead badly enough to kill him and toss him out with the garbage. Because if she could find other possible suspects, that might give Jorge a fighting chance . . . even if he wouldn't fight for himself.

"Ashley, I don't think my mother's gardener did it. I've known him since we were kids, and he's not the kind of guy who would do something like this."

"Well, I don't know him, obviously. I have no idea what did or didn't happen. Just what Ginny told me about the fight and the gardener pulling a gun on Eddie—"

"No, Ashley." She set her mug down on the counter. "It wasn't Jorge who had the gun, it was Eddie," Nikki insisted. "I know. I was there."

"Well, anyway. Did you listen to the radio this morning? They were following the gardener's transfer to the courthouse, where he was going to be officially charged, I guess. Then to prison. It's just so unfair," Ashley went on with the kind of righteousness—and innocence—only the young could possess. "Politicians want to talk about how far we've come with equality for all races and all, but it's just not true."

"The radio? What's been on the radio? You mean the news?"

"Talk radio. My boyfriend is obsessed with those stations and I give him a lift to work in the morning, so I end up having to listen to that crap."

Nikki headed down the hall, taking her tea with her, leaving the cookie, still calling her name, behind. She wanted to slip into her cubicle-size office before the meeting let out and one of her coworkers cornered her and started asking questions about the body found by Victoria's trash over the weekend.

"People are talking about how this is the case," Ashley continued, "that will finally force legislation controlling illegal aliens entering the country. Meaning Mexicans," she intoned.

"But Jorge was born here!" Nikki protested. "He's an American citizen, the same as you or me."

"That's what I mean. My boyfriend's parents are from Mexico, too, but he was born here. He's working on his MBA, he has a full-time job, he pays taxes out the ass, but he still gets attitude from people. But, like, that would matter to one of those idiots on those shows." There was a woman's voice in the background, then Ashley's tone completely changed as she said into the phone, "That's right. Two o'clock. Then you're invited to the Bernards' afterwards."

"Can't talk anymore? Got ya." Nikki walked into her office, which was only slightly larger than a federal prison cell. "I'll let you go. You and your boyfriend enjoy the show, and thank you, Ashley."

"For what?"

"I don't know." Nikki sat down at her desk, placing

the mug of tea in front of her. She glanced at her ex-partner's bare desk. "For being a nice person?"

Nikki checked the time on the dashboard as she backed the Prius into a parking space on the street, only a block from the gym. She was going to be cutting it close if she wanted to make it to her appointment in Malibu on time, but this seemed too important to put off.

"Yes!" Nikki slapped the steering wheel with delight as the car eased into the parking spot on the first try. Her mother had been giving her a hard time about not driving the Jaguar she'd given Nikki on her fortieth birthday, but who could park a Jaguar the way you could park a Prius?

She hopped out and popped the hatch. She always kept her gym bag in her car, just in case the mood struck her to hit the gym. It didn't strike her all that often . . .

At the front desk, Nikki explained to a muscle-bound chick with spiky, orange hair and a sleeve of tattoos that she was shopping for a new gym. She slyly refused to give the name of her current gym, explaining that it belonged to a friend and she *didn't wanna hate.* Five more minutes of nonsensical chitchat and she had learned that Eddie *had* been a member there, that Astro was a trainer there, and she ended up getting her one-day pass for free. After turning down a Jamba Juice date with *Gwen* at the desk (*oh, gosh, sorry, I'm in a relationship*), Nikki hurried into the locker room and was on the elliptical trainer five minutes later.

Another half hour passed and her plan was going well. Except that she'd seen no sign of Astro. (Who named their kid *Astro*? It *had* to be a stage name.) And she hadn't counted on having to actually exercise. While keeping an eye out for the pecs guy, she watched the TV as she pumped her arms and legs.

After forty minutes on the elliptical, and a game show later, she thought she was going to die. But still no sign of Astro. In twenty minutes, she'd have to close down the stakeout, pecs or no pecs, and get her not so rock hard and aching butt to Malibu.

Panting, Nikki hit the COOL DOWN button on the elliptical machine. She'd spoken to several acquaintances and two clients, one past, one present. Maybe she needed to make an effort to go to the gym more often; it might be a good place to find new clients. The clock was ticking on her Malibu appointment and she couldn't get the TV on her elliptical to change channels. She didn't think she could watch a daytime talk show, not even for Jorge.

Just as she grabbed her fluffy white towel to wipe what she was certain was a beet-red face, she spotted Astro at the front desk. He spoke to Gwen, who pointed in Nikki's direction. Nikki waved the towel.

Hunky Astro was wearing gym shorts and a tight, sleeveless tank and carrying a gym bag. He walked toward her. "Ms. Harper, what a surprise! I didn't know you were a member."

"Call me Nikki, please." She jumped off the elliptical, thankfully making a smooth landing.

"Nikki. Sure. And I guess you remembered my name." He grinned. "So crazy what happened the other night, huh? I mean, can you believe it? Sure, lots of people threatened to kill Eddie, but I can't believe someone really did it."

"Lots of people threatened to kill him?" Nikki repeated, wiping the back of her neck with the towel. "Really?"

"Oh, yeah." He dropped his gym bag between them. "Between the guys whose girls he slept with, the guys he picked fights with in bars, and the guys he owed money to . . ." He gave a wave. "It's a wonder people weren't standing in line to kill him."

Nikki knitted her brows. "So you don't think my mother's gardener did it?"

"Does Ms. Bordeaux think he did? Oh my God." His eyes grew big. "Wouldn't that be something? Poor Ms. Bordeaux. She must be so upset."

"No." Nikki frowned, preferring the previous direction of the conversation. "Mother *doesn't* think he did it. As you said, there were plenty of people who wanted him dead." She eyed the clock. "Far more than Jorge Delgado." She looked back at him. "So who *could* have done it? Who all was at the party?" she went on quickly.

"Oh, I don't know. A lot of people. You were there. Things got pretty crazy, pretty fast."

"I didn't really know anyone at Eddie's party. And I was only there for a few minutes." She took a step closer, hoping she didn't stink too badly. "You by any chance an actor, Astro?"

"Me? Nah." He grinned. "I'm a personal trainer. I could get you a good deal on a few sessions,"—he glanced at her bare arms—"if you're interested."

She resisted the temptation to check out her own perhaps less than optimum biceps. "I just thought maybe the name . . ."

"Nope. My mother named me Astro." Another guy, this one super pumped up, walked by and glanced at Nikki, then made eye contact with Astro. "Hey, Kaiser," Astro greeted.

"Hey, man." The guy kept walking. It wasn't until he passed her that she spotted a swastika tattoo on his neck.

"You seem like a person who knows a lot of people," Nikki commented.

"Him? Nah. He's not a friend."

Nikki watched Kaiser walk to an ab crunch machine. The woman on it had been there at least ten minutes. She was super fit, too. Nikki guessed she had to have done a thousand crunches by now.

"Well," Nikki said. "You do seem like a guy people like." She was totally surprised that he wasn't an actor; every nice-looking young guy in L.A. was an actor.

"Well, I *do* know a lot of people in Beverly Hills," he agreed, with obvious pride. "And I usually know what's going on. No better place to hear gossip than a gym."

"So any gossip about what happened that night?" She was still eyeing the guy with the swastika tattoo. What kind of person had a swastika *tattooed* on them? She could only imagine.

"No." Astro frowned. "Not really. Not so far, at least. I mean, most of the people there weren't really anybody; cocktail waitresses hoping to become models or actresses. People he knew from The Python

Club. Guys from here. Kaiser was there." He pointed in Kaiser's direction.

"Kaiser." She glanced at the guy again, only to find him and the woman on the ab machine watching them. "Really?" She looked back at Astro. "That his first or his last name? Kaiser?"

Astro shrugged. "I dunno. Not the kind of guy you ask, if you know what I mean. He was Eddie's . . . you know . . . *supplier*." He whispered the last word.

"*Supplier?*" she repeated.

Astro glanced at one of the big TVs on the far wall. "Steroids," he whispered, not looking at her. "At least that's what I've heard."

"Ah. So . . . Eddie did steroids?"

"A lot of people do. Not me." Turning back to her, he flexed his biceps to demonstrate. "I might not be as buff as Kaiser, but I'm a hundred percent natural. Wanna feel?" He offered his arm. "Go ahead."

She chuckled, waving her towel. "No, no, that's okay." She looked at the clock again. "Listen, I have an appointment, so I better get going. But, could I give you my card? Just in case you think of the names of anyone you know who might have been at the party that night." She lowered her voice. "Or hear any good gossip. My mother loves gossip," she added, almost shamelessly.

At the mention of Victoria, Astro perked up. "Sure. No problem. I'm just getting started on my workout, so I'll be here for a couple of hours. Just come find me when you get out of the locker room."

"Great. Be right back." Nikki hurried to the locker room, took the quickest shower she possibly could, taking care not to get her hair wet, then dressed. She threw on some lipstick and mascara and hurried out into the main gym, business card in hand.

Only to find Astro missing . . .

Nikki asked Gwen at the front desk if she'd seen him. She glanced around the room of probably two dozen people working out. Kaiser was spotting *ab girl* lifting on a bench.

"He's around here somewhere."

Nikki looked at the clock again. She *had* to get to Malibu. "I told him I would give him my card." She slid it across the counter. "But I have to run. Would you mind giving it to him when you see him?"

"No problem." She looked at it, then up at Nikki. She raised one pierced eyebrow. "Real estate, huh?"

"Yeah." Nikki headed for the door. "Didn't you hear? Astro's looking for something in Beverly Hills."

Chapter 11

Nikki was just turning off Pacific Coast Highway, onto Santa Monica, when Marshall rang her. It was almost seven o'clock; traffic was heavy, but she refused to let it get her down. "Wrap up shooting already?" Nikki asked.

"Even saw the dailies. Awesome day. Fire *and* guns." Marshall was shooting the latest James Cameron action film, which explained the fire and the firearms.

"Glad you were able to exercise your pyromaniac tendencies. I sold the house in Malibu. And probably picked up a new client today, even though I had to cancel on her because the Malibu appointment took hours."

"That's my girl! Headed home to Roxbury?"

"Yeah." Nikki groaned. "What I'd really like to do is go home to my own, quiet little house on Wetherly Drive. But, alas, it's not to be."

"Still in painting hell?"

"Dante's third ring, at least."

Marshall chuckled. "Well, if it's any consolation, sweetheart, that's all I want and it's not happening for me, either."

"Aw, what's the matter?" Someone honked a horn at Nikki, for no reason whatsoever. She ignored the woman in the red Mercedes. Everyone knew Mercedes were not supposed to be red. "Big movie star can't go to his little cottage tonight?"

"No." Marshall sounded as if he was pouting. "My publicist says there've been paparazzi in front of the Beverly Drive house for hours. Apparently, someone *leaked* information about my affair with my leading lady—"

"You're having an affair with Scarlett Johansson?" she asked with mock surprise.

"Apparently," he sighed. "Nice girl, but not my type," he added drolly. "Anyway, the paparazzi are all on stakeout, hoping to catch me taking her home tonight. So, I'm Beverly Drive bound. God, I hate that tomb of a house. Why did I let you talk me into buying it?"

"Because you told me you needed a splashy house in a splashy neighborhood." He owned a seven-bedroom neoclassic on three acres: pool, tennis courts, and guesthouse. It was all for show. He spent most of his time in the little Craftsman cottage next door to her, living a quiet life with his Rob. "You could always come out of the closet," she suggested.

"Right." He laughed without humor. "My father would probably shoot an arrow through my heart from his front porch on the reservation in Onondaga."

She smiled. Marshall and his closet was a whole

other subject, one far too complicated for a Monday evening commute. "If it's any consolation, you'll make money on the North Beverly Drive house when you sell it."

"I thought houses weren't selling."

"Yours isn't for sale right now, so it's a moot point. Listen to your publicist. Go home to your big house in the right zip code. Play nice with the media. Callie knows what she's talking about. You've been on the cover of *People* magazine twice in the last six months." She changed lanes and subjects. "So, should I call Rob, see if he wants to stop by Mother's for dinner?"

"That's sweet, but I think he's going to work late." He sighed dramatically. "No need to rush home to an empty house."

The woman in the red Mercedes changed lanes, trying to get around Nikki. Nikki zipped into the right lane, directly in front of her. "Can't your driver just bring him over later tonight, after the paparazzi have gone home?"

"Nah. Callie is getting all Nervous Nelly on me. She wants me to be super careful. We've only got another month till we wrap this film. Then the locusts will likely descend on someone else. Besides, I've got an early call tomorrow. So what else is going on with you? Hear anything from Jorge?"

Traffic suddenly dropped to a crawl on Santa Monica; no zipping to be done, even in her little car. "Um, he went for his arraignment today. I talked to Rosalia, who had talked to Ina. Half a million."

Marshall whistled. Nikki could just imagine him sitting in the back of his stretch limo, surrounded by tabloid magazines (he was a huge fan), diet soda in his hand. He wasn't a teetotaler, but he rarely drank while filming. "Wow," he said. "His mom going to put that up?"

"Apparently, Mother told her not to. Mother says bail bondsmen are crooks. Rosalia says Mother offered to pay his full bail."

"I thought he didn't want anyone's help."

"He was pretty adamant when I talked to him yesterday, but he's been moved to the California State Prison. He might change his mind."

"Can you force someone to accept bail?"

"I have no idea. But we're talking about Mother; you know how persuasive she can be."

"So anything's possible," Marshall agreed. "You ever catch up with Jorge's cousin? The one Eddie was sparring with?"

"Nope. No one has heard from her. She won't answer calls. Jorge's sister sent her husband over to her place to check on her this afternoon. Hector says her roommate says she hasn't seen her all weekend."

"Interesting. Maybe *she* killed Eddie," Marshall suggested. "The police think of that?"

"She's only five feet tall, Marshall. How would she have carried him to the alley after he was dead? He was killed elsewhere, then posed in the alley."

"How do you know that, Detective Smarty Pants?"

"No blood. No sign of a struggle. Just like with Rex. The body was moved postmortem."

"I'm just throwing ideas out there. You're the expert, not me," Marshall said good-naturedly. "I heard the funeral is tomorrow. Should I come?"

"I don't think that's necessary. It's not as if you're close to the Bernard family."

"Or Eddie," he piped in. He paused for a moment. "Okay, so out with it, my little secret P.I. What else did you do today? Who did you talk to about Eddie's murder?"

"I worked today, Marshall. I sold a six-point-five-mil house. How would I have time to—"

"Come on," he teased. "You're a lousy liar."

"Actually, I think I'm getting better at it."

"And?" Marshall asked.

"There was no lying involved . . . not today, at least," she said preemptively. "But I talked to Ginny's assistant, who says Ginny was upset that Eddie was already using—this was days before the party—and that she had given Abe an ultimatum."

"Juicy . . ."

"According to Ashley, Ginny's assistant, Ginny told Abe it was her or Eddie and it was Ginny who ended up at the Beverly Wilshire."

"Oh my God. I knew Abe had a hard time telling Eddie no, but I had no idea . . ."

"I also found out that Eddie was doing steroids . . . or at least *had* been before his last stint in rehab."

"Not that surprising."

"The interesting thing is that the guy he bought from was there at the party that night."

"Ooh! Maybe Eddie owed him money." He hesitated. "Did Eddie look to you like he'd been using steroids?"

"No, definitely not," Nikki said, thinking back to Eddie's soft, flabby body.

"So maybe he owed him money from *before* rehab and the dude came to collect?"

Traffic had begun moving again, and Nikki was

nearly to Wilshire and only blocks from home. "Sounds a little far-fetched. I don't think people are killed over owing their steroid provider money. But it's a place to start. And I talked to a guy who was at the party that night. I think he can give me names of some of the people who were there, so—"

"You're really doing this?" Marshall interrupted.

"What?"

"You know *what.* Again, Nikki?"

"It's Jorge." She groaned. "You know, you sound like Jeremy. He thinks I should mind my own business."

"Good for Jeremy. You should listen to him."

"He says I need to consider the possibility that Jorge could have done it."

"He thinks Jorge could have done it?" Marshall went back to his gossipy tone.

"No," she said firmly. "He doesn't. He just ... thinks I need to take into consideration ... the evidence."

"Meaning the pruning shears."

"Meaning the pruning shears," she repeated, turning onto Wilshire. "Speaking of pruning shears, I was wondering if you would mind if I gave Rob a call? I'd love to know what was in the autopsy report."

"Beyond the fact that Eddie was stabbed through the heart with a pair of pruning shears?" he asked dryly.

"We don't know that." She tightened her grip on the wheel. "We don't know for sure that that was what killed him."

"No, you're right. But I doubt the gardening tool in his heart was good for his health." He sighed. "I'll ask him for you. It's not his department, but you know cops. They're like a bunch of teenage girls. They all talk."

"No, no, Marshall. I don't need you to do that. I can ask him myself."

"I don't mind. Besides," he said conspiratorially, "it'll give me an excuse to call him at work." He sounded like a little kid. "I'm not supposed to call him while he's at work."

"I can do it."

"I know you can, sweetheart. Let me do it for you."

"Okay." She smiled as she turned onto Roxbury. "I'm home. Call me later if you get lonely in that big house."

"I will." He made kissing sounds over the phone.

Nikki pulled through the white wrought-iron gate and watched it close behind her, eyeing a dark van parked on the far side of the street. More ghoulish paparazzi hoping to get a snapshot of one of the Bernards? As she pulled up the circular drive in front of the white Paul Williams Georgian, Stanley and Oliver sprinted around the side of the house, crossed the drive, and raced around the massive, three-tiered marble fountain in the middle of the front lawn. No stone dolphins for Victoria, only sheer elegance.

Nikki got out of the car, slinging her bag over her shoulder. "What are you guys doing out here? I go to work and you two have the run of the place, is that it?"

The dogs barked and leaped and chased each other as Nikki leaned over to give them each a stroke down their silky backs. As she stood up, she realized she smelled a distinct aroma . . . one you didn't often smell in Beverly Hills.

Barbeque?

Nikki followed a stone path around the side of the house, into the backyard. On the terrace, she found her mother lounging in a chaise, reading a magazine. Amondo stood at a stainless-steel barbeque grill, the source of smoke and the heavenly smell.

"You have a grill?" Nikki asked.

"We do now." Victoria didn't look up from her copy of *The Economist*. On the table beside her chair were copies of *Women's Day* and *The New Yorker*. Her mother had eclectic taste. "Amondo bought it for us at one of those do-it-yourself stores. You know, where they sell lumber and such. I went with him."

Nikki could only imagine Amondo pulling up to Home Depot in the white Bentley.

"He put it together himself," Victoria went on, turning the page in her magazine.

Nikki glanced at Amondo, dressed casually in slacks and a polo—polo tucked in, of course. An Italian ex-pat, Amondo had been a member of Victoria's staff almost as long as Ina had. He was not only Victoria's chauffeur and bodyguard, but her assistant and her friend. In light of his appearance Saturday morning from Victoria's bedroom, Nikki wondered, for a brief moment, if she needed to revisit her interpretation of Amondo and Victoria's relationship. The thought passed quickly. Eddie was dead. Jorge was in prison, accused of murder. Nikki's brain could handle only so much stress.

"We'll eat shortly, *mia cara*," Amondo told Nikki, a pair of stainless-steel tongs in his hand. One thing

Amondo did *not* usually do was cook for the household. That was purely Ina's domain.

"Where's Ina?" Nikki asked.

Victoria looked over her reading glasses and took a sip from her glass. Apparently cocktail hour had begun without Nikki. "Working."

Nikki glanced over her shoulder . . . as if Ina might magically appear in the kitchen doorway. "I thought she worked here."

"There was a problem with one of Jorge's employees." Victoria sipped from her glass with great relish. "That Southern boy who works for him. The one with the unfortunate lisp."

"Harley?"

"Yes, Harley," Victoria confirmed. "Amondo, you've outdone yourself." She held up her glass. She liked her margaritas in tall, slender glasses. "This is divine."

"Limes Mr. Hefner sent over, *il mio amore*," Amondo said.

Nikki felt a little like Alice. Was there any escape from this rabbit hole? "Mother," she said firmly. "What are you talking about? Where is Ina and why is Amondo cooking dinner?"

"I'm trying to tell you, Nicolette. The boy with the lisp."

Nikki closed her eyes for a moment, then opened them. "*Harley*. Who's probably thirty."

Victoria nodded. "*Harley*. He had a fender bender with some singer, Britney something. Not the fault of the gardener, I might add"—she raised a finger—"but the Mercedes. Anyway, Ina went to settle the matter with the police and all, and then to get one of

Jorge's *other* trucks up to that Jackson girl's house."
She put her glass down and fluttered her hand. "The
one from the singing family."

"Janet Jackson?" Nikki questioned.

"I don't know who his clients are, Nicolette. Anyway, apparently this young woman was having a dinner party and it was *imperative* that her yard be
trimmed today. She seemed to have no empathy for
Jorge's situation."

"So, Jorge is in jail for Eddie's murder and Ina is
taking up the slack with his lawn care business?"
Nikki asked.

Victoria put down her magazine as if perturbed.
"That would be an accurate assessment, Nicolette.
Would you like to go upstairs and freshen up before
dinner? Amondo and I thought we would eat on the
terrace. We're having grilled fish tacos." She smiled.
"It seems that Amondo has talents of which we were
unaware."

Nikki dropped down to sit on the end of the chaise
longue. "Mother, what are we going to do about
Jorge?" Oliver and Stanley, seeming to sense Nikki's
sudden feeling of inadequacy, both parked themselves beside her. Stanley leaned against her boot
and gazed up at her with big, soulful eyes.

"I know you know that bail was set at half a million," Nikki went on. "That means the DA's office is
serious about this case. He's been charged with first
degree murder."

"I've offered an attorney. I offered to put up bail.
Jorge has refused both." Victoria folded her petite
hands, looking Nikki directly in the eye.

There was something about Victoria's gaze, even

at her age, that could still capture and hold an audience. Even an audience of one. Even her firstborn child. Nikki was still in awe of her, just as she had been as a child permitted to visit on set with her mother.

"I don't know what to do," Nikki said quietly, unable to break the spell or look away.

"Did Jorge do it?" Victoria asked very softly, her pink lips barely moving.

Nikki's eyes stung. "I don't know."

"Then find out, and respond accordingly." Victoria held Nikki's gaze a moment longer and then popped her legs over the side of the chaise and tossed her reading glasses on a table. "Shall I set the table, Amondo?"

Nikki stared at her mother, pretty certain Victoria had never set a table in her life.

"Certainly not." He waved her back onto the chaise and she didn't put up a fight.

"Guess I'll go up and change." Nikki rose.

"Excellent," Victoria said, stretching out again and reaching for her glass. "Over dinner, we'll discuss our plan for tomorrow."

"Our plan?" Nikki turned back. The dogs, hot on her heels, hit their brakes. Oliver was so close, he bumped into her. "We're going to Eddie's funeral. Then back to the Bernards' to pay our respects."

Victoria glanced at her over the rim of her frosty glass. "Which is *exactly* why we need a plan."

Chapter 12

The service at the synagogue and burial at Hillside Memorial Park were just as awful as Nikki had anticipated they would be. Abe and Melinda, dressed all in black, escorted by their daughter, who had made it home in time, looked the part of the grieving parents. Ginny, fashionably dressed in Oscar de la Renta, again was dry-eyed and looked like a third wheel. Her daughter, Lissa, did not sit with her at either of the services.

Because they were private services, only family and close friends were invited, but there were still over a hundred people present. After the burial, Amondo drove Nikki and Victoria back to Roxbury in the Bentley, and left them at the Bernards' front door. Both women were dressed in Coco Chanel black dresses, Victoria's from the previous season, Nikki's, 1950s vintage. Victoria wore her trademark white pearls. Nikki's were a delicate gray, a gift from her father for her twenty-first birthday, which had been a bit of a joke between the two of them at the time, making a slight mockery of his then-twice-divorced ex-wife. After his death, the string of pearls became one of her most prized possessions, and was no longer a mockery of her mother, but a tribute.

"You look lovely today, Nicolette," Victoria said as she led the way up to the Bernards' front door. "Appropriate, elegant, and lovely."

"Thank you." Did a daughter ever outgrow beaming under her mother's approval?

Victoria rang the doorbell and Mozart's allegro chimed. "You'd do well to wear those spiky heels more often," she said, glancing at Nikki's red-soled Christian Louboutin pumps. "They make your long legs even longer." She sighed, presenting herself to the security monitor so she'd be prepared when it came on. "I was always envious of those long legs of yours."

Nikki, surprised by her mother's confession, had no time to respond before the door opened. No video camera today; it was Ashley in the flesh, in a black dress and heels. "Ms. Bordeaux, Ms. Harper, please come in. The family is expecting you in the North Salon."

Victoria tucked her Hermès clutch (ancient, but still quite fashionable) under her arm as she strolled through the front hall. "Thank you so much. I know the way."

"Ms. Bordeaux?" Ashley called after her.

Victoria turned on her kitten heels. "Yes?"

"I just wanted to thank you for the Jay-Z tickets." The assistant clutched her hands to her heart. "The concert was amazing."

"I'm so pleased." Victoria gave her *the smile.*

Nikki hung back as her mother walked into the parlor on the right side of the main hall, opposite the parlor they'd occupied the last time they were in the house. "I'm glad you had a good time, Ashley." She glanced quickly at the young woman. "I hate to ask. You don't have to say anything if you don't want to, but . . . have you heard anything about the case against my mother's gardener?"

"Just that he'd been charged and that he was in jail. Ginny said she couldn't believe bail had been set at all, him being such a danger to society and all. But I don't know," she added quickly. "That detective, Dowbronski . . . Donbroski—"

"Dombrowski," Nikki offered. "Lieutenant Detective Dombrowski."

"Yeah, the hot cop. Looks just like Robert Redford in *Butch Cassidy and the Sundance Kid,*" Ashley said. "I'm not so sure he thinks the gardener did it. He's called a couple of times wanting to speak to Mr. Bernard or one of the Mrs. Bernards. And he was here again yesterday taking statements from all the staff. He talked to everyone, one at a time, in Mr. Bernard's study, with the door closed. Of course, the staff was off the night of the party, so I don't know what the point was. I had to answer questions, too." Ashley moved closer to Nikki. "About Ginny's house staff. And Ms. Bordeaux's," she added in a whisper.

"Detective Dombrowski asked you questions about my mother's staff?" Nikki asked, not bothering to whisper. "How could you answer questions about her staff? You don't know her staff."

"But how would I know that unless I asked?" a male voice questioned.

Nikki looked up to see Detective Dombrowski walking toward them, a plate of canapés in his hand.

"Sorry," Ashley mumbled. "I didn't get a chance to tell you that he asked Mr. Bernard if he could come back to the house after the funeral." She gave Nikki a sheepish look. "I need to check on things in the kitchen. Ginny didn't like Ms. Mar's salmon."

Nikki turned to the detective, offering her hand. If she was caught, she was caught. She might as well make the best of it. "Lieutenant Detective Dombrowski. Nice to see you again."

He smiled, shaking her hand, holding it just a second longer than necessary. "And you as well . . . though, obviously I wish it wasn't under these circumstances."

She fingered her black clutch; it was a no-name found in a little vintage shop in Santa Monica, but it had character. Surprisingly enough, so did this cop. "This typical, Lieutenant Detective? Attending victims' funerals, undercover?"

"Not exactly undercover. I asked Mr. Bernard's permission to be here and I'm wearing my badge." With his free hand, he opened his suit jacket to reveal the gold shield on his shirt pocket.

Again, he was wearing a nice suit; it didn't scream cop salary. It suggested . . . family money? A wealthy wife? She glanced at his left hand. No wedding ring. No white band of skin suggesting he'd worn one recently. But a lot of men didn't wear rings. Her guess, though, was that he was single. He wasn't being overt about it, but, like Saturday morning, he seemed to be cautiously interested in her.

"You, on the other hand," the detective went on, "you could possibly be undercover. The mourning attire, the innocent look on your face."

She frowned. "I have no idea what you're talking about, Lieutenant Detective Dombrowski."

"I think you better call me Tom." He popped a salmon canapé into his mouth. "I know some people at the Hollywood station. There was talk last fall about you being involved in the Rex March case."

"Involved?" Nikki arched an eyebrow, imitating one of her mother's best looks on film.

Finishing his plate, he balled the napkin up and placed it on top. "Sticking your nose in police business."

She chuckled. "You're friends with Detective Lutz from the Hollywood station?"

"I wouldn't call us friends."

Dombrowski's tone suggested he didn't care for Detective Lutz; Nikki hadn't, either. She was intrigued now. "So what did your non-friend say about me?"

"That you were a pain in the ass . . . and pretty clever. He told me you solved the crime before he did."

Her smile was genuine. "Did he really?"

"You're not sticking your nose in *my* police business, are you, Ms. Harper?"

She studied his handsome face, not sure now if he was trying to flirt with her or intimidate her. "I think you better call me Nikki."

He glanced away, chuckling, then looked back at

her. "Look, *Nikki*, I'm not going to give you any information about this case, and I'd really prefer you stay away from my possible witnesses . . . and/or suspects, but I *will* tell you—"

"Yes?"

"Rest assured, I intend to give Mr. Delgado a fair shake." He held her gaze with his Redford blue eyes. "No matter what the media is saying."

"I appreciate that, Tom." Nikki took his plate and walked past him.

He turned to watch her go. "Where are you going with my plate?" He was really good-looking, even when frowning.

"To the kitchen."

"The kitchen?"

She glanced over her shoulder. "Everyone knows, *Tom*, you have questions in Beverly Hills? You go to the kitchen."

Nikki then turned on her Christian Louboutins and walked away.

The Bernards' kitchen was busier than LAX the Wednesday before Thanksgiving. Waitstaff was coming and going with trays of food and drinks. Ashley was pacing, talking on her cell phone, another cell phone ringing in her hand. A young man, who Nikki guessed was Abe's assistant, Jason, was also on the phone, pacing in the opposite direction.

Ellen Mar was at the massive, stone-hooded range, sautéing shrimp with one hand while opening a broiler to check on bacon-wrapped scallops with the other.

Nikki carried the detective's plate to the sink, resisting her urge to rinse it off and place it in one of the two dishwashers. While she had been raised with staff in the kitchen and the house, nannies, and drivers, Victoria had insisted her daughter learn to be self-sufficient. As a teen, while Nikki's friends were sending their jeans out to be laundered, she was home using the washing machine. She could also cook her own meals. Not that Victoria knew a thing about cooking, but she had made sure that Ina had taught her daughter the basics.

"Ellen, good to see you," Nikki greeted.

Ellen smiled, then frowned when she saw Nikki placing the plate in the sink. "I'm sorry, someone should have gotten that for you. It wasn't necessary for you to bring it to the kitchen. Antonio! Could you please get in there and pick up the guests' glasses and plates? I'm paying you to serve, not flirt."

A young man in a black dinner jacket and dreadlocks, who had been talking to a young Asian woman, grabbed a tray off the counter and took off.

"No, no, it's okay," Nikki insisted. "I just—I was on my way to the kitchen. I thought you might be here. I heard you were making some sort of amazing salmon hors d'oeuvre." She hesitated. "And I was avoiding the salon," she confessed.

"Funerals are hard." Ellen grabbed a second pair of tongs and turned the shrimp in garlic and butter sauce with both hands.

"They are," Nikki agreed, casting a glance in Ashley's direction. The assistant walked into the hall, still on the phone.

Emily Bernard passed Ashley and entered the

kitchen: long, blond hair (extensions), black skirt and tunic, and now-obvious baby bump. Nikki must not have noticed it at the funeral because of the black swing jacket she'd been wearing.

Emily looked up from her cell phone. "Hey, Nik." Her dark eyes were lined, top and bottom, in black eye pencil, making her look more like she'd just attended a rock concert than her brother's funeral.

"Hey, Em." Nikki gave her a hug. "Glad you made it back in time for the funeral. Your mom was afraid you weren't going to be able to get home in time."

Emily frowned. Flesh-colored lipstick. "More like she was afraid I wasn't coming at all." She punched a couple of keys on her phone and set it on the counter, next to a bottle of wine and a half-empty glass. "I made Tag pay for a private flight back from Tokyo. No way I was flying commercial carrying this basketball." She ran her hand over her belly, which really wasn't all that big.

So the tabloids were right. Marshall had told Nikki weeks ago that he'd read that Emily Bernard was knocked up by her rock-star on-again, off-again boyfriend, who was more off than on. Tag Thomas MacGee wasn't exactly a rock star. His band, A Lead Balloon, was a Led Zeppelin cover band. They got few bookings in the United States, but they were big in Japan.

Nikki tried not to make it obvious that she was taking in the baby belly. No one in the Bernard household had said a word about Emily's pregnancy either before or after Eddie's murder; Nikki had assumed it was the usual tabloid nonsense. Maybe no one in the family had known. Emily had been gone for at least three months, traveling with the band. At thirty-two, she'd spent almost as many years globe-trotting with various lead singers as she'd lived with her parents. Emily had always been a bit of a free spirit.

Abe's assistant, operating double BlackBerries, wandered out of the kitchen, leaving Nikki and Emily with a little more privacy.

"I know your mother is glad you're here," Nikki said. "I hope you can stay a few weeks. She's going to need you when the shock of this wears off and she has to go back to day-to-day living."

"I don't know if I'm staying *here*. This place had bad vibes *before* Eddie got himself murdered." She picked up a wineglass off the counter and took a sip. She didn't seem all that upset that her brother was dead. "All I know is that I'm not going back to Tokyo. Tag and I broke up."

"Did you?"

Emily rolled her eyes and took another sip. "Tag doesn't know it yet, but he'll figure it out." She gave her belly another rub. "This little rug rat will be better off fatherless than with a loser like Tag MacGee." She finished off the wine, and reached for the open bottle on the counter.

Nikki caught Ellen's eye across the massive granite counter. Nikki had to look away to keep her thoughts to herself. She didn't know a lot about pregnancy, but she didn't think Emily should be drinking *multiple* glasses of wine.

"So it's really something, huh? Jorge killing Eddie?" Emily said as if talking about the weather. "I always liked Jorge. He was nice to me when I was a kid." She started on the fresh glass of wine. "Nicer than Eddie ever was."

The guy with the dreadlocks returned with a tray full of dirty plates and began to stack them in the granite sink, making a racket. Nikki slid over a little closer to Emily, a little farther from the dish action. "Jorge was charged. That doesn't mean he did it."

"From what Momsy says, sounds to me like he did it." She made a sound of derision. "Stabbed him through the heart with a pair of pruning shears. Sounds to me like Jorge finally had enough of Eddie's crap. It's really amazing someone didn't do it sooner."

"Emily." Nikki glanced away, then back at her. "It's unkind to speak that way of the dead. Eddie was your brother."

"Like he ever acted like it." She swirled the wine in her glass, then glanced slyly at Nikki. "It's too obvious, though, isn't it? The gardener's pruning shears sticking out of Eddie's black heart? It was a setup."

"You think?" Nikki asked.

"For sure." Emily lifted a coal black eyebrow. "What I want to know is if the police are taking a look at my stepsister."

Chapter 13

It was a good thing it wasn't Nikki drinking the wine, because she would have choked. "Your sister?"

"*Step*sister," Emily corrected. She spun around. "Can I help you?" she asked sharply.

Nikki looked over Emily's shoulder to see Ashley standing there, looking at them. Nikki had been so intent on what Emily was saying that she hadn't seen Ashley return to the kitchen.

"What's your name again?" Emily asked Ashley.

"A . . . Ashley." She had a cell phone in each hand in a death grip.

Emily could be a pretty scary woman, with or without the black eyeliner.

"Ashley Carter," Ashley whispered.

"Well, *Ashley Carter*, I'm not sure why my father pays for my stepmother to have an *assistant*, since she doesn't work, but it's not to listen in on family conversations." Emily fluttered her fingers. Her fingernails were painted blue and black . . . alternately. One black nail. One blue nail. "So be gone!"

Ashley muttered something that sounded like an apology and ducked out of the kitchen, almost colliding with Abe's assistant.

Feeling badly for Ashley, but not sure there was anything she could do, Nikki returned her attention to Emily. "What makes you say the police should be looking at Lissa?"

Emily rolled her eyes. "I've been in Japan for three effin' months. You live next door. How is it I hear more than you do?"

Nikki's phone vibrated in her handbag, tucked under her arm. She ignored it. "You know me, Em. I never know what's going on," Nikki joked.

"Well, I heard that big brother Eddie tried laying some romantic moves on little stepsister. Only Lissa didn't appreciate it."

"He tried to . . ." Not knowing how to put it delicately, Nikki didn't finish the sentence.

"He tried to get her into bed, plying her with drugs and alcohol, I'm sure. But she put him in his place."

"She threatened him?"

"Oh, she threatened him, all right." Emily's kohl-lined eyes grew round. "I heard she threatened to kill him in his sleep if he ever tried anything again."

"She threatened to kill him?" Nikki murmured. The twenty-year-old was petite. There was no way she could have moved Eddie's body if she *had* managed to kill him with the shears. "But it was just that, right? A threat? You don't think she really did it?"

Emily shrugged. "Maybe she told that big boy-friend of hers. Maybe *he* killed Eddie. Like, to defend her honor, or something bitchin' like that."

"Who's Lissa's boyfriend?"

"Name's Aziz. He's some oil sheik's kid."

"Last name?"

"Ferret. Farah . . . something like that."

Nikki knew the Farah name. Two years ago, Wind-sor Real Estate had sold a thirty-eight-million-dollar house to an Arab named Farah. There were rumors about the guy, about who he was and what he had done in Saudi Arabia. Not nice rumors. Scary stuff. Nikki had assumed it was just gossip. Some people saw a rich man with dark skin and a head covering from the Middle East and made the assumption he made a living torturing and killing his enemies. What if there was a thread of truth to the rumors? What kind of son would such a man have raised? "Was Aziz at the funeral? Is he here?" Nikki asked.

Emily thought for a minute. "I don't remember seeing him. But that doesn't mean he wasn't there. Me being so grief stricken at my brother's funeral and all. Hey, can I have one of those?" Emily pointed to the counter.

Nikki glanced over at Ellen, who was plating the sautéed shrimp. They smelled delicious and garlicky; under other circumstances, Nikki might have nabbed one, too.

"Certainly," Ellen said. "Let me get you a plate."

"I don't need a plate." Emily plucked a shrimp off the silver serving tray, and bit it off down to the tail. "These are delicious." Still chewing, she tossed the tail shell on the granite countertop and grabbed another shrimp off the plate.

"Ms. Harper?" Ellen gestured to the serving tray. "Would you care for a shrimp?"

Nikki knew that before Ellen had won the contest on the Food Network, she'd been working as a private chef in Beverly Hills. She could only imagine the things she had seen and heard in people's houses.

"I have toothpicks," Ellen offered, watching Emily grab another shrimp off the plate.

Nikki's phone vibrated again. "No, thanks." She dug into her bag. "Could you excuse me?"

The first missed call was from Rob. The second, minutes later, was from Marshall. She wanted to ask Emily more about whatever it was that had happened between Lissa and Eddie, but she sensed that Emily's moment of *sharing* had passed. She wasn't entirely sure she believed Emily, anyway. Growing up, Emily had been a notorious liar, and from what Nikki heard, she'd carried the trait into adulthood. "I should return this call," Nikki said apologetically.

"No problem." Emily dismissed her with a wave of a shrimp. "I need to go mingle, anyway. Otherwise, I'll hear about it from Momsy for the next decade."

Nikki walked into the breakfast room with the vaulted ceiling. Since Marshall was probably calling to ask Nikki why she hadn't picked up when Rob called, she called Rob first. It went straight to voice mail. Gazing out through the double French doors onto the stone terrace, Nikki dialed Marshall. He picked up on the first ring.

"Did you talk to Rob?" he asked excitedly.

She glanced over her shoulder. Emily was still feasting on Ellen's shrimp. Ashley was hovering in one doorway, on a phone again, Abe's assistant in another doorway. Ellen was directing waitstaff.

"It went to voice mail." Nikki opened a door and stepped out onto the terrace, which resembled a tropical island with full-size palm trees, banana trees, and giant elephant ear plants. A stone waterfall on the edge of the pool gently splashed.

"You have to call him back," he insisted. "I just talked to him. I know he's available. He must have seen Eddie's autopsy report. Of course, he wouldn't tell me a word," Marshall pouted.

"I thought you were shooting today." Nikki walked around a banana tree in a huge pot. She could smell the scent of spring roses on the warm breeze. Melinda had an amazing green thumb.

"I am. I'm in my trailer, waiting to be called. Watching TV." He sighed. *Bored. Bored.* I should have come to the funeral."

"I don't think you were invited, Marshall."

"Whatever. Call Rob back. I'm dying to hear what the news is."

She stopped in front of the guesthouse, also built in the French Regency style, with a pretty, gold-and-white front door. "Marshall, I just called him. He didn't pick up."

"You want me to call him? I can call him back."

Nikki leaned over to breathe in the scent of tiny roses growing on a trellis. "I'll call him again."

"Oh, good. Then call me!"

"I thought you were headed back to the set to shoot your next scene."

"Nikki, honey, I'm the easiest star in Hollywood to get along with: I'm never late, I always know my lines, I do what the director asks and I *don't* do the leading ladies. I think I can take a personal phone call once in a while."

She was laughing when she hung up. What was funny was that what he said was absolutely true. Marshall was the most un-starlike star she had ever met. She dialed Rob's number again. This time, he picked up.

"Sorry about that, Nik. I'm at work. I had to rough up a punk."

She sat down on a knee-high stone wall that ran down both sides of the guesthouse. "Rob, I never know when to take you seriously and when not to," she said.

"In my line of work, that can be a good thing. Okay, so Eddie Bernard's autopsy report." He hesitated. "I can't believe I snooped around like this for you."

"I'm sorry." She grimaced. "I wouldn't want you to get into trouble."

He chuckled. "I'm always pretending I'm a badass. I need to actually do something badass once in a while."

"Abe's cousin was telling me at the funeral that the autopsy hasn't been released to the family yet. How did you get a look at it?"

"You don't want to know."

"O-kay," she said.

"Okay," Rob repeated. "So before I tell you what was in the report, I have to ask, are you getting yourself involved in this case?"

"Not . . . *involved* . . . per se," she hemmed. "I just want to make sure Jorge's getting a fair shake."

"He could start by having an attorney. Marshall says Victoria offered to pay for one. No one, innocent or guilty, should try to navigate this system without an attorney."

"I tried to tell Jorge that. I'm going to see him as soon as I can. Apparently, visiting hours aren't until the weekend. I'll try to talk some sense into him. In the meantime, I'm just . . . trying to figure out what could have happened. I know the evidence looks incriminating. But I also know Jorge didn't do it."

"You're just protecting the innocent? Not getting your nose into police matters?"

"Mistakes are made, and you know it, Rob. Simple indifference on the part of the police could mean life in prison for Jorge. Or worse."

Rob was quiet for a moment. "I understand you've got problems with law enforcement because of what happened with your father." He stopped, then went on. "But I have to say, we're not all losers. I know a lot of good cops in this town. We're not all out to screw over the little guy. Some of us actually want to protect him."

"Know any bad cops?" she asked. "How about some who just don't give a damn? Then there are the ones actively on the take. You read last week's *L.A. Times*? What about that cop on the vice squad—"

"Point taken." He exhaled.

Nikki heard a door open and watched two men in black suits step from the breakfast room out onto the terrace. One nodded in her direction, but then they walked to the far side of the pool, where there were several tables. A few nights ago, Eddie's friends had been partying at those tables. She remembered the glasses, the ashtrays, all cleared away by the cleaning crew. Only the bud vases remained, with fresh roses in them.

She watched the two men. She really didn't want to share this conversation. Then she saw one of them pull a pack of cigarettes out of his jacket and offer it to the other guy. They weren't on a covert operation for Lieutenant Detective Cutie Pie; they were sneaking a smoke.

"Layman's terms," Rob said, "Eddie Bernard died because something—a sharp, pointy object—was plunged into his heart, stopping his heart from pumping blood to his brain . . . and other vital organs."

"He died from a pair of pruning shears being stuck in his chest?" she said, getting up to pace.

"The heart was severely damaged; it was the only conclusion the coroner could make. There was some blood around the heart and in the chest cavity, which the coroner questioned, but there was no conclusive explanation, from what I could tell."

"The coroner was sure the pruning shears were what killed him?"

"I think that was pretty obvious. The shears were in his heart."

"They find fingerprints on them?" She walked along the side of the guesthouse, toward a little shed behind it.

"Multiple sets. At least five, maybe six. This was a busy pair of shears. The only prints that could be identified, though, were Jorge's, and a Hector Alvarez. You can only identify prints already on file, obviously."

"Hector works for Jorge," Nikki said. "It would make sense that his fingerprints would be on them."

"Right. He had a gang-related arrest years ago. He was questioned this morning by a Lieutenant Detective Down . . . Dow— Wait a minute, I wrote it down. He's out of Beverly Hills."

"Dombrowski," she said.

"That's him. He also interviewed another guy . . ." He paused. She imagined he was reading notes. "A Wesley Butterfield."

Butterfield . . . Butterfield. The name sounded vaguely familiar. "Were his prints on the shears?"

"Nope. Not sure why he was called in. Just know that he was. In fact, he was questioned that Saturday morning."

"He was at the Bernards' Saturday morning?"

"I guess. *Then* he was brought into the police station Monday."

Nikki's thoughts were flying in multiple directions at once. Who was this Wesley Butterfield and why was he still at the Bernards' the morning following the party? She needed to talk to Hector. And she still needed to talk to Ree. If she could find her. And why hadn't her buddy Astro called her? She'd thought he would have taken advantage of her leaving her card. She tried to focus.

"Time of death?" she asked.

"Between one and four A.M."

So had Eddie been killed while the party was going on, or after his *guests* went home? Nikki didn't know what time the party had broken up, but she'd find out. "Did you get to see the tox screen, by any chance?" she asked Rob.

"He was high. Big surprise. Marijuana, cocaine, some serious cocktail of downers and something called Anavar. It's an anabolic—"

"Wait, let me guess," she interrupted. Reaching the shed, she turned and headed back toward the pool. "Steroid."

"How do you know about steroids?" Rob asked.

She ignored the question. "You said Eddie was high. How high?"

"That, I don't know. These were just preliminary lab results. We don't even know everything he was on. Those were just the highlights. The full report hasn't been written because all the results aren't back. Some lab tests take days, some weeks. And I only got a quick look-see at the prelim."

"So cause of death hasn't actually been determined?"

"You mean, did he overdose and die and then someone plunged a gardening tool into his chest afterwards? No, Nikki. This is definitely a homicide. The drugs might have eased his passing, but he was murdered."

"Right." As much as Nikki hated to think about the logistics of it, she wondered if it had been a surprise attack. It would have had to have been, wouldn't it? Otherwise, he would have fought his attacker. "There were no defensive wounds, were there?" she asked.

"Nope."

Had he passed out before he was murdered? Had the cocaine and downers together rendered him unconscious? It would certainly be easier to kill a man with a pair of gar-

dening shears if he was unconscious. Nikki heard male voices in the background.

"Sure, no problem," Rob said to someone. Then to Nikki, "I gotta go."

"I appreciate this, Rob."

"You appreciate what? Who's Rob?" The male voice that came from behind her scared the bejeezus out of her.

Nikki swung around as she disconnected. She knew that voice. How good a detective could she be if she let the same man sneak up on her *twice* in an hour's time? "My boyfriend," she said. *That was quick,* she thought. *And good on the fly.*

"And you were thanking him for . . ." The detective waited.

Nikki smiled up at him. "Oh, Tom, it would be unladylike for me to say."

Tom Dombrowski smiled. "You're good." He pointed at her.

"Thank you." She smiled back. "Now, if you'll excuse me, I should probably go back inside and offer my condolences."

Nikki didn't make it beyond the kitchen. As she stepped into the breakfast room, she heard a voice she knew entirely too well.

"Now that you're a big star, do you still hire out?" Victoria was saying. "My housekeeper's always done our cooking, or we bring a caterer in, but it might be nice to have a private chef for one of my movie nights."

"I'm not exactly a big star," Ellen said as Nikki entered the kitchen. She caught Nikki's eye, her blue eyes twinkling with amusement. "So the answer to your question is that I *do* hire out for special occasions and that I'd love to come cook for you and your guests some night."

"Do you hear that, Nicolette?" Victoria stood at the granite island, looking perfectly at home in her Coco Chanel dress, in her neighbors' kitchen. "Ellen would love to prepare something amazing for one of my movie nights." She looked back at Ellen. "But I'd prefer real food, appetizers that look as they should." She pursed her lips. "No cream puffs in the shape of meatballs or anything on that note."

Ellen chuckled. "I can make whatever you like, Ms. Bordeaux." She left a tray of mushroom caps she was stuffing with crab imperial and reached into a black canvas bag on the far counter. "Here's my card. You can have your assistant call me."

"Oh, I don't have an assistant, dear. What would a retired woman my age do with an assistant?" Victoria accepted the card and held it in the air. "Look, Nicolette, I have Ellen's card. Now you can give her a ring and ask her to lunch."

Chapter 14

Ellen cut her eyes at Nikki as she returned to stuffing the mushroom caps.

"Mother, I don't need you to help me make play dates."

"Don't be ridiculous. Ellen is a nice young woman and she's new to L.A. She'd probably enjoy having lunch with you, maybe making a new friend. Frankly, Nicolette, you could use some nice friends."

Nikki could tell that Ellen was struggling not to laugh. Nikki *did* like Ellen. And she was liking her better by the minute.

Victoria waved the business card as she walked away. "Ellen's mother would probably appreciate it if you asked her daughter to lunch. I'll keep this card for you, dear, and give it to you later." She walked out of the kitchen.

Nikki just stood there for a minute. She and Ellen were alone in the room. Finally, she just said, "I don't know what to say. I'm beyond embarrassed. I'd like to apologize, giving the excuse of poor judgment in a time of bereavement, but the fact is, *this*"—she waved her hand in the direction Victoria had gone—"is my mother on her *good* behavior."

Ellen grinned as she added a bit of curly parsley to the tray of mushroom caps. "I think she's a hoot. She and my mother could be identical twins . . . separated at birth. Except that my mother was born in Nairobi and is black." She looked at Nikki across the counter, smiling. "The truth is, she's right. I don't know many people in L.A. and most I do know, I wouldn't have lunch with if I could help it. So . . . how about lunch?"

It was funny; the older Nikki got, the smaller her circle of friends seemed to become. It was just that, as the years passed, it was harder to make the effort. Maybe harder to trust people. She did need to get out more, make new friends. Wasn't it natural to just hate it when your mother was right? "I'd love to have lunch with you. Tomorrow?"

"Perfect. I heard Villa Blanca has changed up their menu. I've been dying to try it."

"One o'clock?" Nikki asked, turning one ear toward the doorway. She thought she heard Lissa's voice. A phone conversation.

"Sounds good." Ellen glanced toward the front of the house. "I brought six servers with me. You'd think one of them would wander this way, at some point."

Nikki glanced at the tray of delicious-looking crab imperial–stuffed mushroom caps. "Want me to take them in?"

"Don't be silly." Ellen grabbed a pile of white napkins. "If Ms. Bernard saw one of her guests serving food, she'd have a seizure. Mrs. Ginny Bernard, that is. Melinda's a sweetheart."

"You don't get along with Ginny?" Nikki asked. "I just assumed because you and Abe are friends . . ."

"Ginny's . . . shall I say . . . territorial?"

"With?"

"I'm sorry." Ellen picked up the tray of mushroom caps. "I'm being catty and it's wrong of me. Ginny is Abe's wife and Abe's been too good to me for me to talk about her." She offered the silver tray. "Would you like to try one?" She held out the napkins.

Nikki couldn't resist. "Thanks. See you tomorrow, one o'clock. I'll make a reservation."

The crab-stuffed mushroom was incredible. Nikki waited until Ellen was gone, and then headed out of the kitchen, in the direction of Lissa's voice.

She found the twenty-year-old standing in her stepfather's study, on her cell phone. Nikki had only met Lissa a couple of times, and then just to say hello. The young woman had been at boarding school when Abe and Ginny had married. A year ago, she'd moved in with Abe and Ginny . . . and Melinda and Eddie. Nikki heard she was going to UCLA.

Lissa looked up.

Nikki nodded and pretended to be looking at Abe's half a dozen Emmys on a shelf in the study. She scarfed down the rest of the amazing appetizer.

"So . . . I'll see you later?" Lissa said into her phone. She paused. Giggled. "Me, too."

"Pretty impressive." Nikki crumpled her napkin and nodded toward the Emmys.

Lissa glanced over her shoulder. She was wearing a very short, very tight, black knit dress and black, short boots with four-inch spike heels. She shrugged, looking back at Nikki. "I guess. I don't really watch his shows."

Nikki took a step toward her. "I'm really sorry about your brother."

"*Step*brother," she corrected. Again, a shrug. "It's not like we were *close*." She met Nikki's gaze, lowering her voice. "Let's face it, we both know what a shit he was. He hadn't been out of rehab a week and he was doing coke again?"

"I still wouldn't wish that on anyone," Nikki said carefully. "Being murdered, his body dumped like that."

Lissa cut her eyes at Nikki. "Yeah, I know everyone's going on about that gardener doing it, but you and I both know it was only a matter of time before *someone* did it." She held out her hand, checking her manicure. "I mean, it's pretty bad when your own family members are threatening to kill you."

"One of his family members threatened to kill him?" Nikki said. *Was she going to get a confession out of Lissa? Was it really going to be that easy?*

"His mother," Lissa whispered.

Wow. Nikki hadn't seen that coming. It took her a second to regroup and reply. "Melinda threatened to *kill* Eddie?"

"Every time he got out of rehab." She pointed a finger. "*You do drugs again, Eddie, and your mama's gonna kill you*," she mocked. She went back to talking in her own two-pack-a-day sultry voice. "No, seriously. The police might have that gardener locked up, but any number of people *could* have done it. The gardener was just the easiest to pin it on. And have you seen the TV and papers? The press is *loving* it." She looked up at Nikki, lowering her voice to sound conspiratorial. "*Personally*, I was suspicious of the pool boy when I heard."

"The pool boy?" Nikki echoed.

Again, the shrug. "Think about it. He had total access to our shed where all that gardening crap is kept. Maybe he walked in, grabbed a pair of those scissors, and stabbed him in the heart." She demonstrated an overhead stab with an invisible weapon.

Either Lissa didn't hear or didn't understand that the shears had belonged to Jorge. But what she had to say was certainly intriguing. "Why would you be suspicious of . . . the pool boy?" Nikki asked.

Lissa looked up the hall toward the sounds of the gathering. She waved Nikki into Abe's study. Nikki stepped in, tossing her napkin in a leather trash can behind Abe's enormous cherry desk. Lissa went on, no encouragement necessary.

"Didn't you hear? The fight with the gardener wasn't even Eddie's *first* of the night. Rocko, the pool boy, crashed the party and he and Eddie got into it big-time."

Rocko . . . Rocko, the pool boy. Wasn't Victoria's pool boy named Rocko? Surely there couldn't be two Rockos who serviced pools in Beverly Hills? "What were they fighting about?" Nikki asked.

Lissa shrugged. "I don't know. Some ongoing thing. Aziz said he heard that Eddie and Rocko got into a fight at The Python Club months ago, before

Eddie went into rehab this last time, and Eddie still had a beef with Rocko." She thought for a moment. "Or maybe Rocko had a problem with Eddie. Who knows?"

"The Python Club," Nikki repeated. The Python Club was a den-of-iniquity type of bar on Sunset, well known for its hip celebrity crowd and the drugs that flowed freely there. A decade ago, a promising young actor had died of an overdose in the men's bathroom, shutting the place down for weeks. Supposedly, the owners had cleaned up their act before reopening, but Nikki heard rumors and The Python Club still, periodically, made the papers with scandals and arrests involving drugs and sex.

"That's really . . . crazy," Nikki said, not sure what else to say. Or ask. If they were talking about the same Rocko, he was definitely big enough to have moved Eddie's body after he was dead. But how had he gotten the pruning shears? *When* did he get them? Nikki saw Jorge with them around four. The fight had been around five, because Nikki remembered telling Jorge when they got back to Victoria's that it was time to quit for the day and go home.

"You know when Rocko and Eddie had this fight the day of the party?"

"No, but it was early. People were just getting here. There were girls laying out by the pool. I saw them from my window. I was getting dressed to meet Aziz."

"But it was before Eddie had the fight with Jorge?"

"Definitely. I left around four, so it was before that." Lissa's phone rang and she checked the screen. Smiled. "Hey," she said into her phone. She turned and walked away from Nikki, out into the hallway. "I *said* I'd see you later." Her laugh was deep and throaty and so . . . *young.*

Boyfriend again, Nikki thought as she walked out of the study, giving Lissa a wave as she went in the opposite direction. It was time she joined the other guests, anyway, and made her condolences.

After that, she thought she might go for a ride. Ree's cell phone was still going straight to voice mail. Nikki had questions for Ree. Like exactly what was her relationship with Eddie? Were they boyfriend and girlfriend? Dating? It was time she paid her a visit.

"*No sé,*" said the young Mexican woman who answered the apartment door after Nikki knocked, then beat on it. *Politely.* "She not here." She was wearing a waitress's apron that was stained with food and grease. Her English was pretty good, but heavily accented. She glanced over Nikki's shoulder suspiciously.

The hall smelled of fried food, rodents, and . . . desperation. Ree lived in one of the many apartment buildings in South L.A. that should have been condemned years ago . . . along with the owners. Nikki didn't know what the solution to illegal immigration was, but this wasn't it.

"*No entiendo por qué* . . . why people keep coming here and coming here, asking." She looked at Nikki closely. She was a pretty girl. Probably midtwenties. But she looked as if she had already led a hard life. "You're not the *policia?*"

"No. I'm a friend of Jorge Delgado's. Ree's his cousin. I'm sure you know Jorge's been arrested for killing a man in Beverly Hills. I don't think he did it. I know he didn't. Ree's not in trouble, but I need to talk to her. She might be able to help me help Jorge." Nikki frowned and glanced down at the young woman, who couldn't have been much taller than five feet. She wondered who had been here ahead of her, asking questions about Ree. "Have the police been here?"

She rested her hand on the doorknob. "Tall *hombre.* Gringo. Nice suit." She brushed her hand over her stained white blouse. "We don't answer the door."

Had to be Dombrowski. He really *was* investigating the murder. "Have you seen Ree?"

"No. No, since *sábado.* Hector came. Ree, she went with him." She motioned with her hand. "Since this time, we do not see her."

"Wait. Hector was here and Ree left with him on Saturday?" That didn't make any sense. Rosalia told Nikki that Hector had looked for Ree Monday and hadn't been able to find her. That no one had heard from her since *Friday.* "She went with him? When?"

The young woman thought for a moment. "My dinner," she said. "It *es* cooking." She started to back into the apartment and close the door.

"Please," Nikki begged. "I swear. I'm not trying to get Ree into any trouble. I'm trying to help Jorge."

The woman hesitated. "He came here *sábado* . . . Saturday. It was morning. I never liked him. Hector. He has *una cara fea*—ugly face," she said with distaste.

But it didn't sound like it was Hector's face that offended her. Nikki suddenly got a weird feeling. "Has Hector been here before?" Ree was Rosalia's cousin . . . not Hector's. "Alone?"

"We told her it was *muy malo*. Bad. An *hombre* with a wife."

Hector and Ree? So had she been *dating* both men, Hector and Eddie? "Hector came here and then she left with him?"

"*Sí, en* his noisy red car."

Saturday morning, Nikki thought. While his brother-in-law was on his way to the police station to turn himself in for a murder he didn't commit, and while his pregnant wife was lying in her bed, crying, Hector came for his girlfriend . . . and took her somewhere? "Did she say where she was going?" Nikki asked. "When she left with Hector?"

The girl shook her head. "No. But she took a bag. *Y* clothes. And her cell *teléfono,* she leave it here . . ."

Chapter 15

When Nikki walked into the kitchen the next morning, she heard voices on the terrace: her mother's and . . . *Melinda Bernard's?* She glanced at the clock on the kitchen wall as the dogs trotted out the French doors. It was seven thirty-five.

What on earth was Melinda doing here at seven thirty in the morning? The day after her son's funeral?

Nikki had a feeling she needed to fortify herself with caffeine before going to find out. She was pouring herself a cup of coffee from the French press on the counter when Ina walked in. Ina was wearing jeans and a JORGE & SON T-shirt. Nikki had never seen Ina in a pair of jeans, not in all the years she had worked for Victoria.

"Bagels on the counter. Fruit salad in the refrigerator," Ina said, carrying an armful of clean kitchen towels. She moved with businesslike efficiency.

"I'm trying to find out what happened that night

at Eddie's party," Nikki said quietly, not wanting her voice to carry out onto the terrace. "I think I might have a few leads. Jorge wasn't the only person Eddie had an altercation with that night. And Eddie did do drugs that day."

"And this comes as a surprise to who?" Ina asked.

Nikki glanced in the direction of the open French doors, then back at Ina. "Melinda Bernard is outside talking to Mother," she whispered.

"I know," Ina said, speaking at a normal volume . . . maybe even a little louder than usual. "I let her in when she rang the front doorbell. At *seven fifteen* in the morning." She crossed the kitchen. "Mrs. Bernard, she knows how hard it is to be a mother." She crossed herself with her free hand. "My son, he calls last night and says, 'Mom, I don't want you to worry about me. I'll be all right.' He says, 'Mom, I don't want you to come see me Saturday during visiting hours. I don't want you here.' " She pulled open a kitchen drawer and began to stuff towels inside. "He tells me not to worry, but how do I do that?" Ina looked at Nikki, her eyes tearing up. "How do I not worry about my only son, who the police say killed a rich man? My son, who will not defend himself."

Nikki's heart wrenched and she looked away, uncomfortable with her own emotions. But she made herself look at Ina again. Because she owed so much to Ina. Because Ina deserved it. "I want you to know I'm going to figure this out, Ina. I'm going to find out who killed Eddie and then the authorities will have to release Jorge."

Ina closed the drawer and crossed the kitchen. "You're a good girl, Nikki. You were always a good girl." She took her car keys from a wooden bowl on the counter near the door. "There's salad in the refrigerator and my chicken chili in the Crock-Pot for your dinner. I'll be back tomorrow to get ready for Victoria's guests."

"So you won't be here today?" Nikki asked. Not that she thought Ina didn't deserve some time off, but it was just strange not to see her here. Ina was supposed to work five days a week, flexible hours, depending on Victoria's schedule. By choice, Ina worked six days a week, sometimes seven, and was almost always there morning and evening, taking time off in the middle of the day. She had been a permanent fixture in the house for most of Nikki's life. Ina was family.

"I have to go to work." Ina opened the door.

Nikki stood there, coffee cup in hand. "You're going to mow lawns?"

"If I have to. Someone has to keep my son's business going while he sits in jail like a fool when his mother says she'll put up his bail." She headed for the door. "My lazy son-in-law should be here to mow today. Tell your mother not to worry. Her house and lawn will be immaculate for her guests for movie night tomorrow night."

Nikki watched Ina go out the door, then added cream and sugar to her coffee, took a sip, and walked out onto the terrace.

"Nicolette," Victoria called from the round patio table where she was having her breakfast. She always had breakfast on the terrace, weather permitting, and read the paper. "Join us for breakfast."

"Actually, I can't stay," Melinda said. She rose from

a white, wrought-iron chair. "I just needed to speak to Nikki." Her gaze darted to Nikki. "Privately."

Victoria raised her perfectly sculpted eyebrows. She was looking sharp this morning in khaki slacks, a pale blue sweater, and her pearls. She was dressed to go somewhere, looking put together and very pretty. Very movie star–like.

Melinda looked . . . like it was the day after her son's funeral. She was wearing jogging pants, athletic shoes, and a baggy T-shirt. Her hair was pulled back in a ponytail, but it hadn't been brushed. Her eyes were swollen, and without makeup, she looked pale and . . . old.

"Would you like to come inside?" Nikki motioned to the door, curious as to what Melinda wanted.

Victoria started to get up. "I can go inside. I've nearly finished the paper, anyway."

"No, no, please, Victoria." Melinda held up her hand. "I don't want to be a bother." She glanced at Nikki. "I should get home. Abe hadn't come down yet when I went for my walk, but he likes to have his coffee by the pool in the morning." Her mouth stretched tight. "Ginny tends to sleep in, letting Abe fend for himself. She's never taken the role of wife particularly seriously."

"Oh, *really?*" Victoria said, settling down in her chair again.

Melinda closed her eyes, pressing her fingers to her forehead. "That was unkind of me." She opened her eyes, letting her hand fall. "I know this has been difficult for Ginny, too. It could be that she just needs some space from the family. God knows, over the years I've felt that way at times. Abe's so driven;

he's not always an easy man to live with. It's just that I don't think he should be alone right now. He is, after all, sitting *shiva* for his son." She turned to Nikki. "Would you like to walk me home, Nikki? This will only take a minute."

"Sure." Nikki set down her coffee. She was barefoot, in sweatpants and a tee. Her hair was probably a fright, still pulled up in a topknot on her head. But she always grabbed a cup of coffee when she first woke before she jumped in the shower. She hadn't expected guests this early.

Melinda walked off the terrace, into the soft, springy grass. Nikki hustled to catch up.

Melinda waited until they were just out of sight and out of hearing distance of Victoria before she stopped. She looked up at Nikki. "I'm just going to come right to the point because, honestly, I don't have the energy for niceties today."

That didn't sound good.

"I understand your loyalty to your mother's gardener."

"He's not just the gardener, Melinda," Nikki said quietly. "This is Ina's son. He's my friend."

"And my son is dead."

Nikki met the older woman's gaze, her heart twisting. For all of them. She heard a lawn mower start up somewhere on the property.

"I understand that you only want to help Jorge, to make sure he has a fair trial," Melinda continued. "But you can't be going around stirring up rumors about my son. About my *dead* son, who can't defend himself."

Nikki froze, not sure what she was talking about.

"What that little slut, Lissa, said about my boy," Melinda said defensively. "It's not true."

Nikki wondered which part of what Lissa said wasn't true. The fact that he was still doing drugs? The fact that he made a pass at her? Or the fact that he was such a jerk that more than one person wanted him dead?

Or the part about Melinda threatening to kill him herself . . .

And who had told Melinda that Lissa had tattled? Surely not Lissa herself?

"Melinda, I'm not sure what—"

"It was a lie. All a fabrication of her imagination. Lissa was just jealous of Abe's attention to our son. Our son would never have said anything inappropriate to her. Or *done* anything," she added quickly. "And I'd appreciate it if you'd not repeat to anyone what was said." She hesitated. "Including the detective working on my son's case."

Nikki was careful not to respond in any way. She just let Melinda go on.

"Lissa's nonsense has nothing to do with my son's murder, but if it came out, it would be plastered all over the tabloids. I know very well he wasn't an angel." Her voice caught and she took a breath before she went on. "But he's dead now. Surely enough bad things that are true have been said about him. I don't think he deserves to make the front page of the tabloids again, based on lies."

"Melinda . . . please believe me when I say I had no intention of—"

Melinda held up her hand and Nikki fell silent. "I know you mean well. And I understand why you're doing what you're doing. But can't you just let the police do their job? Can't you leave me with what little dignity I have left?"

Nikki thought carefully before she spoke. She still wasn't sure how Melinda had found out that Nikki knew about the possible situation between Eddie and Lissa, but she had a feeling that Melinda wasn't aware that her own daughter had been the one to tell the tale. She took Melinda's hand in hers. It was small, and cool. Her pointy nails were opaque, with only clear polish on them.

"I would never say or do anything to intentionally hurt you, Melinda," Nikki said. "You've always been kind to me, and kind to my mother. I *was* asking questions yesterday at the funeral, but not with the intention of hurting anyone. Or . . . harming Eddie's reputation. I'm just trying to find out what happened that night. And," she added quickly, "no matter what anyone tells me, I'd never go to the press. I'd *never* do that. You know that over the years our family has suffered from things printed in the press, too. True or not."

Melinda slid her hand from Nikki's. "I just hope that when you're asking your questions, you're considering the source." She glanced in the direction of the gate between their two properties. "I should go. Abe will want his coffee." She walked away.

Nikki felt badly. She didn't want to hurt Melinda or Abe. She didn't even want to hurt Eddie, at this point. She just wanted the truth. She caught up to her. "Melinda, please call us if you need anything."

The older woman offered a quick smile. "Thank you. You've always been kind to us, Nikki. You *and* your mother. I appreciate that." She stopped at the gate. "I hope I haven't offended you. Or Victoria." She rested her hand on a wrought-iron bar. "I just feel as if I need to protect my son." She pressed her lips together and glanced away, tears in her eyes again. "I couldn't protect him from himself when he was alive. At least I can try to protect him from others, now that he's dead." She swung open the gate and walked through. "Have a good day, Nikki."

The dogs were lounging under the diving board on the pool deck when Nikki returned to the terrace. Victoria was waiting for her, her paper spread out on the table in front of her.

"Sit down, drink your coffee. And tell me what was so private that Melinda couldn't speak in front of me." She glanced in the direction of the Bernard mansion, obviously annoyed.

Nikki sank into a chair and reached for her mug, feeling like a complete jerk. She'd been so eager to learn anything and everything she could about the circumstances surrounding Eddie's murder that she'd forgotten one of the important lessons she'd learned while investigating Rex March's death: people lie. While Emily's version of Lissa's accusation was interesting, that didn't necessarily mean it was true, and it was wrong of Nikki to have automatically assumed it was.

Nikki sighed and sipped her coffee.

Victoria folded her paper noisily. "Well?"

"There was a nasty rumor going around involving Eddie and Ginny's daughter."

Victoria's eyebrows went up. "I can only imagine."

"Melinda said it wasn't true and she wanted to

make sure I didn't repeat it. She doesn't want anything like that hitting the tabloids."

"Poor Melinda. She's taken a beating all over town over that boy. Has for years. She was always sensitive to what was being said about her, or about Eddie, whether it was true or not." Victoria reached for her glass of orange juice. She liked a glass of freshly squeezed juice in the morning and Ina made sure she always got it.

Nikki took another sip of coffee, mulling over everything she'd learned the day before. She had so many directions to go in today, she wasn't sure what she should do or who she should talk to next. She wished she could talk to Jorge, but there were no visiting hours at the prison facility he'd been taken to until Saturday. She'd already gone online this morning and checked. "The guy who cleans your pool. Isn't his name Rocko?"

"Yes." Victoria sat back in her chair. "Nice young man." Then she whispered. "*Gay.*"

"Mother, that's not a dirty secret these days. You don't have to whisper it." There was a small serving bowl of fruit salad on the table. She picked a piece of fresh mango out of it. "Do you know anything about him having some ongoing argument with Eddie?"

"I know he's a nice young man. He's always polite and he keeps a very clean pool."

Nikki smiled and picked a piece of pineapple out of the bowl.

Victoria slid a small plate and fork across the table to her. Nikki ignored her and plucked another piece of fruit from the bowl. "Do you know a Wesley Butterfield?"

"I do not." She pushed the fork she'd offered closer to Nikki. "Do you think he's a suspect?"

"I wonder if the cops think so. He was interviewed. Along with Hector, whose prints were on the pruning shears. But apparently this Wesley Butterfield's prints were not."

Victoria picked up a small pad of paper and a pen. She was a great one for lists and always kept paper nearby. "I think you should start a list." She wrote across the top of the page in her beautiful penmanship: *People who wanted to kill Eddie Bernard.* She slid the pad of paper across the table. "Write it down." She offered the pen.

Nikki hesitated, then accepted the pen.

"Write down *Jorge,*" Victoria instructed.

Nikki held the pen poised over the paper.

"Write it down," Victoria repeated.

Nikki exhaled . . . and wrote down Jorge's name.

"Who else is a suspect?"

"I haven't been able to locate Ree . . . She apparently left town Saturday and hasn't been seen since. There's no way she could have physically killed him and moved his body, but I guess she could have gotten someone to do it for her." Nikki wrote her name down.

"Who else?" Victoria encouraged. "*Anyone* who might have wanted to see him dead. No matter how far-fetched. Remember in *Tell Me No Lie,* it was my beloved maid of thirty years who tried to poison me. The police never suspected." She held up her finger. "Because they didn't know that I had made her give up her illegitimate child at birth and never tell a living soul."

Nikki loved the way her mother could relate real life to the movies she'd been in. She wrote down *Wesley Butterfield.* She knew nothing about him, but why else would Dombrowski have questioned him unless he was a suspect? Then she added *Lissa.* Then *Rocko.*

"Excellent," Victoria said, looking at the list. "*Ginny.*"

"Ginny?" Nikki glanced up.

"We heard her threaten to kill him the night of the fight. Eddie was driving a wedge between her and Abe. He was a constant embarrassment. And then there's the matter of Eddie and her little girl."

Nikki cut her eyes at her mother.

Victoria raised her hands. "One never knows what goes on behind closed doors. Write down Ginny's name." She sat back in her chair, crossing her arms. "And then add my name."

Chapter 16

Nikki looked up, certain she'd misheard. "Pardon?"

"Write down *Victoria Bordeaux*," her mother instructed. "As a suspect."

"Mother—"

"I'm serious. If you're going to do this, it has to be done right. You can't become emotionally involved. You can't decide, based on your *feelings*, that Jorge didn't kill Eddie . . . or that Jorge's little cousin didn't kill him, or the wicked stepmother . . . or me. Your investigation has to be based on facts."

Nikki set her pen down. Took a sip of coffee. "But you're *not* a suspect."

"Why not?"

Nikki waited, totally perplexed, amused, and intrigued, all at the same time. She thought she knew her mother well, but Victoria was *always* unpredictable; she'd give her that. "You're not a suspect because . . . you had no reason to kill Eddie?" Nikki asked.

"You don't know that. What you *do* know"—Victoria held up her finger—"is that I once threatened to kill him."

"You did?"

"Don't you remember that time I called you in New York and told you I came home from a première to find Eddie and three naked women in *my* pool? And they were smoking *marijuana*." She whispered the word. "On my pool deck. The Bernards' pool had been drained for repairs," she added as an aside. "I told you I told Eddie Bernard to get off my property and take his little floozies with him, and if I ever caught him in my pool, uninvited, again, I'd wring his worthless neck."

"That's not exactly a death threat . . . and it *was* at least ten years ago."

"What time was Eddie killed?" Victoria asked.

"Sometime early Saturday morning, between one and four, according to the coroner's report."

"Where was I between one and four A.M. the morning of Eddie's murder?"

"Mother, this is—"

"Where was I?"

Nikki exhaled. "This is silly," she muttered. But she had little choice but to play along. "You were in bed. Asleep. Wearing that cute little black silk mask"— she drew two fingers across her eyes—"to block any light that might creep in from under the drapes."

Victoria didn't even crack a smile. "Do you have proof I was in my room?" She went on before Nikki could answer. "You don't. And I don't. None that I would be willing to reveal, at least. And I don't have any security cameras monitoring the grounds and neither do the Bernards. For all you know, I could have done it."

Nikki gave her mother a look. "*How* could you have done it?"

"When I excused myself to go to the restroom when I first returned to the terrace with Marshall after the fight at the Bernards', I could have gone in through the kitchen and out another door. While Jorge and Hector were loading their trucks and doing whatever it is they do to pack up to go, I could have taken Jorge's shears that he left in that bucket beside the house. I could have then hidden them until I had the opportunity, in the middle of the night, to slip out. I could have killed Eddie while he was immobilized by whatever alcohol and drugs he had consumed and then transported his body to the alley."

"Mother—"

Victoria threw up her hand, silencing Nikki. "I could have moved the body. I'm strong for my age and size"—she held up one finger—"and you know it." She shrugged. "Or maybe I got Amondo to help me. He'd kill for me if I asked . . . and go before a firing squad without ratting on me. Then I could have returned to bed, all in time for Ina to find the body." She opened her arms and let them fall. "So, like it or not, I'm a suspect."

What Victoria was saying was so preposterous that Nikki didn't know what to say. She would have laughed, but she could tell by the look on Victoria's face that she was serious.

"Write down my name." Victoria tapped the piece of paper.

Nikki hesitated, then wrote *Victoria Bordeaux*.

"Excellent." Victoria picked up her paper, took a sip of her orange juice, and glanced at her daughter again. "Shouldn't you be getting ready for work? Or are you taking the day off? You've got a lot of leads to follow up on today." She began to scan her newspaper. "Did you know the president of the United States is coming to California today? His helicopter lands at Stanford University at three. Isn't that interesting?"

Nikki picked up her list of suspects and her cup of coffee and headed inside. She hadn't thought about taking the day off, but maybe it would be wise. "Have a good day."

"You, too, darling." Victoria's attention remained on her paper. "Say hello to Ellen when you see her for lunch."

Nikki grabbed a second cup of coffee, then a shower, and sat down on her bed in her robe, hair piled up on top of her head in a towel, and opened her laptop. She Googled Wesley Butterfield. A little trick Marshall had taught her. He was always Googling friends, acquaintances, what have you. She got a couple of hits for Facebook and MySpace pages, but it was a prepubescent in New Jersey . . . not the right guy.

She Googled the name again, and found a *Wezley* Butterfield. In his early thirties. Resided in Los Angeles. *Bingo*. A Wikipedia page. She scanned it.

He was the son of a man named Colin Butterfield, who was the founder and leader of a large independent church in L.A. That's how Nikki knew the name! The Church of Earth and Beyond followed beliefs that involved self-improvement through various means of counseling and health practices and . . . *alien life forms.* Colin Butterfield had been a Scientologist and had broken off—or maybe been kicked out, she couldn't tell—from the group a few years ago, forming his own church. The previous year, the church had been recognized by the federal government as a religious organization and given tax-free status.

Nikki scrolled down to the middle of the page to check out a grainy photograph. The caption read *Colin and Wezley Butterfield, 2011.* She recognized the father right away. He'd been featured on the cover of a magazine recently. But the thirtysomething young man with dark, curly hair looked vaguely familiar, too.

Nikki grabbed her Cheaters off the bedside table and slid them on. She leaned closer to the computer screen, then pulled her glasses off in surprise. Wezley Butterfield was the disheveled man she'd seen in the alley Saturday morning.

Nikki Googled Wezley Butterfield, this time with a z, and on the second page of results, found a blurb from the *L.A. Times* from the year before. He'd been arrested for a D.U.I. . . . and for possession of cocaine—Eddie's favorite party drug—with the intent to sell. Was that why the police had questioned Wezley multiple times? Obviously, he must have been at Eddie's party. How else would he have ended up in the alley that morning, looking the way he had? Did they suspect he provided the cocaine Eddie used the night he was killed? Or had he just been *with* Eddie that night? Could he account for Eddie's final hours?

Nikki closed her laptop and went to her window. Before she left for work, she wanted to speak to Hector, but she hadn't heard the mower in a while. She couldn't see him from her window. He must have gone.

She got dressed, thinking her mother was right; there was no way she'd have time to work today. She'd take a personal day. Her first stop would be Astro's gym. She was curious as to why he hadn't contacted her. He'd seemed like such a fan of Victoria's that she thought for sure he'd take advantage of having Nikki's personal number. She wanted to see if he knew anything about Wezley, and if he knew what time the party broke up that night. Had Eddie been murdered during the party, or after?

Dressed in black jeans, short boots, and a cute Matsuda cardigan sweater over a tank, Nikki hurried out of her bedroom. On impulse, she stopped at her mother's bedroom door and knocked. No answer. She slipped in. Victoria had no privacy issues; Nikki was welcome in any room in the house, but she always felt strange in her mother's pink boudoir without her being present.

Nikki opened the top drawer of a pretty little French acacia wood dresser and grabbed three signed glossy photos of her mother. Surely Astro would love to have one, and there was just no telling when extras would come in handy. She'd throw them in the trunk of her car. Next to the photos, she located a manila envelope of gift certificates and coupons Victoria received in swag bags. These gift bags were given to her and other celebrities in green rooms, at premières, and at fund-raisers. The two bottom drawers held more swag gifts: perfumes and colognes, watches, cashmere pajama bottoms, jewelry, makeup, and who knew what else. And Nikki was sure there were several small appliances like toasters in a closet somewhere. Victoria regifted the gifts, and encouraged Nikki to do the same.

Nikki flipped through the gift cards. She was sure she'd seen one for Villa Blanca. She'd treat Ellen to lunch. She found gift cards for all sorts of restaurants, gyms, and golf courses. There were also gift cards for manicures, facials, a *surf butler*—whatever the heck that was—at a hotel on the beach. Even a five-hundred-dollar gift card at a tattoo parlor that had been featured on the TV reality show *LA Ink*. Nikki chuckled. Her mother could certainly use *that* one. . . . Finally, at the bottom of the pile, she found the one she was looking for. She closed the drawer with her hip.

Next stop, B. H. Fitness . . .

Nikki walked into the gym through the double-glass front doors, her handbag slung on her shoulder with the signed Victoria Bordeaux eight-by-ten glossy inconspicuously tucked inside. She'd even had her mother personalize it. The Sharpie signature on Astro's bare chest would eventually fade, but glossies on acid-free paper could last decades.

Nikki was disappointed that she didn't spot Astro

in the open workout room. She didn't see Kaiser or his female sidekick, either. However, Gwen, with the spiky orange hair, greeted her with a grin at the front counter.

Gwen folded her hands and leaned on the counter. Leaned close. "Change your mind about that Jamba Juice?" she asked seductively.

The smile. "Sorry. *Still* have that boyfriend," Nikki said sweetly. She glanced around. "I . . . I was hoping to find Astro."

Gwen was wearing tiny, tight, black boy shorts and a pink tank top that accentuated her muscular arms and the tattoos that ran from the shoulder to just below the elbow of her left arm. Nikki tried not to stare; there were bright green vines, big flowers in pink and blue, and . . . were those *monkeys?*

"You like?" Gwen asked, running her hand down her arm.

"It's really . . . something," Nikki said enthusiastically. "I don't think I've ever seen anyone with monkey tattoos."

"It's an original design." She turned sideways so Nikki could get a better look. "This one's a tamarin." She pointed to an orange monkey that was entirely too realistic-looking to be on a woman's arm. "And this one's a snub-nose."

That one's creepy, is what it is, Nikki wanted to say, but she pretended to be interested.

"You have any?"

Nikki looked up. "Any?"

"Tats."

"Me? Oh, no." Nikki shook her head. "I have a hard time ordering lunch. I'd never be able to come up with something I wanted on my body permanently." She took a step closer, placing her hands on the countertop. "So, Gwen . . . have you seen Astro?"

"He, um"—she glanced up, in the direction of the open gym—"called in sick today."

"So he didn't come in at all? Not even for client appointments?"

Gwen shook her head.

That was weird. Astro didn't seem like a guy who called in to work sick. "Was he here *yesterday?*"

Gwen looked around again, obviously checking to see if someone was there. A particular someone. "Called in sick yesterday, too."

Nikki frowned. That seemed doubly odd. "So, have you seen him since Monday, when I was here?"

The young woman looked uneasy. "No. He left Monday. Kind of suddenly."

"Do you know why?"

Gwen hesitated. "I'm really not supposed to talk about employees. You know. HIPAA and all."

"I think that pertains to medical records."

Gwen nibbled on her lower lip.

"Did you give Astro my business card the other day? When I couldn't find him?"

Gwen grimaced. "Look, I really like you. I think you're super cute, in a conservative kind of way."

Conservative? Nikki glanced down at the tight black jeans that were practically jeggings, her cool Japanese designer cardigan, and semi-high-heeled boots. She thought she'd left the house looking modern and hip.

"I *really* don't want any trouble," Gwen said in obvious discomfort.

"And I'm not here for trouble." Nikki held up both hands. "Definitely not trouble. I'm just trying to find Astro."

Gwen looked like she wanted to say something. She just needed a little nudge. Nikki glanced at the jungle of tattoos on her arm. *Tattoos* . . . She leaned on the counter. "You plan on getting more tattoos? You know . . . finishing up that sleeve?"

"Ah . . . I'd love to finish my sleeve right to the wrist." Gwen ran her hand down the length of her arm. "But tats are pricey. Good tats."

"Would you like a gift card for five hundred dollars for that tattoo parlor on *LA Ink*? Free?"

Gwen looked at Nikki. "Are you trying to *bribe* me?"

Nikki felt her face flush. She stood up to her full height. "I . . . it wasn't so much—"

"I love it!" Gwen declared, slapping the counter with her palm. "I swear to God, you ever dump that boyfriend of yours, you give Gwendolyn a call." She curled her finger, beckoning Nikki.

Nikki stepped closer, again.

"I tried to give your card to Astro," she whispered, keeping an eye on the gym floor and its occupants. "But Kaiser snatched it right out of my hand."

"He *took* it?"

She nodded. "Then he and that weird girlfriend of his and Astro talked over at the incline press. Kaiser seemed hot. Then Astro took his bag and left and he hasn't been back since."

"Weird," Nikki said, thinking out loud.

"*Right*," Gwen said.

Nikki looked at the orange head again. "You have a home address for Astro?"

Gwen hesitated.

"Look, I won't tell Astro how I found him and I sure as heck won't be saying anything to Kaiser." Nikki waited. "And I was serious about that gift certificate. Someone gave it to me." (Barely a lie. And totally harmless.) "It's just lying in a drawer. Someone might as well use it."

"You sure *you* won't use it?"

"Fairly sure," Nikki said.

Gwen thought for a minute, then turned to the computer on the counter. "Hang on." She hit a couple of keys, then grabbed a notepad and jotted an address down. She ripped off the top page and slid it across the counter to Nikki. "If anyone asks—"

"I didn't get it here." Nikki glanced at the piece of paper, then slipped it in her bag. "Thanks, Gwen. I appreciate this. I'll drop off the gift certificate tomorrow."

"Cool. Thanks."

A young woman in matching shorts and a bra top approached the front desk. "Excuse me," she whined.

"Have a good day," Nikki said cheerfully to Gwen, and walked out the door.

In her car, Nikki pulled the photo of Victoria out of her bag—she didn't want to wrinkle it. As she closed the door and tossed the photo on the passenger seat, she spotted an envelope sticking out from beneath a folder she'd planned to drop off with her client.

The unfamiliar business-size envelope had been between the mail she'd picked up at her house the day before and the comparative analysis for a client she'd dropped on the seat that morning. The envelope had her name written across it . . . in letters that appeared to have been cut from a glossy magazine, à la ransom-note style.

NIkKI

"What the heck?" she muttered. And ripped open the envelope.

Chapter 17

Nikki unfolded the piece of ordinary printer paper. Like the outside of the envelope, cuttings from a newspaper or magazine were glued together to make the words.

CuRI●si7ÿ kILLeD... tHe reaL eStaTe AgeNt

Oh my God! Was this a death threat?

Nikki dropped her hands, with the paper, to her lap and looked around. Cars passed on the street. A woman dressed in a navy blue suit hurried down the sidewalk in heels, a gym bag in one hand, a cell phone in the other. No one was paying any attention to her.

Nikki hit the LOCK button on her car door. Then she hit it a second time, just to be sure . . .

Then, she realized she was being silly. The car had been locked when she just got in it. It had *not*, however, been locked at her mother's overnight. There was no need. The property was gated.

Heart pounding, she opened the letter and read it again.

It still said the same thing.

Hands a little shaky, she folded it carefully and slipped it inside its envelope. She set the envelope on the passenger's seat and started the engine of the Prius.

But then she just sat there, hands on the wheel.

What should she do now?

She was scared, but probably not as scared as she should have been. The threat made her angry. All she was doing was looking out for Jorge's best interests.

Who the heck had gone to the trouble of writing that note and leaving it in her car? The *why* was pretty simple—because she was on to someone.

But who *could* have left it there?

Only someone with access to her car, parked in her mother's driveway, in the last twelve or so hours. The envelope hadn't been there when she left her car in the driveway the previous night. Only someone with access to the security code to the front gate could have done it.

She ran quickly through the short list of names: her, Victoria, Amondo, and Ina. Then there were those who provided services to Victoria, but, unlike many celebrities, her mother was very selective as to who could gain access without permission. Many people in Beverly Hills had florists, manicurists, even massage therapists coming and going as they pleased. But not Victoria.

Besides those who lived in the house, and Nikki, the only people who could get through the front gate without someone in the house unlocking it were Jorge and his crew . . . and the pool boy who came every other day or so. *Rocko.* Who Eddie had fought with the day of the party.

Nikki took a deep breath, exhaled, and took another.

She'd heard a mower earlier . . . when Melinda was there, but by the time Nikki got out of the shower, he was gone.

Melinda had been there. Obviously, she didn't do it. Her son was the one who had been murdered. Besides, she'd walked right up to the front door and rung the doorbell. Ina had said so. But that meant if Melinda could have walked from the Bernards' to Victoria's, through the side-yard gate, anyone else in the Bernard household could have walked through it, too. Anyone on the Bernard property could have entered the Bordeaux property by the unlocked gate, left the note on Nikki's front seat, and gone back through the gate without being seen.

Had Ginny *really* been sleeping in, as Melinda had thought? Could *she* have left the note? Was Lissa at the house? And who else had access to the Bernards' security code at the front gate? Not Ashley because she had been waiting at the gate when Nikki gave her the Jay-Z tickets. Maybe Abe's assistant? And Rocko, who also cleaned the Bernards' pool. And who knew how many other service people?

Nikki decided, at that moment, that she was calling a security service *today* and making arrangements for cameras for Victoria's property, whether she liked it or not.

Nikki glanced at the envelope on her seat again. Should she call Dombrowski? No. He would tell her to stop talking to people, and to keep her nose out of cop business. She'd keep it to herself . . . at least for now.

Nikki punched the address Gwen had given her for Astro into her GPS and pulled away from the curb.

Nikki expected Astro to live in a condo, or maybe an apartment, a bachelor pad for a good-looking, muscly guy. She did *not* expect the little bungalow she pulled up in front of, south of Pico Boulevard, or the white picket fence. Or the fluffy, white toy poodle that barked at her from a window as she walked up the sidewalk to the front door.

Nikki rang the doorbell. The little dog barked wildly from the other side of the door. She heard it growling as the door swung open and a tiny woman with long, thin, blue-rinsed hair, pulled back in a ponytail, looked at her from behind big Edith Head glasses. She was wearing a calf-length gauze skirt and wooden beads. Nikki couldn't tell if it was supposed to be a costume or not.

"Yes?" the woman inquired. Her voice was squeaky.

Nikki wondered if she had the wrong house . . . or if maybe her buddy Gwen and the monkeys had sent her on a wild-goose chase.

"Hi," she said, looking at the older woman

through the screen door. "I'm Nikki Harper. I'm looking for Astro."

The woman looked up at Nikki; her crazy glasses seemed to magnify her eyes and the wrinkles around them. The poodle continued to bark, bouncing up and down.

"Astro Wharton?" Nikki said. "He works at B. H. Fitness on North Bedford."

"I know where he works," the woman said, still taking Nikki in.

"Oh, so you *do* know him?" Nikki smiled warmly.

"I should. He's my son." Her reply was not warm.

The poodle jumped up against the door and growled. It appeared to be foaming at the mouth now.

"Does . . . does Astro live here with you?" Nikki asked.

"He does. Do I know you?" She squinted from behind the glasses.

"Um, I'm Nikki Harper—"

"You said that."

"Maybe you know me because of my mother?" She had to speak louder to be heard above the mad dog. "Victoria Bordeaux?"

The older woman thought for a moment. "Nope. Don't know her."

"She's an actress. *Was* an actress. She's mostly retired now. *Sister, Sister; Fifteen Green Street?*"

"Nope."

Nikki smiled again. "Is Astro here?"

"You his girlfriend?"

Nikki noticed for the first time that a station

wagon in the driveway had suitcases in the back. "I'm not Astro's girlfriend."

"Because you're better-looking than the last one." She squinted. The dog continued to bark. "Is that really the color of your hair?"

Nikki ran her hand over her head. "Really the color of my hair."

"I used to be a redhead."

"Did you?" Nikki glanced at the car again. There was a cooler on the backseat. *Road trip.* "Are . . . are you taking a trip?"

"Why do you want to know, Miss Nosy Nikki Harper Parker?"

"Um . . ."

"To see my sister," the woman said. "She lives in Scottsdale. That's in Arizona. She has a pool."

Nikki glanced at the poodle, still jumping up against the screen door, still barking, still growling. She wondered how long the dog could keep it up before collapsing in exhaustion.

"Is . . . Astro going with you? To see your sister?"

"Is this it, Ma?" The male voice came from inside.

Astro appeared in the doorway behind his mother, carrying two more suitcases. He halted, obviously startled to see Nikki. And maybe a little bit afraid . . .

The dog was still barking. "Ms. Harper."

"I stopped by the gym. I heard you were out sick."

He stared at her for a second, then looked at the dog. "Peaches! Enough!"

Peaches fell silent at once and trotted out of sight.

"Sorry about that," Astro said. He seemed nervous. He was wearing a plaid short-sleeved shirt, shorts, and a ball cap. He hadn't shaved in a couple of days. She might not have recognized him on the street.

"Is this your girlfriend?" his mother asked.

Nikki made eye contact with him. "I told her I wasn't your girlfriend, but I'm not sure she believed me," she said with amusement.

He seemed to relax a little. "Go finish packing, Ma. I'll load these in the car." Astro opened the front door and Nikki backed down the steps.

She followed him to the car. "Are you okay?"

"You were looking for me at the gym?" He opened the hatch of the station wagon and slid the suitcases in with the others.

"You going somewhere?" she asked. It seemed like a lot of luggage.

"To see my aunt."

"In Scottsdale. Your mother told me." She hesitated. "Is everything okay, Astro?"

He cut his eyes at her and again she saw the nervousness in them. "What would make you ask?"

Nikki glanced at the door. His mother was standing there, watching them. She returned her attention to Astro, now genuinely concerned. "Are you leaving town?"

"I told you, I was—"

"I mean, are you *leaving town*," she said, lowering her voice. "Like in a hurry . . . like getting away from someone? Something?" She was concerned, but also suspicious.

"Did someone at the gym say that?"

"No. I'm just . . . *curious.*"

"Don't be. Why were you looking for me?"

"I wanted to give you this." She reached into her bag and pulled out the glossy photo of Victoria.

"Wow," he said, accepting it. "Autographed and everything."

"Autographed and everything," she repeated. "I got worried when I found out you'd called out sick, two days in a row. And Monday, I looked for you when I came out of the locker room. To give you my card, but you were gone."

He glanced at the door. "Ma!"

Nikki looked up to see Astro's mother still standing at the door watching them, trying, no doubt, to listen in on the conversation.

"All right, already," she grumbled.

He waited until she disappeared from sight. "I can't talk to you."

"According to who? That Kaiser guy?"

He exhaled, letting the hand holding the photo fall to his side. "Look, I don't want any trouble."

He was the second person to say that to her today. "Neither do I."

He held on to the photo of Victoria, as if it were a true treasure. It had been taken years ago, back in her golden days of cinema. It was one of Nikki's favorites.

"You should stay away from Kaiser," he said.

"I went to the gym looking for you, not Kaiser."

"He's dangerous."

Nikki hesitated. "Do you think he had something to do with Eddie Bernard's murder?"

"I don't know." He was holding so tightly to the photo that Nikki was afraid he was going to crease it. Not that she cared, but she thought he would.

Nikki laid her hand on Astro's arm. "Do you know if Eddie owed Kaiser money? For drugs?"

He shook his head. "I don't know. Eddie and I, we didn't talk about that kind of stuff. We just worked out."

"So if you don't know anything, why do you think Kaiser doesn't want you to speak to me?"

He didn't answer.

Nikki tried to think . . . fast, because she had a feeling she might not get another chance to speak to Astro. There were *a lot* of suitcases in that car. "You said Kaiser was at the party that night. Did you see any trouble between Eddie and Kaiser . . . or even see them talking?"

"They talked, for sure. I was coming out of the bathroom in the pool house. They were talking. Kaiser seemed pretty angry, but Eddie just walked away."

Nikki knew that drug dealers killed clients who didn't pay, to serve as a reminder to other clients to pay their tabs. But Eddie had only been out of rehab a week when he was killed. How big a tab could you run up in a week?

"You know where he lives?" Nikki asked. "Works?"

"I'm almost ready!" Astro's mother shouted from the front door. "I just have to water the cactus."

Astro looked at the door, then back at Nikki again. "I don't know where he lives. He works at The Python."

"The Python Club?" That set off all kinds of alarms in her head. She knew Eddie had once frequented The Python Club, and the alleged fight between Rocko and Eddie took place there.

But Kaiser couldn't have left that note in her car . . . could he? There was no way he could have gotten onto Victoria's property.

What if he had some way of getting into cars? Picking locks or something? Had he seen her go into the gym? She hadn't seen him. The idea sounded a little crazy. There was no way he could have known she was going to the gym. That note was premeditated.

She looked at Astro again. "Do you know a Wezley Butterfield?"

"Wesley?"

"It's actually Wezley . . . with a z."

"Eddie was talking about him last week when we worked out. How they got to be good friends in rehab. I never really met him. But he was at the party."

"Did you speak to him at the party?"

Astro shook his head. "No, but I saw him. Weird guy."

"Weird how?"

"I don't know. Just weird—"

"Astro!" Mrs. Astro opened the front door and Peaches flew down the steps, barking.

Nikki froze.

"Peaches! Back in the house!" Astro ordered. "Ma. Keep control of the dog. We don't want her biting someone again."

"I'm ready to go," *Ma* announced. She had an orange backpack, that could easily have been made in the 70s, slung over one shoulder. She held open the door and Peaches retreated back into the house.

"I'm sorry. I gotta go," Astro said to Nikki. "It was really nice of you to bring me this. It means a lot to me. Please thank Ms. Bordeaux. I'm gonna frame it right away."

"Thanks for talking to me. For taking heat from Kaiser over it."

He shrugged. "He's a jerk."

"Do you think he would . . . hurt someone?"

"No. Maybe. I don't know." Astro tugged on the brim of his cap.

Nikki met his gaze. "If someone has threatened you, if Kaiser threatened you in any way, you should call the police."

"No one threatened me," he said, pretty unconvincingly. "Let me walk you to your car."

Nikki headed for the gate, then stopped and turned back. "Just one more question, and then I'll go. I promise. Do you know what time the party ended at the Bernards' house that night?"

"Early. Like midnight. Some woman came out to the pool deck and said if we didn't all clear out, she was calling the cops."

"A woman? His mother?"

"I think so." He held open the little gate in the picket fence for her.

"And did everyone leave?"

"As far as I know," he said.

Nikki walked to her car. "But you don't know for sure?"

He shook his head. "As soon as she said *cops*, I took off. It wasn't that good a party, anyway."

Nikki unlocked her car door and he opened it for her.

"How long are you going to be gone, Astro?"

He looked out over the car's hood rather than at her. "I don't know. A week, maybe two. Maybe longer."

"You're sure Kaiser . . . or anyone else, didn't threaten you in some way?"

"I'm taking my mother to see her sister," he said.

"I don't suppose I could have your cell phone number?"

"I don't have a cell phone." He smiled. "You have a good day, Ms. Harper. Be safe."

She watched him as he walked away. Didn't have a cell phone? Who didn't have a cell phone these days? She guessed she couldn't blame Astro for being hesitant, especially if Kaiser had threatened him.

But why would Kaiser threaten Astro? And, more importantly, what did it have to do with Eddie's murder?

Chapter 18

"Thanks so much for lunch," Ellen said to Nikki as they walked out of the restaurant to wait for their cars on the corner of Brighton and North Camden. "I could have sat here all day and talked to you."

"I feel the same way." Nikki slipped her bag over her shoulder. "So, you're coming tomorrow night for Mother's movie night?"

"Are you sure it's okay?"

"Absolutely. You can meet Jeremy." She laid her hand on Ellen's shoulder. "And, who knows, maybe Will and Jada can set you up with a friend."

"Oh, no, not after the last loser." Ellen laughed. "I think I'm ready for a man-break."

"Fine. No setups. But I'd really like you to join us."

"Only if you promise to come by my shoot Monday."

"Are you sure? I don't want to get in the way."

"You won't be." Ellen looked up as the valet pulled a white BMW M3 convertible up to the curb. "This is me." She stepped off the curb in front of the car. "I have to warn you, shooting cooking shows for the Food Network is a lot different than shooting scenes for a Victoria Bordeaux movie. Things will be crazy. We shoot like . . . four or five half-hour shows in a day in this little bungalow in the valley they rented."

"It sounds like fun." Nikki waved to her as the valet held her door open. "See you tomorrow night! Cocktails are at seven."

"See you then!" Ellen waved and climbed into her car, but instead of pulling away, she put the passenger side window down. "And call me if you need me." She looked at her meaningfully. "I'm serious. I agree with Jeremy."

Nikki chuckled and leaned down to talk to her through the window. "You don't even know him!"

"I agree with him anyway." She lowered her voice. "You *should* leave this murder investigation to the police." She gave Nikki a stern look. "That being said, you call me if you need someone. Or if you just need to talk."

"If I shouldn't be involved, I certainly shouldn't be dragging you into it."

"Promise me," Ellen said.

"Okay. I promise. Have a good day." Nikki stepped back and waved and this time Ellen pulled away from the curb and into the traffic on Brighton Way.

As much as it pained Nikki to admit it, her mother had been dead-on. Ellen was terrific. They had a lot in common and they'd just . . . clicked. Nikki had the feeling that lunch today was the beginning of a great friendship, which made her feel good.

The valet pulled her car up to the curb and she fished in her bag for a tip. She was still contemplating whether or not she was going to The Python Club later on, but she knew her next stop: The Church of Earth and Beyond.

Nikki checked the addresses on Sunset; according to her Google search, she was two blocks west of the church. Fortunately, traffic was moving slowly, giving her time to think. She didn't have a plan as to what she was going to do once she found the church. Should she go in and just ask to speak to Wezley? Or should she just inquire about him?

According to the Internet, he was an employee of the church and some sort of financial administrator. He might very well be there. And if he wasn't, that might be even better. There might be other people at the church more willing to talk about Wezley than Wezley himself.

Nikki slowed for a yellow light ahead and spotted a sign for the church on the next corner. Then, out of the corner of her eye, she saw someone on the sidewalk in front of a used-car lot jumping up and down, waving a sign. As she got closer, she realized it was Elvis Presley waving the No MONEY DOWN placard. L.A. was full of Elvis impersonators.

Then, when she stopped for the red light, she realized this wasn't just any Elvis. It was *her* Elvis. And he was trying to wave her down.

For a moment, Nikki considered just pulling away. Unfortunately, there were cars both in front of and behind her, so there was no escape route. She groaned aloud, signaled, and pulled over. Taking a breath, she put down the passenger side window.

Elvis propped his sign against her Prius and leaned in the window. "Hello there, little lady," he crooned.

"Oh, E. Not the black rhinestone jumpsuit," she said.

He shook his head in shame; his inky black pompadour stayed perfectly in place.

"Frankly, I'm disappointed in you," she teased. "You're generally more creative."

He sighed, pushing his sunglasses back up the bridge of his nose. "At least it's not the *white* jumpsuit. A personal request from Billy himself." He pointed toward the enormous sign that said BILLY'S BARGAINS.

"Personally, I always liked the white pants, white shirt, and red sash from *Blue Hawaii*."

"Very understated," he agreed, turning the corner of his mouth up just the way Elvis had. "Very classy."

She nodded. "So, you're working?" She continued to nod. Most of the time, he just panhandled on the street. Tourists loved a good Elvis. "That's good. I'm glad."

"Been working a lot. Got myself a little place," he said.

His impersonation was good. It always had been, as long as her little brother didn't try to sing. Carry a tune, he could not. Which had proved to be a bit of a problem when his life's work had become impersonating The King.

"Read about Eddie turning up in her trash," he said. "She must be horrified."

He always referred to their mother as *she*. Elvis, a.k.a. James Mattroni, had had a falling out with Victoria years ago and they didn't speak. Their mother maintained it was because her son refused to seek help for his schizophrenia, help she was willing to pay for. Jimmy, who refused to answer to any name but Elvis, insisted it was because she was jealous of his talent. And other semi-crazy reasons. Nikki tried to remain neutral; it was hard for her to see him ill. Beyond the Elvis thing. She was glad he was looking so good. He looked good when he took his meds. It just never lasted long.

His father, James Mattroni Sr., had been schizophrenic as well, and had committed suicide when Jimmy was a freshman in college. Jimmy had never forgiven Victoria for not fighting harder to get custody of him when his parents had split, when he was a toddler. If it was any consolation, even though Victoria rarely spoke of the matter, she'd never forgiven herself, either.

Nikki pushed her Persol sunglasses up on her head. "She was pretty upset about Eddie."

"Jorge really kill him?"

"No," Nikki said firmly. "Jorge didn't kill him."

"I thought as much." He looked up and down the street. "I read the Warren Commission Report."

Nikki furrowed her brow. It was always this way with Jimmy. He'd seem perfectly normal for . . . minutes. Then the crazy would begin to spill over. She didn't say anything, though she had to admit she was a little curious as to what her brother thought was the connection between JFK's murder and Eddie Bernard's.

"So, where you headed?" he asked, saving her from stepping into his pit of crazy.

"Um . . . across the street." The glass-and-cement building that was the Church of Earth and Beyond was on the opposite corner from Billy's Bargains. Along with its parking, the building took up almost a full block.

Someone honked their horn and yelled out the window as they went by in a car, "Viva Las Vegas, baby!"

"Viva Las Vegas!" Jimmy shouted back, standing up and fisting the air.

Nikki clung to the steering wheel. She wasn't exactly *embarrassed*. She just felt awkward when she was around Jimmy. Maybe inadequate, because she had never been able to help him.

Jimmy leaned back in the window. "So exactly where *across the street* are you going?"

"The Church of Earth and Beyond."

"Planning on becoming a friend of the fruit trees?" he asked . . . in his Elvis voice.

She lifted her brows. He grinned.

"I . . . I need to speak to someone there."

"This have anything to do with Jorge being locked up?" His gaze fell to the pile of paperwork on the car seat. The crazy, scary death threat note had somehow slid out and her name in cutout letters was visible.

Nikki smiled and reached for the envelope to tuck it out of sight. "What if it did?"

"If it did . . ." He reached into the car and grabbed the envelope before she had a chance to get it. "I'd say you ought to mind your own business. You're in real estate, right?" He held the envelope just out of her reach. "Not an officer of the law?"

"Give that to me, E." She held out her hand.

Elvis opened the envelope, pulled out the note, and read it. "This a joke or for real?"

She hesitated. "I don't know."

He glanced up at the church across the street. "You think this letter came from one of those whack jobs?"

A pecan calling a filbert a nut? "No . . . *no*," she said.

"Would it do any good for me to say you shouldn't go in there?"

"Probably not."

He looked at her through his amber-colored aviator glasses.

"I'll be fine, E. I'm just going to have a look around." She put her hand out for the note again.

He slowly tucked the note back into the envelope and handed it to her. Then he stood up and picked up his sign.

"It was good to see you," Nikki said out the window, assuming their visit was over.

Until he opened the back door and stuck the big yellow sign in her backseat.

It took a second for her to realize what he was doing. "No, E," she said. "No way. Absolutely not."

He closed the back door and opened the front.

"E!"

"You almost got yourself killed last time you couldn't let the police do their job," he said. He scooped up the paperwork and files on the seat and tossed them in the back.

"E, that stuff's important." She looked at him. "And how the heck do you know anything about that?"

"*She* told Celeste. Celeste told me. Celeste and I talk sometimes. I have a cell phone now."

Celeste was their half sister, the daughter of Victoria and her fourth husband.

"You have a phone? E, that's great! You haven't had a phone in years."

"Never had a cell phone," he said proudly. He pointed across the street. "Let's go. I'm only supposed to take a fifteen-minute break."

"You really don't have to go with me." What she meant, of course, was that she didn't want him to go with her.

"You're wasting time. Now I only have fourteen minutes." He put on his seat belt, taking care not to disturb the rhinestones on his jumpsuit. "Who are we questioning?"

"*We're* not questioning anyone." She groaned, signaled, and pulled away from the curb. "Wezley Butterfield was at Eddie's party that night." She inched her way from the right lane to the left. "He's been questioned several times about the murder, by the police."

"Wezley Butterfield? His father runs the church. Wezley's an alcoholic and probably a druggy. Got arrested last year."

"How do you know that?" she asked with surprise.

"I *read*," he said, and looked at her as if she were stupid. "Recycling bins are full of newspapers and tabloids. He a suspect in Eddie's murder?"

She went through the intersection and darted across the lanes to pull into the parking lot. "I don't know. But the police must know something." Surprised that there were so many cars there in the middle of the afternoon, she pulled into a parking space.

"You have a plan?" E asked, looking up at the glass-and-cement weird pseudo-art-deco-style building.

She looked at him.

"No problem." He got out of the car and swaggered away.

"E!" Nikki grabbed her bag and jumped out of the car. She hurried after him, darting in front of a young woman carrying a stack of books, headed for her car. "Sorry! Excuse me!" She caught up to Jimmy. "You really, *really* don't have to do this with me," she said in a loud whisper.

Jimmy halted at the double glass doors. "Come on, little lady," he said in a voice that was pure Elvis. "Don't tell me you're embarrassed by your brother." He opened the door for two middle-aged women and they passed between him and Nikki.

She looked at him; she knew she should hold her tongue. Jimmy was sick. This wasn't his fault. "Of course I'm embarrassed!" she heard herself say. "You think you're Elvis Presley!"

He looked away, then back at her, with pain evident in his eyes. "I don't *think* I'm Elvis," he said quietly. Then came the famous upper lip sneer. "I just wish I was."

The emotion in his voice made her feel small. She wanted to hug him, but Jimmy didn't really like to be touched. Instead, she met his gaze through the amber glasses. "So, Elvis, you have a plan?"

He winked at her and held open the door. "Oh, I got a plan, little lady."

Chapter 19

Jimmy walked into the Church of Earth and Beyond as if it were the International Hotel in Vegas. He *owned* it. He swaggered into the large, two-story lobby and greeted several other visitors who glanced at him curiously.

This didn't look like any church, synagogue, or mosque Nikki had ever seen. The room was filled with display boards providing written and video information on the church and its beliefs. The open, airy lobby hummed with activity as visitors chatted, watched videos, and drank coffee from a coffee shop in the building.

Elvis swaggered his way to a large, curved reception counter that looked like a hotel check-in. Nikki hung back.

"May I help you, sir?" a girl in her late twenties with a sharp, asymmetrical haircut asked. Either she didn't notice it was Elvis Presley approaching the desk, she'd been trained not to notice the oddballs, or she didn't care.

"I certainly hope you can," he said, resting one elbow on the counter and posing. "I'm on a . . . *spiritual journey.*" He drew out his last words, sounding like a boy from Tupelo, Mississippi.

"You've come to the right place, then," she answered.

"I'm interested in speaking with someone about what the church has to offer. I was wondering if I could make an appointment. One of those personal counseling sessions I read about on your website."

Nikki was impressed that Jimmy even knew people surfed the Web. He'd lived on the streets a long time. Maybe he really was getting better. Maybe he really was taking his medication.

"Generally, we encourage newcomers to take a class, to study with us and get a feel for our beliefs before entering auditing sessions. That's what we call the one-on-one sessions."

"Well, is that right, sweetheart?" He adjusted his sunglasses.

Nikki slipped away. She didn't know what Jimmy was up to, but while he chatted, she thought she'd take a look around. She passed the reception desk and followed a wide hall. There was a directory listing the "Purity Center," the "Audit Center," the chapel, and various classrooms. She stopped at a water cooler beneath the directory and plucked a paper cup from a stack. She poured herself some water and looked at the sign again.

According to the directory, everything was on

floors one, two, three, or four. But she remembered seeing five floors from the parking lot. The directory didn't list the private offices of the founder, Colin Butterfield . . . or his son, the financial administrator.

Nikki finished her water and tossed the cup in a trash can. Then she walked to the nearby elevator and stepped in. She looked at the panel inside the door. Only four floors. She stepped back off the elevator and followed the hall, turning down a smaller hall near the chapel lobby. Beside a janitorial closet, there was a smaller elevator. She stepped on. Sure enough, this elevator listed five floors. She hit the button and the doors closed.

Nikki walked out of the elevator on the fifth floor to a nicely carpeted reception area with artwork hanging on the walls. *Expensive* artwork. A woman in her forties seated at a curved maple wood desk looked up from her computer screen. "Sorry, this is the fifth floor. No public classrooms." She was attractive, with honey-colored hair knotted at her neck and fashionable blue-green glasses. "What room were you looking for? I can give you the floor."

Nikki glanced down the hallway. Nice offices. Private secretary. Bingo. "Actually"—she stepped off the elevator—"I was looking for Mr. Butterfield . . . Wezley." As the words came out of her mouth, she wondered . . . where the heck was she going with this? If she did find him, what was her plan? What was she going to say? Even her crazy brother knew she needed a plan.

"I'm sorry, Mr. Butterfield doesn't see anyone without an appointment."

"I . . . I spoke to Mr. Butterfield." Nikki approached the desk and lowered her voice. "This is about Eddie Bernard's death."

The woman looked at Nikki, seeming startled . . . or upset, or something. "Are . . . you the police?"

Nikki shook her head.

"A reporter?"

"No. I was there, too," she confessed. "With Wezley." Not exactly a lie. More like a half-truth. "The night Eddie died."

"Wezley was there, too?" The woman sat there for a moment, then threw her hands up as if she'd crossed some threshold. "Never mind." She rose and adjusted her navy skirt, then gestured with her hands again. "I don't want to know. I told Mr. Butterfield, *senior*," she clarified, "that I wanted nothing to do with any of this."

"With any of . . ." Nikki let her sentence trail into silence.

"His son's nonsense," she whispered harshly. "*Whatever* Wezley's involved with. He needs help." She strolled down the hallway, knocked on a door, and entered at the sound of a male voice.

Nikki crept a little closer; she couldn't make out what was being said. The office door opened and the receptionist hurried out, head down. The man Nikki had seen in the alley Saturday morning appeared in the doorway. He was dressed in black pants and a black shirt and tie. He looked a heck of a lot better than he had the last time she saw him. His dark hair was neatly combed, his clothes pressed; he looked like a hipster exec now, not a hungover party boy.

"Mr. Butterfield . . . Wezley . . . ," Nikki said, walking toward him, offering her hand. "Nikki Harper. It's good to see you again."

He stared at her with a strange look on his face for a moment, then took a step back. He looked almost paranoid. "I don't know you. I've never seen you before in my life." He looked at the receptionist. "Monique! You know our rule. I don't see anyone without an appointment." He stepped into his office and closed the door.

Did he really not remember speaking to her? Or was there some ulterior motive for the performance he'd just given?

Nikki just stood there for a moment, not sure what to do. Not sure what Wezley or the receptionist were going to do. Were they going to call the police?

Call the police? She chastised herself mentally. And say what? Say people were trying to make false appointments?

Nikki took a deep breath, turned, and strode back toward the receptionist, who was taking her chair again. "Okay . . . ," she said to the woman. "That was really odd. He didn't remember meeting me . . . *or* speaking to me." She left it at that, hoping Monique would get the impression that Nikki and Wezley *had* had an appointment.

"Not all that odd." Monique's tone was cynical.

Nikki glanced down the hall again, her mind racing. "This . . . this has happened before?"

Monique moved a mouse across a mouse pad, glancing at her computer screen. "Happens all the time." She looked up at Nikki. "He's an alcoholic. He blacks out."

"But he was talking to me. I thought people *passed out* when they black out," Nikki said.

Monique looked up. "Oh, he does that sometimes, too. At first, I just thought he was a liar. After awhile, I realized he really can't remember things he says and does when he drinks. Which is a lot of the time." She returned her attention to her computer monitor. "There was this one time, I asked weeks in advance for a Friday off. I was taking my son to a Justin Bieber concert. The tickets cost a fortune and we had to drive up to San Fran. Come Thursday, he says I can't have the next day off. Swears he never gave me the day off and insists I come in or he'll fire me. I'm a single mom. I can't get fired." She shook her head. "But it wasn't right. It wasn't fair."

"But . . . he's been in rehab, right?"

Monique looked in the direction of the offices. "I don't know that that always works."

Nikki walked toward the elevator. "Did you know Wezley was at Eddie Bernard's party the night he died?"

"I heard rumors, in the break room." She looked up. "But how do you know what's true and what isn't, you know?"

Nikki smiled. "It was nice talking to you, Monique."

The woman smiled back. "You, too. I hope this won't give you a bad impression of our church. There are some really good people here. And good ideas."

"I'll keep that in mind." Nikki hit the CALL button and the elevator doors opened. "Have a good day."

"You, too," Monique called as the elevator doors closed.

Nikki found Jimmy in the lobby, watching a video on the church's belief in a Supreme Being. He was listening intently and didn't see her. "E," she called.

He turned to her. "I was afraid you went out the back door to get away from me. Where'd you get to?"

She headed for the door, glancing around at all the people in the lobby as she went. "I tried to talk to Wezley Butterfield."

"What were you going to say to him?"

She shrugged. "I don't know. It didn't matter because he took one look at me and said he'd never seen me before. It was really weird. He practically slammed his office door in my face."

Jimmy held a glass door open for her. He was always the perfect gentleman.

"He didn't recognize me. He didn't remember speaking to me in the alley. His secretary says he suffers from blackouts."

Jimmy made a motion as if drinking from a bottle.

She nodded. "At the very least." She looked at him. "How about you. Find out anything?"

"No . . . but I got an appointment with his *sister*. She's going to talk to me about what the church has to offer a man like me."

"His sister." She raised her eyebrows. "I'm impressed. I didn't even know he had a sister."

"Gets better." He went to the driver's side of Nikki's Prius, waited for her to unlock it, then opened the door. "Apparently Jennifer and Wezley Butterfield don't get along all that well. Sounds like she has Daddy issues, from what Erica said. And she blames it all on her brother."

Nikki slid into the car. "*Erica?*"

"At the front desk. She had an Elvis poster on her bedroom wall till she was eighteen," he said as if that was all the explanation Nikki needed.

"And you're really going to do this? Have this appointment with the sister?"

He shrugged. "Why not? Maybe the Church of Earth and Beyond really does have something to offer me."

"You think she'll talk to you?" She looked up at Jimmy, for once seeing past the Elvis persona. "You think you could get her to tell you something about her brother—better yet, her brother and Eddie?"

"With my charm?" He opened the back door and grabbed his BILLY'S BARGAINS sign.

"You don't want a ride back?"

He shook his head. "Nah, I'll walk. It's just across the street." He closed her car door. "Give me your cell phone."

She hesitated.

"I'm not going to steal it, Nik. I just want to put my number in."

She handed him her BlackBerry.

"My appointment's Friday afternoon. I'll have to talk to Billy and see if I can take an hour."

She looked up at him as he punched his number into her phone. "This is really nice of you, Jimmy. You don't have to do this."

He handed it back to her and adjusted his amber glasses. "It's the least I can do for my big sister," he crooned. He made eye contact, which he rarely did.

"That note." He pointed to the envelope tucked between her seat and the center console. "Should I be worried for your safety?"

She shook her head and smiled. "No worries, Jimmy." She watched him walk across the parking lot, toting the bright yellow sign, and wondered if she was being overly optimistic.

That night, Nikki was getting dressed in her drop cloth–draped bedroom when her cell phone rang. Rather than returning to Roxbury and then having to give a reason to her mother as to why she was going out at eleven P.M., she'd just come home to her own house to get ready. She needed to check on the paint job, anyway. Which had, apparently, not progressed. She'd have to call the painters in the morning.

The call was from Marshall. She put him on speakerphone so she could continue getting dressed.

"OMG! Did you see the video?"

"What video?" She slid her foot into a boot that sported a four-inch heel. She'd bought them in a phase of her life when she'd felt the need to look sexier. She'd worn them twice, then decided that a cast and crutches were less sexy than a safer heel height.

"Of Ginny Bernard!" Marshall gushed. "It's all over the Internet! Do you live under a rock, Nikki?"

She zipped up the boot. "So what's Ginny saying now?" Ginny, unlike Melinda, had always been vocal with the press. She enjoyed the attention, at least when it was focused on her and not on her loser stepson.

"Nothing! That's what's so crazy. You know Claudio Rune, the guy with the bad toupee who sold those god-awful pics of me to *Us Weekly* last year?"

Nikki *didn't* know Claudio, but she saw no need to slow the conversation with that information. She pulled on the other boot. "Uh-huh."

"Well, he apparently tried to speak to her about Eddie's murder and how Jorge was an immigrant—"

"But he's not an immigrant!" Nikki groaned. "And whether he is or isn't has nothing to do with his guilt."

"You're preaching to the choir, babe. How long will my people have to carry the drunken Indian thing around? But that's not the point of my story," Marshall insisted. "May I continue?"

"Sorry. Let me jump off my soapbox." She paused, with a nod. "Please continue."

"Well," he went on, obviously not really offended, "as she was leaving Starbucks, the paparazzi approached her, asking questions about Eddie and the family and such. Ginny didn't want to say anything, so Claudio got pushy. Ginny got in his face. There was a tussle and she grabbed Claudio's video camera. Elmer Weiss, the short guy with the crooked nose, *he* got it all on camera. Supposedly, he was working out something with *Entertainment Tonight*, but then his girlfriend, who he was fighting with, leaked the tape to the Internet."

Nikki pulled a paint tarp off her freestanding full-length mirror and checked out her outfit: short black skirt, high-heeled boots, and a black tank. She hadn't been clubbing since the late 80s . . . could she pull it off? "Did anyone get hurt?"

"Oh, I don't think so. Ginny was wearing Jimmy Choos when she attacked him. But Claudio went to the emergency room. Said Ginny had injured his back in the altercation."

"*Right,*" Nikki said, walking into the bathroom and flipping on the light.

"Where are you?" he asked. "You sound funny."

"I'm home. I had to pick up some clothes."

"At ten thirty on a school night? You're usually in bed in your jammies at nine."

She opened a drawer and began to dig through her makeup. She knew she had shiny blue eye shadow somewhere. "It's best I not answer on the grounds I might incriminate myself." She pulled out a tray of assorted eye and lip pencils.

"What are you up to?" Marshall demanded. "Does Mother know where you are?"

"I'm forty-one years old, Marshall. I don't have to tell my mother where I'm going."

"This is about Jorge, isn't it? Did you ever find that cousin of his?"

"No, I didn't find Ree. I'm going to see Jorge during visiting hours on Saturday. Maybe he knows where she could have gone."

"You're going to the prison? I wish I could go."

"Marshall." She began to darken her eyebrows with a pencil. "You can't visit someone in prison. You're a star. There'd be a mob scene."

"I know. You're right," he pouted. "Rob wouldn't like it, anyway. He likes to protect me from the big, bad world."

She smiled at the thought. If only everyone had a

Rob in their lives. "I gotta go. Have a good day tomorrow."

"You, too," he said. "Enjoy movie night and tell Will and Jada I said hi."

Chapter 20

Nikki walked into The Python Club at eleven thirty P.M., *way* past her bedtime. It was all she could do not to cringe as a bouncer let her through the nightclub door and the pulsing music and flashing lights assaulted her senses.

She'd tried to dress like she belonged there: the shortest black skirt she could find in her closet, the skimpiest top, and the highest heels. She'd flat-ironed her hair and lined her eyes with enough black eye pencil to outline the fine state of California. And as she squinted in the semidarkness of the room, checking out some of the other women, she saw that she fit in just fine. She just didn't feel it.

There was a live band on the stage playing heavy metal. The place was packed, probably beyond occupancy limits (had anyone given the fire marshal a ring). It had taken some sweet talk *and* the promise of an autographed picture of Marshall for the bouncer at the door to let her in. She slowly made

her way to the bar, excusing herself along the way as
she bumped into people. There was a dance floor in
front of the stage, filled with young, lithe bodies moving to the pounding music. To the rear of the club,
near the bar, were small tables with people seated at
them, sometimes two to a chair. It was a popular
nightspot for young celebrities; Nikki recognized several Hollywood faces.

Trying to stay balanced on her stiletto boot heels,
she reached for the support of the bar. There were
two bartenders: a young woman with blue-black hair
down to her waist and shorts that appeared to be
leather, and a fifty-year-old metrosexual guy in a tight
black Python Club T-shirt and tighter jeans. He was
pretty fit for his age, but he still looked out of place
in the nightclub.

"What can I get you?" the guy asked, sliding a
cocktail napkin toward her as he eyed her. Metrosexual? Maybe. Heterosexual for sure.

Nikki had to turn sideways to fit between a bar
stool with two blond girls perched on it, and some
guy's back on the other side. "Tonic water with a
twist."

He smirked. "AA? Me, too. Two and a half years
sober." He grabbed a glass from under the bar,
added ice, and shot tonic water into it from a hose.
"Here alone?" he asked as he added a slice of lime to
the glass.

"I was supposed to meet my girlfriend, Ellen," she
lied smoothly. She made a show of looking around.
"I think I've been stood up."

He took a small towel and began to wipe the bar
top in front of her.

"You worked here long?" she asked. She thought it was odd that he worked here at all. A recovering alcoholic tending bar?

"Almost two years."

"So . . . you probably knew my friend Eddie. Eddie Bernard? He was a regular here." She knew that from the tabloid news covers. Checkout at the market.

He leaned on the bar. He had a long nose. Victoria would have called it aristocratic. But he was nicelooking: full head of salt-and-pepper hair, just a touch of an afternoon shadow. "*You* were friends with Eddie Bernard?"

She could tell by his tone of voice that he was not a fan.

"Well, childhood friends. We sort of . . . grew apart." She looked at him through her mascaraladen lashes. "Eddie was a troubled soul, but I guess you already knew that, if you knew him from here."

He grimaced. "You can say that, all right."

She took a sip of her drink. "Was Eddie here last week?"

"Didn't see him. I heard he was in rehab. Haven't seen him in about three months."

"Three months," she repeated, inching a little closer to him. The music was so loud, she could barely hear him. "So . . . you were here when he got in the fight with Rocko?"

"Rocko St. Clare? Yeah. It was like last November or something. The two of them were talking, and all of a sudden Eddie just throws a punch." The bartender lifted a fist in the air to demonstrate.

Nikki leaned back.

"Sorry." He offered his hand. "John Boden. My friends call me Johnny B."

"Nice to meet you, Johnny B. Nikki." She shook his hand, then reached for her glass again. "Did someone call the police that night? I know Eddie got arrested over the incident."

"No, no way. No one here called the police. Got arrested later, after Rocko filed a complaint. Or so I heard." Johnny B. began to wipe the bar again. "Nothing ever came of it, though. People said Rocko dropped the charge." He leaned on the bar again and looked both ways before speaking again. As if anyone could *possibly* have overheard their conversation. "Crazy thing was, Rocko shows up on a brand-new Ninja the same week the charge gets dropped." He raised his brows.

Nikki leaned closer. "So you think Eddie bought Rocko the bike in exchange for him dropping the charge?" It sounded like something Eddie would do. Not with his own money, of course. Abe had to have paid for the motorcycle; Eddie hadn't had any money of his own.

"Just seemed awfully suspicious," Johnny B. said.

Nikki nodded, sipping her tonic water as she looked around. A familiar face caught her eye and she did a double take, then looked quickly at her newfound friend. Astro had said Kaiser worked here; she didn't know why she was surprised to see him. "You know that guy? The one near the door, with the swastika tattooed on his neck?"

Johnny B. didn't even look up. "Kaiser. He's one of our bouncers. Another A-hole in a whole barroom of A-holes." He picked up his bar mop, lowering his gaze. " 'Scuse my French."

Nikki snuck another look at Kaiser.

"Owners do the hiring," Johnny B. explained. "If it were up to me, we wouldn't have guys like that here."

"So . . . you don't care for Kaiser?"

"My mother was Polish. Jewish. She got out of Poland in time, but the rest of her family didn't."

She nodded in understanding.

"But even if he didn't have that tattoo, I wouldn't hire him. A guy like Eddie, he's a jerk, but he's harmless. A guy like Kaiser—he leaned on the bar, looking in Kaiser's direction—"he's dangerous."

"Dangerous how?" Nikki asked.

Johnny B. scowled and put both elbows on the bar so he could get closer to Nikki. "Drugs," he whispered. Then he looked at her. "You're not a party girl, are you? You don't look like a party girl."

She picked up her glass as if to toast him. "I'm drinking tonic water in a nightclub."

He chuckled. "Yeah, you look like too nice a gal to be in a place like this."

"So . . . he's bad news, is he? Kaiser?" she asked, trying to steer the conversation back in that direction. She was pretty certain Kaiser had seen her. She kept her back to him.

He gave a humorless laugh. "Yeah, I'd say so. He killed a man. Ended up getting away with it."

Nikki's heart felt like it skipped a beat. At the very least, sped up a little. "You're kidding," she murmured. "Who?"

"I don't remember. Another dirtbag. Drug-related."

"So . . . if Kaiser killed this guy, why isn't he in jail?" Nikki asked. She saw Kaiser move away from the front door.

He shrugged. "I don't know. Our fine criminal justice system at work?"

"But you're sure it was Kaiser?"

"Absolutely. Apparently, he was a draw at the club for a while, due to his *fame*."

"Johnny B., could I get some help over here?" the other bartender called. She was pouring drinks from vodka and gin bottles with both hands. "I'm drowning." She eyed Nikki.

Nikki smiled at Johnny B. She was done with him anyway. At least, for now. And her head was beginning to pound to the beat of the music. "I'm sorry. I didn't mean to keep you. Guess my girlfriend's not going to show up." She sighed and looked back at Johnny B. "Really nice to meet you."

"You, too." He gave a wave as he reached for a customer's empty glass. "Stop back another night."

Not if I can help it, Nikki thought as she spotted Kaiser near the stage and made a beeline for the door.

The next morning, Nikki walked off the elevator into the lobby of Windsor Real Estate to find Wezley Butterfield, of all people, waiting for her. He was sitting in a chair, but popped up as she walked through the door.

"Ms. Harper." He was wearing a black Dolce & Gabbana suit and Italian loafers. He looked sharp . . . and sober.

She removed her sunglasses and tucked them into their case inside her bag. "Mr. Butterfield."

"I brought you a latte, skim milk, one Splenda. Carolyn, here"—he smiled at the receptionist at the desk, who smiled back—"told me what you like."

Nikki glanced at Carolyn and noticed she also had a coffee. "What can I do for you, Mr. Butterfield? Is the church in the market for another property?" The previous night, unable to sleep, Nikki had done some Internet surfing, digging up details on the Church of Earth and Beyond. She had found out the church owned quite a few commercial properties in the Los Angeles area.

Nikki looked at Wezley as she accepted the cup of coffee. Something didn't feel right here. Maybe it was the about-face from yesterday. Yesterday, he'd never seen her before in his life; today, he's buying her *and* her receptionist coffee?

"Could we . . . ," he lowered his voice, "go somewhere more private? Your office, maybe?"

Nikki took a sip of her latte; it was perfect. She cut her eyes at Carolyn. "The conference room?"

"Open," Carolyn sang. She was still smiling at Wezley.

Nikki also noticed Carolyn had a small brown bag from the coffee shop on her desk. The kind of bag where one hid a high-calorie pastry.

Wezley smiled. This guy wanted something.

"This way, Mr. Butterfield." Nikki slung her handbag on her shoulder so she could balance her soft-sided leather briefcase and the coffee cup. She led him down the hall and into the conference room where the Monday Morning Meetings were held. She set her bags on the end of the table. "What can I do for you, Mr. Butterfield?"

"Please." He indicated a chair. "Let's sit. You should enjoy your coffee while it's hot."

Nikki tried not to let her suspicion show as she took the chair and reached for her coffee. She let him begin the conversation, figuring she was in the catbird seat now that he obviously wanted something from her.

"I wanted to apologize . . . for yesterday." He folded his hands on the conference table. "I don't know what happened. I—"

"Mr. Butterfield—"

"Wezley. *Please.* I insist."

The guy was smooth. Which made it all the more interesting to her that he and Eddie could have been friends. Eddie had none of the social refinements of this guy.

"Wezley," she agreed. "There's no need for an apology. I completely understand how you could have forgotten we'd spoken. Saturday morning was crazy—"

"That was exactly what I was going to say." He touched his forehead. He saw a manicurist; his nails were perfectly square and buffed. "I was so upset that morning. Disoriented, I think. By the terrible shock."

Maybe still drunk or high? Nikki wanted to ask. But the guy had brought her a latte. To not bring up his addiction before nine A.M. was the least she could do.

"It wasn't until later that I remembered speaking to you in the alley. Nikki Harper. How could I not

have remembered Nikki Harper?" He was smiling
again. "I loved the piece you wrote for *Architectural
Digest* on Paul Williams. The photos of your mother's
home were stunning." He tented his fingers. "It was
the July issue, wasn't it?"

So he had Googled her, as well. "It *was* July. Thank
you. I didn't take the photos, of course." She sipped
her latte, still not exactly sure why he was here, but
trying to figure out how to use it to her advantage.
Surely this wasn't just about an apology. He could
have phoned for that.

"I just felt so awful after you left yesterday." He
looked her right in the eyes. "There's no excuse for
my behavior. But I've been so upset since Eddie's
death. I haven't been myself. We were good friends,
you know."

"I heard that." Nikki scooted closer to the table . . .
closer to him. Now they were getting somewhere.
"Which made me sort of wonder why you weren't at
the funeral."

He exhaled and looked away. "I'm not sure how
much I should say."

"About the *funeral?*" she asked.

"About Eddie." He looked at her again. "You
know the police have questioned me."

"About . . . Eddie?"

He grew somber. "About what went on that
night."

She noticed that he didn't answer her question as
to why he hadn't attended the funeral. "Detective
Dombrowski questioned you?" she clarified. When
he hesitated, she said, "Because, you know, he questioned me, too."

"He seems very thorough." Wezley's gaze darted toward her again. "What . . . what kind of things did he ask you?"

"About finding Eddie's body. About the party the night before and my mother's gardener's involvement."

"The fight was pretty frightening."

"So you were there?" She didn't remember seeing him, but there were so many people there that evening and, of course, she hadn't known what would transpire later. She couldn't have known that she'd later wish she could recall all the people she had seen.

"I *was* there. I tried to talk to Eddie afterward." He shook his head. "I told him the party was a bad idea from the beginning. I told him to kick them all out. Those people weren't his friends. They didn't care about him."

"But it was Melinda Bernard who actually kicked them all out, wasn't it?"

"Yes," he said slowly. "It . . . it was. How did . . . how did you know that?" He seemed genuinely surprised.

She lifted one shoulder. Took a sip of her latte. "I was just talking to somebody I knew who was there. I heard Eddie was . . . under the influence."

Wezley hung his head. "I feel so guilty about that. I should have been a better friend." He looked up again. "Addiction is a terrible monster. It eats your soul."

"You knew Eddie from rehab, right?"

He seemed stunned she knew that. He took a moment to answer. "I did. Eddie and I . . . we'd hoped to stay on the path of sobriety together."

"So, you guys stayed friends after rehab?"

"To offer each other support. His family, I don't know that they fully understood the demon that possessed Eddie." He looked away, deep in thought. "I guess Eddie wasn't ready to leave rehab." Then he looked back at her. "You . . . you said you spoke to someone who had been at the party. Do you mind if I ask why?"

She hesitated. "I'm not convinced my mother's gardener did it," she said carefully.

"Interesting." He looked up, offering a handsome smile. "Well, I'm glad we have this cleared up. I have to run because I have a meeting, but I just felt awful all night." He rose. "I just couldn't have lived with myself if I hadn't straightened things out between us, Ms. Harper."

She rose. "Nikki."

He nodded. "Nikki. Well, it was nice to see you again." He offered his hand and shook hers. "Have a good day."

She raised her cup to him. "You, too," she called. And wondered what he was really up to.

Chapter 21

Nikki had such a busy day, with two houses to show in Holmby Hills and a potential client meeting in Bel Air, that she barely had time to catch her breath. She certainly had no time to actually think about Wezley Butterfield's visit, or everything she'd learned about Eddie's death.

Which seemed to be nothing.

When she'd investigated Rex March's murder, she'd felt as if she'd moved from clue to clue, but this seemed to be a big pile of unrelated incidents. Or maybe it was a pile of puzzle pieces and she simply needed to put the pieces together.

Despite Nikki's busy day, she hoped to make it back to Roxbury in time to catch Rocko, and allow a few minutes to dress, do her hair, and put on makeup for the evening.

Nikki walked in the front door to find Victoria discussing, with Amondo, the kind of glassware she wanted at the bar that evening. She had a beautiful, expensive collection of colored Depression glassware that she used only on special occasions. Or when the mood struck her. Tonight, apparently, it did.

"I don't know that we need to serve martinis," she was saying. "Do we know if the Pinkett Smiths even drink martinis?"

"I can call one of his assistants, if you like," Amondo offered. He turned to Nikki. "You're home early. You won't be in such a rush."

"For once," her mother put in.

"Mother, do you have any connection to Justin Bieber?"

"Beaver? What an unfortunate surname."

Nikki snickered. "Bie-ber. He's a young singer. Preteen fan base."

Victoria didn't crack a smile. She'd been to the hair salon and her face was already made up for the evening. She wore a white jogging suit and pristine white canvas sneakers. Her "get things done" outfit.

"I've no idea. Amondo?" She turned to him. "Do we have Justin Bie-*ber* associations?"

"I can check into that."

"Please don't tell me you've become a fan," Victoria said.

"No." Nikki headed down the hall. "But I know someone who is. I think he's in town next month. Is there any way we can get a couple tickets?"

"I'll look into it tomorrow," Amondo offered.

"Thanks!" Stanley and Oliver greeted her halfway down the hall, but didn't seem all that excited to see her. They were on their way to the kitchen; Cavies on a mission. Nikki could smell something delicious before she even walked into the room.

"Ina, how are you?" The dogs trotted past Nikki, knowing they had a better chance of getting a treat out of Ina.

"Tired," the housekeeper said, pulling cartons of cream and sticks of butter from the refrigerator. "I had two mowers break down this morning, one worker call in sick, and another who went for lunch and didn't come back. I don't know if he got hit by a bus or went to Mexico to visit his mother." She passed Nikki the butter and cream. "On the counter."

Nikki felt so awful for her. She could see the stress of her son's being in prison, all over her face. Ina was still in jeans and a JORGE & SON T-shirt with an apron thrown over it.

"Is there something I can do for you?" Nikki asked.

"Not unless you can make mini artichoke-and-Gruyère quiches," Ina quipped, snapping a piece of carrot from the refrigerator in half. The dogs ran to her and sat at attention.

"Is the pool guy still here?"

"Should be. Here or at the Bernards'. His van is still in the back." Ina tossed pieces of carrot to Oliver, then Stanley.

"Let me know if there's anything I can do for you to help you get ready for the evening, Ina." Nikki stopped at the closed French doors. "I'm serious."

Ina turned to her. "That detective was next door again today."

"Was he?" she asked. "How do you know?"

"We housekeepers, we have our ways." She turned around. "Don't dawdle. Your mother will want you to greet her guests at the front door."

"I'm not dawdling," Nikki called. "I just want to speak to the pool guy for a sec."

Seeing that snack time was over, the dogs trotted to Nikki.

"Stay here, guys," she ordered, giving them each a pat. Then she slipped out onto the terrace, closing the doors behind her. No sign of Rocko, but she saw his white van parked next to Ina's Honda.

Nikki wandered out to the pool. It was a beautiful spring afternoon. The lawn looked immaculate; the pool sparkled. She walked around to the side yard and peeked through the gate.

Rocko was vacuuming the Bernards' pool. Lissa was lying out in a very tiny yellow bikini. Nikki hesitated. She needed to talk to Rocko, but privately. She hadn't been expecting anyone to be outside at the Bernards'.

She could wait for Rocko to come back to get his van, but she didn't know how long he would be at the Bernards' and she needed to get upstairs and get ready. She didn't have a lot of time. She walked through the gate.

"Lissa," she called.

The young woman had been reading *Cosmo*. She glanced up, through big, dark glasses. "Hey."

"Hey." Nikki spotted Melinda's bathing cap on a lounge chair. (She wore it to protect her blond hair; she swam laps every morning.) "Um . . ." She looked at Lissa. "Do you know if Melinda's home?" she asked casually, knowing very well she wasn't, as they'd passed on Roxbury on Nikki's way in.

"Nope. You just missed her." She reached for an icy glass and turned a page in the glossy magazine.

She was reading an article entitled "10 Ways to Drive Your Partner Wild in Bed."

Nikki glanced in Rocko's direction. Like anyone who provided services in Beverly Hills, he knew how to pretend he wasn't listening . . . even if he was.

"So . . . how is everyone? How's your mother?" Nikki asked.

Lissa shrugged. "Not sleeping at the Beverly Wilshire. So, fine, I guess."

Nikki nodded.

"You mind moving a little this way?" Lissa waved Nikki in front of her.

"Oh, sorry. Am I blocking your sun?" Nikki side-stepped.

"Nah. Mr. M.'s view." She lifted her chin in the direction of the property across the street. "He's up in his little perch watching us. He has a telescope. *Creeper.*"

Nikki glanced over her shoulder. Mr. M. had agoraphobia and hadn't been out of his house in at least twenty-five years. He made a hobby of watching his neighbors from a third-story cupola on the house. Victoria had known him in the fifties when he'd been a handsome, rising film star, and they had once costarred in a movie. He kept himself busy by watching the comings and goings of his neighbors, and supposedly photographing them. Victoria wasn't all that fond of him of late. She suspected he'd been the culprit when an unflattering photo of her without makeup, hair standing on end, had been published in a tabloid.

Nikki spotted Mr. M. and raised her hand and waved.

"Oh, God," Lissa groaned, slumping down in the chaise. "Please don't encourage him."

Nikki glanced at Rocko, who was still paying them no mind.

"Is he taking pictures?" Lissa squinted. "Can you tell?" She sat up. "Because if he's taking pictures of my cellulite, I swear to God, I'll sue." She got up, grabbed her glass, and pranced away. "I'm having another vodka and tonic. You want one?"

"No, no, I'm good." Nikki watched as the young woman went into the house. If Rocko noticed, he still didn't respond.

"Kids today." Nikki chuckled.

Rocko glanced up for the first time. He was maybe thirty years old and looked like a pumped-up surfer: blond hair, board shorts and flip-flops, a tight tee with a hibiscus on it. Very good-looking.

"Nikki Harper," she introduced. "Victoria Bordeaux's daughter." She hooked a thumb in the direction of Victoria's house. "I think we've met before." She walked around the pool toward him, eyeing the Bernards' house. Lissa had disappeared inside. "At least said hi."

"Nice to meet you." He had scooped a couple of bugs from the pool with a net and was dumping them into a white bucket.

"Crazy week here, huh?" Nikki remarked.

"Always crazy in Beverly Hills," he said.

"Yeah, but this was worse than usual. Eddie's murder. Do you know Jorge? I mean, have you met him? The police have the wrong guy." She glanced back at the Bernards' house.

He followed her gaze. He seemed to have become nervous. "I gotta get something out of my van."

Nikki followed. "I heard you were here the other night. At the party."

"Where'd you hear that?" He turned around. The look on his face wasn't exactly menacing, but he wasn't happy, either.

"Jorge's my friend. I think the police are pinning the murder on him because everyone in Beverly Hills wants a quick answer. I'm trying to find out what happened."

He started walking again.

"You were here that night," she said.

Rocko halted and turned around again. "So what? You think I killed him? I'm sure you heard about the fight Eddie and I had months ago at The Python Club. But I was done with that. It was over."

"So you didn't fight with him Friday night?"

He frowned. "No. No way."

She glanced back at the Bernards' house. Lissa had definitely said Rocko and Eddie had fought the afternoon of the party.

"You didn't . . . *exchange words* Friday?" Nikki asked.

"No." He exhaled. "Look, I don't know where you're getting your information, but you're going down the wrong path. We had words that day, yes, but I wasn't at the party. That morning, Mrs. Bernard called and left a message saying there was something wrong with the pool filter. I stopped by to take a look at it and people were already starting to arrive. It was like three in the afternoon." He gestured. "There were girls lying all over, you know, sunbathing."

"Okay," Nikki said.

"I was checking the filters poolside and Eddie comes over, he's wasted, and he wants to pick a fight. He accused me of crashing his party."

"But you weren't?"

"I didn't want anything to do with his dumb-ass party. I came because my client called."

"So . . . you and Eddie?"

"He got in my face. He pushed me."

"You push him back?"

"No. I walked away." He wiped his mouth with the back of his hand. "Now, if you'll excuse me." He stepped through the gate, onto the Bordeaux property.

Nikki really needed to speak to her mother about locking that gate. And a security system. She heard a door open and saw Lissa exiting the back of the house . . . carrying a fresh drink.

Nikki stood there for a minute, debating what to do. She really needed to get dressed and the ponytail wasn't going to do for evening attire.

She marched back across the yard. "Didn't you tell me that the pool guy got into a fight with your brother the day of the party?" she asked Lissa.

Lissa sat back down on the towel stretched over the chaise. "What?"

"You told me the other day that the police ought to be looking at Rocko, the guy who cleans your pool, because he had a fight with your stepbrother the afternoon he was murdered."

"So?" Lissa said, and took a sip of her drink. "I saw Eddie shove him."

"Did you see Rocko shove him back?"

Lissa rolled her eyes and took a sip of her drink. "I

don't know. Whatever. Did Rocko tell you what the
fight at The Python Club was about?" she asked with
a snicker.

Nikki hesitated. "No."

"Eddie punched Rocko during an argument after
Eddie and Rocko had sex."

"Eddie . . ."

"Yup," Lissa said with great satisfaction.

"I didn't realize Eddie was—"

"He said he wasn't."

"So . . . why the fight at The Python Club?"

Lissa adjusted her sunglasses. "I guess Rocko was
running his mouth and Eddie got pissed because he
didn't want anyone to know he had sex with a guy.
Eddie was the one who started it. My girlfriend
Clover saw the whole thing. She was there that night.
Eddie punched Rocko."

Nikki didn't know what to believe and what not to.
"Then Rocko had Eddie arrested?"

"Yeah, but Rocko dropped the charges after
Daddy Warbucks paid Rocko off with a Ninja motorcycle."

"Daddy Warbucks?"

"Abe." She smiled. "I love *Annie.* The musical."

"Ah." Nikki nodded. "You happen to know Rocko's
boyfriend's name?"

She shook her head, reaching for a magazine.
"But he works at that coffee shop on Sunset in West
Hollywood, the one near The Roxy."

Nikki glanced at her watch. She needed to dress.
She glanced up at the house across the street and Mr.
M. As she watched him watching her, she wondered
if he had been up there the night of the party. Had

he seen anything? There was only one way to find out.

Nikki crossed back to her mother's property, then out the front gate, which was open because the servers assisting Ina had just been let in. She walked across the street to Mr. M.'s lovely three-story home. Built in the forties, with his widow's walk, it looked like it should be on a spit of land jutting out into the ocean in Maine, rather than in Beverly Hills. Mr. M. had no gate; he had no security system.

Nikki walked up and rang the doorbell. She didn't expect Mr. M. to answer his door, but she didn't expect a gal who looked like she belonged at the Playboy Mansion in Holmby Hills to answer, either. She was wearing a short, tight black dress with the body to fill it out, black stiletto heels, and a tiny, frilly white apron.

"Hello," the young—barely out of high school—woman said cheerfully.

Nikki smiled *the smile.* "Hi, I'm Nikki Harper. My mom lives across the street." She pointed in the direction of the house. "Victoria Bordeaux."

There was no recognition on the blonde's face.

"Mr. M.," Nikki chuckled, "that's what we call him—"

"That's what I call him, too," she said in a ditzy voice.

"I was wondering if I could speak to Mr. M.? Just for a minute?"

"Please wait."

Nikki was hoping she might be invited in, but the young woman closed the heavy black-and-gold door.

She was back in a matter of minutes. "Sorry," she said. "Mr. M. isn't seeing visitors."

"You told him it was me?" she asked.

The young woman bobbed her head. "He said he wouldn't see you."

"Did he . . . say . . . *why* he wouldn't see me?" Nikki asked.

"He doesn't see guests," the blond bombshell said sweetly.

"I see." *The smile* again. "Well, could you please send Mr. M. my regards and tell him I'd really like to speak to him? That I'll only take a moment of his time."

"I'll tell him," she sang. "Have a nice day!" She started to close the door, then opened it again. "Oh! Mr. M. asked me to ask you how Ms. Bordeaux is. I didn't realize she's the woman we watch on DVDs all the time. Mr. M. loves Ms. Bordeaux's movies. He once starred in one with her, did you know that?"

She was so sweet and seemed so . . . dumb . . . that Nikki couldn't help but smile. "Actually, I did." She started to back down the steps. "Please tell Mr. M. that Mother is doing well and that I'll call on him again."

"Okay." The woman smiled and closed the door.

Nikki sprinted down the steps and out the driveway. If she wasn't home and downstairs before Will and Jada arrived, she'd be in big trouble.

Chapter 22

"Ellen, so glad you could make it," Nikki said when Ellen approached her and Jeremy. Victoria had just called for her guests to join her downstairs in the screening room, so everyone was on the move.

Victoria had built the screening room in the basement of her home in the days before media rooms were all the rage. There, she held movie night weekly, hostessing celebrities and political and social icons. The room sat twenty-five privileged viewers and was a thing of beauty, imitating the grandest theaters of bygone years. Decorated tastefully in an art deco style, with gilt trim and comfortable velvet seating, Nikki still felt a little thrill every time she joined her mother and her guests there. Some of her best childhood memories centered around the screening room. It was there where she had seen her mother's first movies and shared her first real kiss with Jeremy when she was fourteen.

Nikki was glad she could finally catch a minute with Ellen. She'd waved to Ellen earlier, but had been so busy chatting with Victoria's guests that she hadn't had the opportunity to do more than wave across the room. "This is my Jeremy," she introduced. "Jeremy, Ellen Mar."

"Nice to meet you, Jeremy." Ellen shook his hand. She was wearing an elegant jewel-blue sleeveless sheath dress that matched her eyes and sexy nude-colored heels. She looked like a runway model tonight in her chic dress; she reminded Nikki of Naomi Campbell.

Ellen gave Nikki a quick hug. "Thanks so much for inviting me," she said, her blue eyes sparkling. Then she whispered under her breath, "Will and Jada were so nice. So . . ." She couldn't seem to find the right word.

"Normal?" Nikki offered and then chuckled. "I know. I ran into Jada outside the powder room. She was complaining about her shoes being too tight." She and Ellen laughed.

"My son is a big fan of the Food Network," Jeremy said. "He's excited about your new show. He's fascinated by the way you can make sloppy joes look like pumpkin pie."

They all chuckled.

Nikki slipped her arm through Jeremy's. He was tall, with a full head of dark, wavy hair and warm, brown eyes. He wasn't movie star handsome like Marshall, but good-looking. And so darned nice that Nikki sometimes felt she didn't deserve him. "I was telling Ellen at lunch that you got us reservations at

The French Laundry next month. A weekend get-
away."

"I'm so envious," Ellen said. "I've heard reservations there are impossible."

Victoria appeared in the doorway, dressed in an
amazing floor-length Vera Wang gown of spun silver
silk. "There you are, Ellen. Don't let Nikki keep you.
I want you to sit with me." She held out her hand.

"See you later," Ellen whispered.

"*Nicolette?*" Victoria beckoned.

"Coming, Mother." She turned to Jeremy, and he
caught her hands. "Are you coming to Marshall's
party Saturday night?"

He groaned. Jeremy, who had been a child actor,
hated the Hollywood scene and avoided it whenever
possible. It annoyed him that even after twenty-five
years, he was still considered a celebrity when the paparazzi were out. "Do I have to?"

"No. You don't have to." She looked at him. "But I
do." She lowered her voice. "I thought you said the
kids were going to spend the night with their grand-
parents. I thought we were having a sleepover."

He pulled her closer, bringing his nose inches
from hers. "They are and we are," he said in his best
imitation of a sexy voice.

"You don't want to come to Marshall's?" She
whined, giving him her *please, just for me* pout. "Just
for a little while?"

"Black-tie? Hoards of people? Paparazzi?" He gave
her a quick kiss on the lips. "No."

She laughed. "I do have to go. I promised Marshall. You know how he hates these dog and pony
shows."

"So why does he have them?"

"Because his publicist insists they're necessary."

"Nicolette? Jeremy?" Victoria called from the doorway.

"You go to Marshall's, then come over," Jeremy whispered. "I'll have a bottle of wine open and the hot tub bubbling. Deal?"

"Deal." They kissed again.

"We better go," he said with a chuckle, glancing in the direction Victoria had gone. "Otherwise we're both going to be in trouble with Mother."

Nikki was sitting at her desk Friday afternoon, trying to concentrate on a contract she was looking over on her computer, but her attention kept straying to the list of suspects that lay on her desk. She'd thought it was silly when her mother made her write the names down, but she'd been carrying the piece of paper around with her now for two days.

She wasn't ready to cross anyone off the list yet—aside from her mother—but she had added Wezley's name and that's the one she kept coming back to. Something wasn't right with him. It was just a feeling she'd gotten when he'd paid her a visit. This morning, she'd called the rehab facility where Wezley and Eddie had gone, but she'd hit a dead end there. No one would speak to her about either client. Which was, honestly, what she expected. The way it should be.

Now, Nikki was eager to talk with Jimmy to see if he'd come up with anything from the sister in his counseling session, or whatever it was supposed to be. She checked the time. She'd give him another twenty minutes and then call him.

She forced herself to look at the contract in front of her again, but when her cell phone rang, she picked it up. Victoria.

"Mother."

"Just checking in," Victoria said.

"You're never *just checking in*. What's going on?"

Victoria sighed loudly. "I taught you better conversation manners."

"I'm at work, Mother. Working."

"Two things. Those tickets for the Beaver concert. Not easy to come by. Amondo is picking them up at my agent's office this afternoon."

"That's wonderful! Thank you so much." Nikki sat back in her desk chair and kicked off her heels. They were black snakeskin, old Bruno Maglis and very cool, but not the most comfortable she owned. "They're for this kid; his mom works for the Butterfields. Long story, but I think they'll be appreciated."

"I'm glad to be of assistance," Victoria said warmly. "The other thing is I ran into Ginny at Chanel. I was returning that little sweater. Too much money for such a tiny sweater. The cost of clothing is just getting outrageous. It's no wonder young ladies wear so little clothing."

The mention of young ladies not wearing much clothing made Nikki think of the young woman who had answered the door at Mr. M.'s the previous day. "I know what I wanted to ask you. Have you seen Mr. M. lately?"

"How on earth would I see him? He's a recluse. Silly question, Nicolette."

Nikki chuckled. "Let me rephrase. Have you *spoken* to Mr. M. recently? I know you give him a call once in a while."

"I think he was attracted to me once upon a time. Maybe still is. It's the least I can do. We did work together."

"But you haven't spoken to him lately?"

"No," Victoria confirmed. "That photograph he sold was unflattering."

"I doubt Mr. M. was the culprit. I stopped at his house yesterday to speak with him. I wanted to find out if he happened to see anything last Friday night, but he wouldn't see me." She hesitated. "Would you mind?"

"He won't see you unless I come as well," Victoria said tartly.

"Ginny's daughter says he has a telescope and that he watches her with it."

"Not surprising."

"Just give him a call, please?" Nikki asked, rereading a line on the contract. "Oh, you were saying something about Ginny, earlier?"

"Yes. I saw her at Chanel and she was acting odd. She asked me if I'd heard anything about Abe having lunch yesterday with Ellen Mar at The Palm in West Hollywood."

"I thought he was staying home this week. Sitting *shiva*."

"Apparently not, if he was having lunch with Ellen."

Nikki frowned. "So . . . why didn't Ginny just ask Abe? Why would she be asking you?"

"Because she knows I'm good friends with the maitre d'," she whispered.

Nikki had no idea why Victoria was whispering. Didn't ask. "She thinks you see him regularly . . . or he calls you to tell you who had lunch with whom?"

"Oh, for heaven's sake, it's Ginny Bernard. Who knows what she was thinking?"

"What did you say to her?" Nikki asked.

"I told her I hadn't heard anything and then I told her how attractive the tweed jacket she was trying on was. Then, when I got the car, I called Charles at The Palm. I used Amondo's cell phone. They're really quite handy."

Nikki wanted to remind her mother that she'd bought her a cell phone, more than one, and Victoria either misplaced them or declared them inoperable. Meaning *she* couldn't operate them. "What did Charles, the maitre d' at The Palm, say?"

"Abe did have lunch with Ellen!"

Victoria acted as if it were a shocking piece of information.

"So? Abe is producing her cooking show. Maybe they had business to discuss."

"Perhaps," Victoria said.

"Did you call Ginny and tell her?"

"Certainly not, Nicolette. I called you. I've been suspicious of her since day one. If I were you, I'd have a closer look at Ginny Bernard. Maybe she's the one trying to frame Jorge."

The phone clicked in Nikki's ear. Not surprising. Victoria rarely said good-bye when she completed a phone conversation.

Nikki set down her phone; it rang again almost immediately. *Elvis* appeared on the caller ID screen. "Hey," she said into the phone. "I thought I was supposed to call you." She ran the mouse over the mouse pad and corrected a misspelling on the contract. "How'd you get my number?"

"You afraid I'm going to start stalking you?" he asked.

The thought had crossed her mind. "No, no, of course not, E."

"I saw your number when I put mine in. You know me. I have a thing for numbers."

He had a thing for *repeating* numbers when he got upset. "So how was your session at the Church of Earth and Beyond?" she asked.

"The sister, Jennifer Butterfield, was really nice. I was very impressed. And she had a lot of interesting things to say about the church's beliefs. It made a lot of sense. I'm going to a service on Sunday."

Somehow, Nikki wasn't surprised. But Jimmy was who he was, and it had really been nice of him to try to help her out. "So the sister, could you get anything from her about her brother?"

"Not a fan," Jimmy said. In Elvis's voice, of course. "Erica was right. They're barely civil. Serious sibling rivalry between her and Wezley. She's a year older than he is, but he's been the blessed child from the beginning. Because he's a boy, the only son. You know. That nonsense. Wezley has been a screwup his whole life, and Jennifer's been the one who has worked tirelessly for her father. With no credit. Her father barely gives her the time of day."

"Wow. I'm surprised she opened up to you like that."

"I wore the gold suit," he said. "1957—"

"The concert at International Amphitheatre in Chicago," she chimed in.

"She found me irresistible."

"As many women do. So, did you find out anything about Wezley with regards to Eddie? Or the party?"

"She had another appointment, so we didn't get to talk as long as we wanted to. And I was fascinated with the whole concept of multiple lives and humans being alien life forms."

Here we go, Nikki thought. Down the slippery slope . . .

"But?" she interrupted.

"But, she did say one thing. She didn't even know until later about Eddie's murder and Wezley being there that night, but she said that when Wezley came home—apparently they both still live with their father—he was really upset because he was wearing Eddie's clothes."

"He was wearing Eddie's clothes?" Nikki repeated. She thought back to Saturday morning. Wezley had been in a pair of ordinary shorts and a T-shirt. But . . . at his office, and yesterday at her office, he'd been wearing black, head to toe. Sort of like a priest—minus the collar. "Interesting," she said.

"I thought so. We're meeting again next Friday. I'm fascinated by the whole idea that alien spirits could be negatively affecting us today, right here in Los Angeles."

And down the slope he would go. "I really appreciate this, E," Nikki said. "Listen, I need to run, but it was good to talk to you." She paused. "And it was good to see you. Good to see you doing so well."

"Good to see you, little lady," he crooned. "Call me anytime you need me. Or anytime," he added in his own voice.

Nikki left the office a little after six and took the elevator to the parking garage. She was checking her e-mail on her phone as she stepped off the elevator into the poorly lit, slightly creepy parking garage. She knew better than to look at her phone in a place like this. She knew she should have her bag held tightly to her body, keys in her hand, ever vigilant. So she deserved what she got.

Less than three steps from the elevator, she almost walked right into a guy. As she looked up, startled, she realized he wasn't moving. "Sorry," she mumbled.

He still didn't move.

Nikki took a step back, her heart fluttering in her chest. She knew him.

"Rocko," she said.

He was wearing jeans and a T-shirt and sunglasses. People didn't generally wear sunglasses in parking garages at six at night unless they were coming from or going to the Oscars and were big celebrities . . . or they didn't want to be recognized.

"Ms. Harper," he said.

She clutched her phone, wondering how good a weapon it would make. Not as good as a key in her hand, for certain. Of course, all she had was a key fob for the Prius, so that wouldn't have helped.

The elevator closed ominously behind her, making it seem darker in the garage.

"Rocko," she repeated, her gaze darting in search of another human being. The garage was nearly empty. Friday night. Who stayed at work late other than her? "Can I . . ." She narrowed her gaze, deciding the best thing to do was to look right at him. "Were you . . . looking for me?"

He looked away, then back at her, stuffing his hands into his jeans. "I was. Sorry if I startled you. I didn't think I should come to your . . . Ms. Bordeaux's house."

She waited.

"I wanted to talk to you because . . . because you were asking about Eddie and me and . . . and I really feel guilty. With him, you know, being dead and all now."

"You feel guilty?" She tried not to get too excited. He said he *felt* guilty, not that he *was* guilty.

He was now looking down at his boots as if he were a kid, shuffling his feet. This was not Eddie's killer. Nikki didn't know if she should be disappointed or relieved. At least she wasn't going to be murdered in a parking garage.

"I lied," he said.

Chapter 23

"To me?" she questioned.

"To everyone. My friends. Mr. Bernard. That detective." He looked as if he might cry. "Worse thing is, I lied to Mac."

"Mac?"

"My boyfriend. It was last November. We were going through a rough patch." He massaged his temples. "I was hanging out at The Python a lot. Mac didn't like it. And he didn't like Eddie."

"But you did?"

He looked away, then back again. "Please don't say anything to Ms. Bordeaux. I'd hate for her to be disappointed in me. See, I liked the free cocaine. I liked hanging out with Eddie because he had cool friends. Not really *friends*," he corrected. "But you know, the guy with the free drugs is never alone. I liked being a part of that scene."

The elevator behind Nikki opened and she stepped

aside. She wasn't afraid to be alone in the garage with Rocko anymore. She nodded to the guy getting off the elevator as he walked past them. She waited until he disappeared into the rows of cars. "So what did you lie about?"

"About everything." Rocko scuffed his black boot. "The whole thing with Eddie."

"The . . . *affair?*" she said, for lack of a better word. She heard a car's engine start.

He nodded. "Mac and I were fighting a lot and there was this cute guy at the coffee shop who kept asking him out and I was jealous. I was jealous," he repeated. "And I wanted to make Mac jealous, so I told him that Eddie and I had sex."

Nikki actually felt badly for Rocko. He really *was* upset.

"After that, the lie sort of took on a life of its own. Mac told someone at work, who told someone else. It got back to Eddie."

Nikki tucked her phone into her bag. "That's how you ended up in the fight at The Python Club?"

"It wasn't really a fight. I tried to talk to Eddie. He punched me. Then I got all pissed and called the police." He exhaled. "It was all the drugs I was doing. Coke to get high, then downers so I could sleep. I wasn't thinking right. I kept *wanting* to tell the truth, but the lie snowballed. Next thing I know, I'm meeting with Eddie and Mr. Bernard and Mr. Bernard is offering to buy me a new motorcycle to keep my mouth shut."

"About a liaison that never took place?"

Rocko nodded.

"But . . . you said you met with Mr. Bernard *and* Eddie. Didn't the fact that Eddie hadn't had sex with you come up?"

He shook his head. "It wasn't Eddie's money. He didn't care. He just wanted me to keep my mouth shut. He didn't want people thinking he was bi, or whatever."

Nikki thought for a moment. "So what you said about the argument with Eddie this last Friday was true? You *didn't* crash the party?"

He shook his head. "No. Everyone in town was talking about the party, about going. Eddie e-mailed a lot of people, inviting them. I had no intention of going. I only stopped by because I had to make the service call. I couldn't find anything wrong; the filter was working fine. Then I left."

"And you didn't go back later that night?"

"No, ma'am," he said firmly. "I went home and had a Lean Cuisine and watched a *Big Bang Theory* marathon on TV with Mac."

"You didn't kill Eddie."

He shook his head again.

"And you don't know who did?"

Again, she got a no.

Nikki squeezed his muscular forearm. "Go home, Rocko. Have a nice evening with Mac."

He gave her a half smile and walked over to a green crotch rocket parked near the elevator. She watched him put on his helmet, start the bike, and drive away before she walked to her Prius, two rows over. She tossed her bag onto the passenger seat and was climbing in when movement caught her eye. Someone lunged toward her. She was almost in the car, prepared to slam the door, when Kaiser caught her by the arm and pulled her back out.

"I need to talk to you," he said in a gruff voice.

She tried to jerk her arm from him. "Jeez! You scared me half to death." She backed up against the car, feeling like an idiot. Her phone was now *in* the car, in her bag. How was she going to call the police to tell them where to find her dead body? "What do you want?"

He reached around her and closed the door, pressing up against her and pinning her against her car. She looked up at him. Up close, the swastika tattoo wasn't any more attractive.

"You need to stop asking questions about me."

"Do I?" She sounded braver than she felt.

"Yeah, you do, because, otherwise, you're going to end up in the same place as Eddie. In the cemetery."

Nikki was pretty sure she was shaking. "Are you saying you killed him and you'll kill me if I don't drop it?"

He frowned. "I didn't kill Eddie. Eddie killed himself with drugs."

She glanced in the direction of the elevator. The light was blinking. It was headed down again. *Please, oh, please, let someone be going to their car.* She looked at Kaiser. He smelled good, like Calvin Klein cologne, which didn't seem to fit with the tattoo and the intimidation. "Eddie didn't die from a drug overdose. He died because someone stuck a pair of gardening shears in his heart."

"But it wasn't me. And that detective cleared me." He pointed at her angrily. "Which means *you* need to stop asking people about me, and stop bringing my name up around town."

"What detective? Dombrowski?" She dared to look him in the eye. "He talked to you?"

"I got an alibi. He checked it out."

What Kaiser was saying didn't make any sense. He was a known drug dealer. He'd killed a man. Allegedly. He'd threatened Astro.

"But you." He pointed again. "You're stirring up trouble and I don't like it."

"But . . . you're a drug dealer. People like you—"

"I said, let it go!"

He slammed the heel of his hand against her car and she jumped . . . but she didn't burst into tears. She was scared, but she was more angry than scared. Jorge's very life could be at risk and she wasn't going to let this tattooed, anti-Semitic jerk get in the way of her finding the truth.

She looked him in the eye, trying to look as tough as she could. "You say Lieutenant Detective Dombrowski cleared you. You mind if I call him and confirm that? With my cell phone . . . in the car." She pointed behind her.

He cursed under his breath and turned slightly away from her as if in indecision. Then he reached inside his leather jacket.

Nikki trembled. He was reaching for a gun. She saw the handle inside his coat.

Was this it? Was she going to die in a parking garage?

It's funny how the mind works when you think you might die. Time really did slow down . . . almost stop. But the darnedest things go through your mind.

She thought of her mother.

As Kaiser slid his hand slowly out of his jacket, Nikki debated whether or not to close her eyes. Was it better to not know it was coming, or did she want the satisfaction of making him see the light die in her eyes?

"You need to stop asking questions about me," Kaiser repeated, almost in a whisper. "You could cost me my life and the lives of others." Then he opened his hand and flashed a badge.

She only saw it for a second. The first thing she saw was the *U.S.* in the center of the shiny gold shield. Then, the words *Special Agent*, then *Drug Enforcement Administration*.

Holy crappoli! By the time Nikki realized what he had shown her, he was walking away.

"But the tattoo," she called after her.

He touched his neck. "Airbrushed. Hollywood make-believe."

She took a deep, shaky breath, got into her car, and locked the doors. Why, she had no idea. Only then did she exhale.

So . . . she guessed she could cross Special Agent *Kaiser* off the suspect list. As soon as her heart slowed down.

Marshall's party, the following night, was every bit the dog and pony show he'd said it would be. His mansion on Beverly Drive was lit up like a Christmas tree, complete with gushing fountains, moving searchlights . . . and a red carpet to greet the limos. Had there been trumpeters in tights announcing the arrival of the guests, she wouldn't have been surprised.

As Nikki waited in a line of cars for valet parking, she considered doing a donut in Marshall's yard and going back the way she came. It had been a rough day. A rough week. And as much as she hated to admit it, as unfeminist as it seemed, all she wanted right now was to curl up in Jeremy's arms, in his bed, and let him whisper sweet nonsense in her ear.

The trip to prison to see Jorge had been worse than she'd imagined. When she'd arrived at the visitors' center, she'd learned that while Jorge *could* have visitors, she would not be one of them today. Apparently, the only way to visit a prisoner in the state system was to receive a questionnaire, signed by said prisoner, and submit it to prison staff for consideration. The female guard (who looked like one of Tolkein's hobbits) denied her access to Jorge and had made a point of telling her she would be required to list all convictions and arrests, even arrests not leading to a conviction. Nikki had wondered if there was a statute of limitations on the arrests. She didn't bother to ask; she had a feeling Jorge himself was going to be more of a hindrance to her visiting than her juvenile run-ins with the law.

Nikki had left the prison frustrated and annoyed. With Jorge. With herself. A week had passed since Jorge's arrest, and she still didn't know who had killed Eddie. She only knew who hadn't: Rocko was off the list, as was DEA Agent Kaiser.

And then there was the matter of the threatening note left on her car seat. She didn't know what to do about it. Her solution, for now, was to pretend it didn't exist. She had more slippery fish to fry.

She had left a couple of messages on Hector's cell phone, but had gotten no callback. She'd also called his house and talked to Rosalia. Rosalia had promised that her husband would return Nikki's call, but she still hadn't heard from Hector. If Hector didn't get back to her in the next day, she'd track him down at work on Monday. She really didn't think Hector was responsible for the note. It just wasn't his style and, honestly, he wasn't that clever. But she was trying to follow all her leads and, as her mother had suggested, not allow personal feelings to get in the way.

Next in line, Nikki pulled up and a valet in a tuxedo opened her door. "Ms. Harper. Good to see you this evening."

"Thank you." She didn't recognize him, but that often happened to her. She grabbed her silk handbag off the seat and struggled to get out of the car. Why in heaven's name Marshall had to make these things black-tie affairs, she didn't know. Her dress was a navy blue satin sleeveless number with a splash of Swarovski crystals on the left hip: a Chanel copy of a 1930s original and one of her favorite gowns. She was quite sure that tomorrow the media would be commenting on the need for Victoria Bordeaux's daughter to expand her wardrobe, but she didn't care what the press thought. She liked the dress and she intended to continue wearing it.

The young man offered his hand to help her out of the car. Nikki's heels had barely reached the red carpet when she heard the familiar whirr and snap of dozens of cameras. In this age of digital cameras, the press no longer flashed and popped. Instead, they sounded like a swarm of clicking insects.

Nikki flashed *the smile*.

"Ms. Harper, would you like to comment on the arrest of your mother's gardener for the murder of Eddie Bernard?" someone shouted. A big microphone loomed in front of her.

Nikki strolled down the red carpet, smiling left, then right.

"Ms. Harper! You were seen going into the Los Angeles County State Prison today. Did you visit with your mother's gardener?"

"Will Jorge Delgado confess?"

The questions came faster and Nikki tried to walk faster . . . with grace. And not fall in her heels.

"Do you think Mr. Delgado's case will result in changes in immigration laws?" someone shouted.

"Does your mother feel responsible for Eddie Bernard's death?" another demanded.

Nikki kept *the smile* plastered on her face and hurried through the front door, escaping the press as she crossed the threshold. As she entered Marshall's enormous foyer, she realized her heart was pounding and she was breathing in short, shallow gasps.

"Ms. Harper!"

"Nikki!"

They were still calling after her.

"Nik, you okay?"

There were people everywhere. The room was loud and voices echoed off the Carrara marble floor.

"Nikki."

She felt someone touch her bare arm and she spun around.

It was Marshall . . . with blond, bodacious twins at his sides. "You okay, hon?"

She looked up at him and had to laugh. At herself. What was wrong with her? She'd spent her whole life in the public eye. Why would she let a couple of cameras and microphones spook her? The media fed on controversy and the discomfort of others. They couldn't sell papers, magazines, and advertising spots on TV without sensationalizing events. "I'm fine." Her smile was genuine. "I'm good."

"It's about time you got here. I was afraid you were going to stand me up. Champagne?" He waved to one of the hunky guys in tuxes carrying silver serving trays of drinks and hors d'oeuvres.

His dates were tall and skinny and blond . . . just the way his publicist liked them. They each took a glass of champagne.

"I better not," she said, pressing her silk clutch to her.

"Long day?" Marshall leaned down and kissed her cheek.

He smelled delicious. And safe.

"You sure you're okay?" he asked, his handsome face suddenly serious. He was wearing an Armani tux; diamond cuff links sparkled at his wrists.

"I'm fine. I'm fine." She laughed again and stroked his freshly shaved cheek. "Mother?"

"Already here. Holding court in the salon." He pronounced it, black eyebrows arched, the French way Victoria did: sa-*lon*.

"Ah, well, I suppose I should go pay homage." She nodded to both young women. "Nice to meet you, ladies."

"Ella and Bella," Marshall introduced.

Nikki nodded again and walked away. She stopped to speak to several people on her way to the sa-*lon* . . . people she knew and some she didn't. She had her hand shaken, both cheeks kissed, and, as she slipped past a group of men, she was pretty certain someone tried to caress her back-end curves. She was crossing the hall and trying to protect her derriere when she heard a familiar voice call her name above the buzz of the room. A tipsy voice.

"Nikki! Oh, Nikki!"

It was Ginny Bernard. She wore a beautiful black-and-white Yves Saint Laurent gown and a long string of pearls. She held a full glass of champagne. Apparently, not her first.

"Nikki."

"Ginny." They air-kissed. "It's good to see you. I'm *surprised* to see you." She looked around. "Is Abe here?"

"No. He just wasn't up to it, but he insisted I attend. We can't stop living, you know." She took a sip of champagne.

"No, of course not. I agree." She looked into Ginny's face. "How are you? I mean, *really*."

Ginny closed her eyes for a moment. "Hanging in there." She opened her eyes. "The press has been brutal. And everything on the news about Jorge and immigration . . ." She shook her head. "It's just stupid."

"It's ridiculous," Nikki agreed. "Everyone seems to keep talking about him as if he's an illegal. He was *born* here."

"You know," Ginny lowered her voice as she took another sip—*gulp*—of champagne, "that detective has been at our house several times this week." Her gaze darted around them, then back to Nikki. "I don't think he thinks the gardener did it."

"No?" Nikki whispered. She had considered that the threatening note could have come from Ginny, but would Ginny have brought up the investigation if *she* were the one who killed Eddie? It seemed highly unlikely. "Who does he think did it?" she asked.

"God only knows." She pressed her hand to her stomach. "God, my girdle is tight." She took another drink. "Look, I need to tell you something. I don't know how to say it, Nikki, so I'm just going to come out with it."

"Okay," she said.

"Ellen." She punctuated the name with a hiccup. "I think you need to be careful with her."

Ginny looked up. Spotting someone she apparently knew, she grabbed Nikki's arm and pulled her into the library; the room was floor-to-ceiling books, books Nikki doubted had been touched since they'd been unpacked when Marshall "moved in" two years ago.

"Careful with Ellen? How so?" Nikki asked.

Ginny took another sip. "She's not the little innocent she appears to be. I know the two of you have become friendly, but I think you need to watch her."

"Watch her?" Nikki frowned. "I don't understand."

Ginny guzzled the last quarter of her glass and waved to a passing waiter to bring her another.

"She may have befriended you for ulterior motives."

Nikki waited for Ginny to take a fresh glass and

hand the empty one to the server. He offered Nikki a glass, but she declined. Ginny waited until he stepped out of the library before she spoke again.

"Ellen was at the house that night." She tipped her glass. "I bet she didn't tell you *that*, did she?"

Nikki was beginning to wonder if she should have taken the waiter up on the offer of alcohol. "Okay, she was at the party?"

"Not really." Ginny frowned. "She was at our house while the party was going on. She was with Abe, down in his man-cave in the basement. He thought I was at the Beverly Wilshire, so I guess she waltzed right into my home."

Nikki didn't know what to say. It didn't matter; Ginny needed no encouragement.

"That's right," Ginny went on. "Sweet, gorgeous Ellen, who my Abe got that job for at the Food Network, was alone with my husband the night Eddie was killed."

"Are . . . are you suggesting that Ellen might be a suspect in Eddie's death?" Nikki asked incredulously.

"No, of course not. Aren't you listening? What I'm suggesting is that your friend Ellen is having an affair with my husband!"

Chapter 24

"I'm sorry." Nikki leaned closer. The voices coming from the hall were so loud, she could barely hear Ginny. "What did you say?"

"I think Abe is having an affair with Ellen," she said louder. "I'm afraid . . ." Tears filled Ginny's eyes and she took a sip of champagne, but tentatively this time. "I'm afraid Abe's going to divorce me for Ellen."

"Oh, I'm sure this is a misunderstanding." Nikki rubbed Ginny's shoulder.

"No, I'm sure of it. A woman knows these things."

Nikki considered the information for a moment. Had she again misjudged a friend? Could Ellen be the kind of person who had an affair with a married man, right under his wife's—and ex-wife's—noses?

"I think you've got it wrong. I think you should talk to Abe. Abe loves you. I'm sure this is all just a misunderstanding." Nikki went on faster than before, trying to convince herself as she tried to convince Ginny. "They were getting ready to shoot Ellen's show. I'm sure this is about work. Ellen isn't having an affair with Abe. He wouldn't do that to you."

Ginny looked away. "He did it to Melinda," she said softly.

"Nicolette, there you are! It's about time you arrived." Victoria glided into the room in a floor-length, dove-gray, beaded gown that was simply stunning with her blond hair. For a woman her age, she still had amazing feminine curves. She wore no jewelry, other than a pair of gray pearls in her ears. An entourage of men and women in gorgeous gowns and handsome tuxedos followed her.

"Mother." Nikki walked to Victoria to give her a quick but real kiss on the cheek.

Victoria looked surprised, then pleased, by the small token of true affection. "Ginny," she said, tearing her gaze from her daughter, offering her hand to her neighbor, as only a queen would.

"Good to see you, Victoria." Ginny smiled, but couldn't hide her sadness. She squeezed Victoria's hand. "If you'll excuse me, I see Rob Reiner. I should say hello."

Seeing Victoria having *a moment* with her daughter, Victoria's admirers drifted away.

"You all right, dear? You look pale." Victoria peered into Nikki's face and touched the corner of her mouth. "You should touch up your lipstick."

Instead of taking her mother's words as criticism, as she often did, Nikki took them for what they were: Victoria's way of expressing concern. "Are you having a nice evening, Mother?"

"I am." She tapped Nikki lightly on the arm, turning as if to go, then turning back. "By the way, I called M." (She always called him M. rather than Mr. M. His last name was very long, very Swedish or Norwegian and very difficult to pronounce.) "I told him we needed to speak. We've been invited to brunch tomorrow."

"Mr. M. invited us to his home? I thought he didn't receive visitors." Nikki considered the young woman who had answered the door there, and the services she might be providing, but *she* didn't really count as a visitor, did she?

"He receives *me*, dear. I told you, he fancies himself in love with me. Has since . . . well, since ages ago. We'll have a nice brunch, we'll catch up, and you can conduct your inquiry." She looked at Nikki more closely. "Are you certain you're not ill?"

"I'm fine." Nikki sighed, tucking her bag under her arm. "I'm upset. Ginny just told me something, something awful. About Ellen. But I don't think it can be true."

Elsewhere in the house, an orchestra struck up a waltz. Later in the evening, Marshall had said, James Taylor would be singing in the garden.

"Whatever did Ginny say?"

Nikki looked at the floor, then back at her mother. "That Ellen was at the Bernards' that night. The night Eddie was murdered. Not working. *Visiting.*"

"Good heavens, don't tell me Ellen wanted him dead, too?"

Nikki pressed her lips together, not sure if she wanted to laugh or cry. "Ginny wasn't insinuating that Ellen had killed Eddie." She met her mother's

Bordeaux blues with her own. "Ellen didn't tell me she was there. We've talked several times. About Jorge. About the party. About the circumstances of the murder. We had lunch together. Why would she not mention she was there?"

"If Ginny wasn't suggesting that Ellen killed her stepson, what *was* she suggesting?"

Nikki hated to even say it out loud, but Ginny was right. It was suspicious that Ellen hadn't told Nikki about being there that night. Why would she keep it a secret . . . unless she had *another* secret? "That Ellen and Abe are having an affair."

Victoria burst into laughter. "That old geezer? Ellen is gorgeous. Why would she want Abe? He's got to be thirty-five years her senior and six inches shorter."

"He's done a lot for her since she came to L.A.," Nikki argued. "Stranger things have happened."

"Well, there's only one way to find out, isn't there?" Victoria patted her already perfect coiffure. "Ask her."

A different, young, beautiful, top-heavy woman greeted Nikki and Victoria at Mr. M.'s door the following morning. Again, dressed like a naughty maid.

Victoria looked her up and down. "Good morning, darling," she said with a cheerful smile.

"Good morning! Mr. M. is waiting for you in the sunroom. I'm so tickled he's having friends over." She giggled.

Victoria looked at Nikki, arched her brows, and smiled again at the blonde as she walked in the door.

"Champagne." She handed over the bottle she carried in her arms. "I told M. I'd bring it for mimosas. Can you make a mimosa, dear?"

"I can." Another giggle. She closed the door behind Nikki. "Right this way."

Nikki had never been in Mr. M.'s house. Her jaw dropped as they walked down a well-lit white hall that looked more like it belonged in an art gallery than in a home. The walls were lined with amazing photographs that had to have spanned forty years, most of which appeared to have been taken from his perch atop his house. Nikki stopped at a nearly life-size picture of Victoria, twenty years ago, getting out of her white Bentley in her driveway. Victoria was wearing a little Jackie O. suit and her pearls, and was smiling at someone in the distance.

Nikki stopped to stare at the photo. "Mother," she said softly.

Victoria stopped and looked back at the photo. "Isn't that nice?" she said. Then, under her breath, "I told you he was in love with me."

Nikki continued down the hall. There were photos of Rosemary Clooney, Lucille Ball, Gary Morton, Maureen O'Sullivan, and Mia Farrow, all of whom had lived on Roxbury at one time or another. And more photographs of Victoria. Photographs of her when she was young . . . and photographs that appeared to be quite recent. In a small rectangular frame, there was a series of shots of Victoria beside the Bernards' pool. In one, she was lying on a lounge chair; in the next, rising and taking off a white robe; in a third, she was diving into the pool in a pretty sapphire one-piece bathing suit, a swim cap on her head. Nikki recognized the bathing suit; Victoria had bought it a year ago.

There was a photo of Nikki, too. From many years ago. She was in shorts and a T-shirt, barefoot, reading on a bench that had once been in the front yard. She studied it for a moment, and decided she liked it.

"Mother, I had no idea," Nikki said, stunned by the amazing photographs . . . and the Victoria Bordeaux shrine.

"A little unnerving, isn't it?" Victoria continued to walk down the hallway, her loafers tapping on the polished chestnut flooring. "I just don't look at them."

"You . . . you come here? I thought you said you and Mr. M. weren't speaking . . . because of that photograph that was published last year." Nikki followed her mother and the blonde, but was still gazing at the beautiful photographs that lined the walls.

"Perhaps I was exaggerating a little." She pursed her lips. "For heaven's sake, he's a recluse. Someone needs to visit him other than—" She cut her eyes meaningfully at the young woman leading the charge.

All Nikki could do was smile.

They were led to a double-eaved, curved sunroom filled with tropical plants and white wicker furniture. A beautiful table had been set with white china, flowers at each place setting.

"Mr. M.," the blonde cooed.

Nikki was so busy taking in the amazing room that she didn't see, at first, the elderly gentleman standing beside a large, potted, banana palm. He was on the short side and thin, with a head of silver hair . . .

and was wearing a silk robe and silk pajama pants, à la Hugh Hefner.

"M., darling." Victoria walked to him and presented her hand.

He bowed and kissed it as if she were royalty, then kissed her cheeks, one and then the other. "Victoria, I'm honored. And your daughter, Nicolette." He walked to Nikki and offered his hand. "I'd recognize those Bordeaux blues anywhere."

Nikki shook his hand.

"I'll make up a pitcher of mimosas," the blonde called from the doorway, then disappeared with the bottle of champagne.

"I'm so honored you could join me." Mr. M. led them to the table and pulled out a chair for Victoria, then one for Nikki. He took a chair next to Victoria.

"Your photographs are incredible, Mr. M. I've never seen those pictures of Mother."

"All part of my private collection."

"You took them all? Even the one with her in the little blue hat with the veil?"

He flashed a handsome smile at her mother. "I took that on the set. I was interested in amateur photography, even as a young man."

Another blonde arrived with a plate of eggs Benedict, salad, and fresh fruit, followed by the first blonde with a big pitcher of mimosas made with freshly squeezed orange juice and Victoria's excellent, but not ridiculously expensive, champagne.

As they shared the meal, Nikki mostly listened to her mother and Mr. M. talk as they recalled past events on Roxbury Drive, and in Hollywood and Beverly Hills. Mr. M. was gracious, well spoken, and amazingly entertaining. Nikki could have sat there and listened to the two of them all day. It wasn't until after the dishes were cleared from the table that Victoria worked her way to the true reason for their visit.

"M., I know you're aware of the unfortunate incident that occurred last weekend on our street."

"I was shocked, Victoria. And for you to find him in your trash." He shook his head. "I would have given anything to have spared you that sight."

Victoria waved her hand as if to say *whatever*. "I'm sure you're also aware that my gardener was implicated in the crime."

"He was charged." Nikki looked to Mr. M. "Jorge is a longtime friend, and the son of Mother's housekeeper. But you probably already know that," she added. "Anyway, he didn't kill Eddie, Mr. M., but he's in jail and refuses representation."

"Why is he refusing representation?" he asked.

"Because he's young and foolish, that's why," Victoria put in.

Nikki looked from her mother to Mr. M. "I'm trying to figure out who *did* kill Eddie."

The elderly man looked at Nikki. "Are you certain he didn't do it? I saw the fight that night. I feared for the Mexican's life."

Nikki knew not to be offended by Mr. M.'s reference. He was eighty years old, if he was a day. The world he had lived in was not the world of today. "You saw the fight?"

"I did, although there was so much to observe that night, it's a miracle I didn't miss it. The gunshot drew my attention." He frowned. "Eddie Bernard was a foolish young man. I always felt badly for Abe and Melinda."

"That night," Nikki said, trying to steer the conversation back to the party again, "how much did you see?"

"Oh, I got an eyeful." He adjusted his horn-rimmed glasses.

Victoria smiled at Nikki slyly, then looked back to Mr. M. "Do tell."

"Drugs, alcohol, nakedness," he muttered, seeming embarrassed.

"We were there, at one point." Nikki pushed away slightly from the table.

"I saw you. Very brave of you to go to the Mexican's rescue." He glanced at Victoria and winked. "Nut doesn't fall far from the tree."

Nikki was beginning to feel a little weird about Mr. M.'s compliments to her mother, but Victoria didn't seem to be in the least bit disturbed. "It's really what happened after the party that I'm interested in. Did you . . . see the party end?"

"Heard it. I was watching a movie in my bedroom. Eddie Bernard's parties bore me after a while. Always the same."

Nikki sighed. "So . . . you didn't see anything after midnight?"

"I . . . think I wandered upstairs once after midnight. I have insomnia."

"Did you see anything, M.," Victoria questioned kindly, "that might help Nikki with her investigation?"

He hesitated.

"M.?"

"It was late . . . actually, early morning. I was only

up there a moment." He stopped, and started again. "There was a man in the pool and then he got out. It was . . . three thirty . . . four, maybe."

Victoria arched her brows. "Do you know who it was?"

He shook his head. "I didn't have the right glasses on. I do that sometimes." He chuckled. "He was bald, I think." He touched his head.

Victoria looked at Nikki.

Nikki thought for a minute. Some of the photos on the wall . . . they had been in a series, as if one had been taken right after the other. "Mr. M." She looked him in the eye. "I know you have a telescope."

He cleared his throat.

"I don't care. I don't judge you," Nikki said quickly. "But do you also have cameras set up? Do they take pictures of your neighbors when you're not watching?"

He cleared his throat again. "I . . . I don't—"

"Mr. M.," Nikki said as gently as she could, "the pictures of my mother in the hall, the series of photos of her in the blue swimsuit. They were taken at the Bernards', last Labor Day."

"A very attractive swimsuit, I might say," he told Victoria.

She smiled flirtatiously. "Why, thank you, M."

"The camera that you used to take those pictures of my mother, is it on a tripod, or were you holding a camera?"

Again, he looked nervous. "I took those pictures with my Nikon D7000, and a telephoto zoom. It was a beautiful day. I was in my perch for hours."

"Okay." Nikki thought for a moment, then looked

at him. "But you also have cameras on tripods, too, don't you? For when you're not on your perch. You take pictures of your neighbors. Of all of us. A lot of pictures."

Victoria touched his arm. "It's all right, M. I'm rather flattered."

"I do have cameras set on tripods," he answered sheepishly. "So . . . so I don't miss anything."

"Do you have a camera set on the Bernards' yard?"

"I . . . have one that shows the Bernards' pool area. Part of it."

"Do you have pictures from the night Eddie died? After the party was over?"

"Possibly," he answered.

Nikki smiled kindly. She supposed she should have been upset; after all, Mr. M. *was* sort of a stalker. But he was harmless, that was obvious. And his voyeurism could possibly be helpful in figuring out who killed Eddie. "Have you looked at the photos from that night?"

He shook his head.

"Could you?"

He hesitated.

"Maybe you could print them for us, M. Just off your printer here, however it is you do that." Victoria gave his hand a squeeze as she rose. "Could you do that? For me, M.?"

He looked at Nikki, then back at Victoria. "For you. Maybe I could print them. But, they're probably not very good."

Nikki got up. "That's okay. There's probably nothing to see. I just . . ." She looked at him as he, too, stood. "It's worth having a look. Did . . . did a detective happen to come speak with you? Detective Dombrowski?"

"Tall chap? Nice suit?"

"That would be him."

"He's come by. We don't answer the door to strangers," Mr. M. said.

Victoria kissed his leathery cheek. "Thank you so much for brunch, M. It was wonderful seeing you." She looked into his eyes. "And thank you for helping my daughter. I can't tell you how much this means to me. We'll let ourselves out."

Victoria walked away. "Nicolette."

Nikki took a couple of quick steps to catch up, praying Mr. M. would have the lead she needed.

Chapter 25

It took Nikki the remainder of the day to get up the nerve to call Ellen, even though she spent the afternoon on the phone. She listened to Marshall talk about who had come to his party, who hadn't, and what the latest gossip in town was. She chatted with Jeremy. She, again, tried to get a hold of Hector; there was no answer on his cell or at his house. She even called her painter and chewed him out about the delays on her house, just to postpone her conversation with Ellen.

Finally, sitting alone in her room in her mother's house, the dogs lounging on the bed (where they were not allowed to be), she hit Ellen's name on speed dial. By the third ring, she was ready to chicken out and hang up. What kind of message could she possibly leave? Just as she was about to hit the END button on her phone, Ellen picked up.

"Nikki! How are you?"

"I'm . . . I'm well."

"I'm really looking forward to having you come to the set tomorrow. Friday was crazy. I was making these cream puffs that were supposed to look like individual servings of mashed potatoes, but they were a total fail. I bet I've made them a dozen times, but once I was in front of the camera, I was all thumbs."

Nikki stroked Oliver, the Blenheim.

"I was mortified," Ellen went on. "But, oh my gosh, you should have seen the pizza that looked like cherry cobbler. It was divine."

Oliver made little grunting sounds of contentment as Nikki rolled him over and rubbed his belly. Jealous, Stanley inched across the duvet, wanting his share of the attention.

"I was thinking, if you came at noon *and* we're running on time, you could watch me tape one episode and then we could have lunch together. The house Abe rented has this cute little patio with a table and lounge chairs . . ."

The mention of Abe made Nikki feel sick to her stomach. "Ellen," she said. "I need to . . . talk to you about something."

"Sure," she said, cheerfully. "Sorry, I'm running on. Too much coffee. I've been trying to make this chocolate dessert in a martini glass and it—oh, gosh, here I go again." She inhaled, then exhaled. "What's up?"

Nikki laid back, resting her head on the upholstered headboard. "I have to ask you . . ." She stopped, then started again. "Last Friday night, were you at the Bernards' house?"

Ellen was quiet on the other end of the line.

Not a good sign.

Nikki waited, a sinking feeling in the pit of her stomach. The worst thing was, she really liked Ellen.

"I'm sorry," Ellen said finally. "I should have told you." She paused. "But . . . it was personal."

"Personal?" Nikki echoed.

"Yes. I didn't want to share because . . . I wasn't comfortable sharing. Someone else was involved."

"You were with Abe."

"I . . . How do you know that?" Ellen asked.

"It doesn't matter." Nikki sighed. "But I need the truth."

"Oh, God, Nikki, please don't tell me you think I killed Eddie."

Nikki looked into Ollie's big, dark eyes. "No. I don't think you killed Eddie. But I have to ask, what were you doing with Abe?"

"What was I *doing*?" Ellen's voice took on a prickly tone.

"Yes, what were you doing with Abe?"

"Nikki, I don't really think that's any—" Ellen stopped midsentence. "We were discussing business."

"Alone. In Abe's basement, with him? In his . . . private room?"

Ellen was quiet again for a second. "Nikki, it's not what you think."

"No?"

"No. I can't tell you what we were discussing. It was confidential. Between Abe and me."

Nikki groaned. "Ellen, I'm just going to come out and say it. Are you having an affair with Abe Bernard?"

"No," she said quickly. "God, no, Nikki. Do I seem to you to be that kind of person?" Now she sounded angry.

"I don't know, Ellen." Nikki ran her hand over her face. "I don't know what to think." She exhaled. "I'm beginning to think I'm not as good a judge of character as I once thought."

"Listen to me, Nikki," Ellen said, enunciating each word. "I am not having an affair with Abe Bernard. He's married."

"But something *is* going on," Nikki intoned. "You were seen at The Palm, having lunch."

"He's my producer. We had lunch. In a public place. If I was banging my boss, do you think I would have gone to lunch with him at The Palm?"

Nikki was quiet.

"Look," Ellen said after a minute. "I'm not going to tell you what's been *going on* between Abe and me. You're just going to have to take my word on it that it's not . . . inappropriate. Between the two of us." She was quiet again for a moment. "You're not coming to my set tomorrow, are you?"

Nikki bit down on her lower lip. "I don't think so."

"Okay, I understand. No, no, I really don't." Again, Ellen paused. "Have a good evening."

She hung up.

Nikki tossed the cell phone onto her bed and scooped Ollie up into her arms and cuddled him. "So now what do we do?" she asked, feeling just awful. She'd probably just lost a friend with that phone call.

Stan nosed his way into her lap.

"Track down Hector? Find out where the heck

Ree is? Is that what you say?" She rubbed one soft head and then the other, feeling worse with each passing moment. "Okay," she said firmly. "Okay, I can do that."

And if Hector couldn't give her any helpful information? If Mr. M.'s photos didn't offer any answers? Then what? she wondered.

Then she had to pray that Dombrowski was doing a better job investigating than she was, or Jorge might really have to stand trial and take his chances.

Monday morning, Nikki tried Hector's cell phone one last time. When he didn't pick up, she headed to Brentwood. Ina had been more than happy to tell Nikki where Hector was working and asked Nikki to remind him not to waste time because she needed him in Bel Air in the afternoon.

Nikki knew the house; she'd sold it to the present owners. It was a lovely two-story home with an enclosed front courtyard that separated it nicely from the street. She pulled up behind the JORGE & SON utility truck; this was the truck Jorge usually drove. Nikki spotted Hector from the street; he was in the courtyard, trimming palm fronds. She walked up the sidewalk.

"Hector."

From the look on his face, she was afraid he might run. He knew she'd been looking for him. He really *was* avoiding her. The obvious question was *why*.

"You're a hard man to catch," she said. She pushed her sunglasses up on her head so she could look him in the eye. Because of the retaining wall between the sidewalk and the courtyard, he was standing a few feet above her. She squinted in the sunlight, her hand over her eyes. "You want to come down here and talk to me, or do you want me to come up there?"

He dropped the bag he'd been using to dispose of the brown fronds and jumped down. "I . . . I can't really talk. Work." He hooked his thumb in the direction of the palm tree.

"This will only take a minute; I don't want to keep you from your work. Ina asked me to pass on a message, by the way; she says not to waste any time today. She needs you in Bel Air when you're done here. And she says 'answer your damned cell phone when she calls, the first time'."

He gave her a look that made her hold up her hands.

"Ina's words, not mine," she said.

He adjusted his ball cap, though it didn't really need to be adjusted.

"Okay, Hector, so on to business. The business between you and me." She gestured. "You've been dodging me for days. What's going on?"

He crossed his arms, his posture defensive. "Nothing."

She wasn't in the mood for this today. She was still upset about her conversation with Ellen. Ellen had made it sound as if she were protecting a confidence with Abe by not sharing that she'd been there that night. But what secret could she possibly be keeping?

"You're avoiding me, Hector. What is it that you're not telling me about the night Eddie died?"

"I don't know what you're talking about." He didn't meet her gaze.

So maybe he did have a conscience.

"Do you know where Ree is?"

"No."

"That's funny, because the last time her roommate saw her, she was leaving her apartment with *you* Saturday morning. Saturday morning, while your brother-in-law was turning himself in for a murder he didn't commit, and your pregnant wife was sitting home alone crying."

Hector stroked his pockmarked cheek.

"Hector, did Ree kill Eddie? Did someone kill Eddie *for* her?" She didn't give him time to answer. "Did *you* kill him for her?"

His head snapped up. "No," he said ardently. "I did *not* kill Eddie Bernard. Not that I wouldn't have liked to," he added under his breath.

"Where did you take Ree Saturday morning?" She waited. "Hector, do you understand that there's a real possibility that Jorge could spend the rest of his life in jail? That he could end up on death row if convicted? If you had something to do with Eddie's death, or you know who did, you have to tell me. You can't let Jorge take the fall for this. He's been too good to you."

Again, she waited.

"Ree had nothing to do with Eddie's death," he finally admitted. He looked away again. "I took her to the bus station Saturday morning. She went to Mexico."

"Why?" Nikki demanded.

"Because . . . because it was over."

"What was over?"

She was surprised to see his eyes fill with tears.

"The affair," he said miserably. "She asked me to go with her to Mexico. That night. Friday night. She swore there was nothing between her and Eddie anymore and she wanted me back. I had my bag packed. But then I couldn't do it. I met her and I told her so."

Nikki remembered the morning she was at Jorge's . . . the duffel bag beside the door. She'd been afraid Jorge was about to run. "That was *your* bag by the door that morning, wasn't it?"

He nodded. "I told Rosalia what I'd done. That I was sorry." He ran his hand under his nose. "I'm not proud of myself. But I love Rosalia. And I love my kids. That morning . . . before you called to tell Jorge about Eddie, me and Rosalia, we talked. She told me to go if I wanted to, but I didn't want to. So I took Ree to the bus station and I said good-bye."

"Wait a minute. You said you were out with her Friday night? *After* you got home from work. How late?"

He shrugged. "I don't know. Late. I didn't leave until after Rosalia went to bed."

"Did Jorge know you were having an affair with Ree?"

He stared at his shoes. "No. No, of course not. Rosalia didn't want him to know. She said it was between us. I think she was afraid Jorge would kick me out of the house if he found out."

"So Jorge might have known you were gone that night, but not known you were with Ree?"

He looked up at Nikki. "You think Jorge thinks I killed Eddie? That I packed a bag because I was going to run?"

"It's possible. It would make sense. He wouldn't even provide the police with his own alibi—that he was home with you and his sister."

"Because I wasn't there," Hector whispered.

"Jorge wouldn't say anything to defend himself." She met his gaze. "Maybe because he thought he was protecting you . . . for his sister's sake."

Hector stuffed his hands into his pants pockets. "I didn't mean to do this to my family. I didn't mean to get Jorge into trouble."

"The gardening shears. Do you know what happened to them that day?"

He shook his head. "Jorge asked me to grab them after he said we should go home. We were in the back, putting tools in the shed. He was doing things to clean up. I was doing things. I thought he got the pruning shears."

"So they were *missing?*"

"I . . . I don't know. I guess they were."

"Could someone have come through the side gate, taken them, and gone back to the Bernards' without being seen?"

Hector thought for a moment. "I guess. We were walking back and forth from the truck to the shed."

"Which would explain why you thought Jorge picked up the shears."

"There were a lot of people at Eddie's that day. Anyone could have done it," he said.

Yes. But no. Her list of suspects was now short: Wezley, Ginny . . . Victoria. But Wezley was looking more suspicious to her by the minute. And what about Abe? As preposterous as it seemed, had he lost his patience with his son? Was that the secret Ellen was protecting? Of course, if she added Abe to the list, did she need to include Melinda? *Maybe Melinda and Victoria did it together . . .*

She groaned inwardly. This was making her crazy. She was making herself crazy. She returned her attention to Hector, who seemed to want to say something.

"Are . . . are you going to tell Jorge?" he asked. "About me and Ree?"

She shook her head. "I can't even get in to see Jorge. It's not my business, anyway, Hector. It's up to you and Rosalia what you tell her brother."

He hung his head. "I tried to get in, too. You got to have this form filled out. Ina talked to him on the phone. He doesn't want any visitors. He won't sign to have anyone come."

Nikki slid her glasses back on. "I should let you get back to work," she said. She looked up, remembering the threatening note that was still riding around in her car. "Wednesday morning, you were at Mother's house. Someone left something in my car. You know anything about it? Did you see anyone in the yard when you were mowing that morning . . . someone who could have come from the Bernard property?"

He shook his head and asked, "What did they leave?"

"Doesn't matter," she said, as much to herself as to him. There was always the possibility that Hector was still lying about something, but she didn't think so. He was too upset. Her gut told her that while he was the kind of guy that would cheat on his pregnant wife with her cousin, he wasn't a killer. The pain was too obvious on his scarred face. She walked away. "You have a good day, Hector."

"You, too." He pulled his ball cap off and ran his fingers through his scraggly, dark hair. "Nikki?" he called after her.

She looked back.

"Me and Rosalia, we appreciate what you're doing for our family. For Jorge. But if it don't work out, you can't blame yourself."

She offered a quick smile. "Thanks, Hector."

Nikki got in her car and, as it purred away from the curb, she checked the clock on the dash. She had to get to work for the Monday Morning Meeting, but her day was pretty open after that. Maybe after lunch, she'd hit the Church of Earth and Beyond and sniff around Wezley's office again. She had the perfect excuse: Justin "Beaver" tickets.

Chapter 26

Nikki was just getting into the elevator at the Church of Earth and Beyond when her cell rang. She checked the screen. It was Ellen. She considered not answering it.

She stepped back off the elevator, into the deserted hall. "Hello?"

"I was afraid you weren't going to pick up," Ellen said.

Nikki chewed on her lower lip for a moment. She stared at her shoes. She was wearing what was fast becoming her uniform on bad days: black boots and skirt and short-sleeved sweater. Victoria said she was very New York City. It may not have been a compliment.

There was a scuff on the toe of one foot.

Nikki looked up again. "I seriously considered not answering," she confessed. The elevator door closed behind her. "I thought you were taping your show."

"I am. Lunch break one thirty to two thirty. I'm

calling because I was upset by our phone conversation yesterday. I really wish you'd come by today."

"Sorry," Nikki said. "My afternoon is busy."

Ellen exhaled. "Okay. Look, Nik, I really want to be friends. I like you and I think we're a lot alike. I could use a good friend like you. I didn't want to tell you what Abe and I have been talking about, what we were talking about last Friday night in private, because I was hoping he would change his mind."

Nikki was quiet for a moment. "Ellen, if this is something Abe's asked you not to repeat . . ." She exhaled. "I wouldn't ask you to divulge something told to you in confidence."

"I was just hoping I wouldn't have to. It doesn't matter, now, because he's going to do it, anyway. Everyone will know in a few days."

Ellen had Nikki intrigued now. "Okay . . . ," she said.

"Abe has decided to divorce Ginny and remarry Melinda."

"What? You're kidding." Nikki began to pace in front of the elevator. This was as crazy and unexpected as the tattooed gym-rat/bouncer turned DEA agent. "Have . . . Melinda and Abe been . . . seeing each other?"

"No. Melinda doesn't know. Things haven't been good between Abe and Ginny since the beginning. Apparently, he immediately regretted divorcing Melinda and marrying Ginny, but he didn't know what to do. Then the problems with Eddie—"

"Didn't help matters," Nikki interjected.

"Exactly."

"So . . . there's no affair, between you and Abe or Abe and Melinda?"

"No affair," Ellen said. "I told you, I've sworn off men. Unless, of course, Jeremy becomes available."

Nikki laughed, feeling immensely better. "Sorry. He's not."

Ellen laughed with her, then grew more sober. "I really am sorry about this whole thing. I just didn't know what to do. Abe has been so good to me and—"

"You don't have to say any more." Nikki turned to face the elevator that would take her up to the fifth floor. "I shouldn't have jumped to conclusions so quickly. I knew what kind of person you were the minute I met you. I should have followed my instincts." She pushed a lock of hair behind her ear. "It's just that this thing with Jorge and Eddie . . . It's got me so rattled. I don't know what to think about anyone anymore."

"I understand completely. I shouldn't have gotten upset with you yesterday. If I were in your place, I would have reacted the same way." She paused. "So, friends?"

"Friends," Nikki agreed.

"Great. So what day can you come by the set? Tomorrow? Wednesday? We'll be taping the rest of the week."

Nikki hit the CALL button on the elevator and slid her favorite Prada bag up farther on her shoulder. "I'll have to check my calendar, but I think I have lunch open both days."

"Great. Then come by. Both days. Listen, I have to run," Ellen said.

Nikki heard commotion in the background. "Me, too. How about if I call you tonight?"

"Perfect." Ellen paused. "I'm really glad you picked up. Have a good day."

Nikki was smiling when she got on the elevator. "You, too."

She was still smiling to herself when she got off the elevator. Monique was at her post at her desk. Monique did not look happy to see her.

The receptionist glanced down the hallway in the direction of Wezley's office, then back at Nikki. "Ms. Harper."

"Hey, Monique. I came by because . . ." Nikki took a step closer, glancing down the same hallway. "Is he in?" she whispered.

Monique nodded.

Nikki took another step, now standing right in front of Monique's desk. "I kept thinking about what you said. About you not being able to take your son to the Justin Bieber concert." She reached into her bag. "My mother's agent has some connection with his agent or something." She pulled out an envelope. "So I got you four tickets for next month here in L.A." She shrugged as she offered the envelope. "Maybe he could take two friends?"

"Oh, my gosh. For me? For us?" Monique took the envelope and peeked inside. "I . . . I don't know what to say." She looked up. "Thank you so much. My son will be thrilled. How much do I owe you?"

"Oh, no. No, they're yours." Nikki touched her desk. "My mother didn't pay for them. They're yours to enjoy."

Monique fanned her face with the white envelope.

"I can't believe you did this. You don't know me. You don't know my son."

Nikki grimaced. "I felt badly when you told me the story about him going back on his word." She tilted her head in the direction of Wezley's office. "He's an odd duck, that one." She went on before Monique could say anything. "He came to see me last week, after I was here. To my office, apologizing profusely because he remembered that we *had* met. Do you think that's strange?"

Monique set the envelope on her desk. "Not any stranger than half the other things he does."

Nikki waited.

Monique exhaled. "Like putting a security code on his e-mail so I can't get in." She laid her hand on the mouse and dragged it, then pointed at her computer monitor. "It's my job to look over his and Mr. Butterfield's e-mail and mark what's a priority and what isn't." She put up both hands. "I haven't been able to get into his in days. But he's checking his e-mail constantly."

"I wonder why?" Nikki asked. She thought she heard a door open down the hall, but when she looked, she didn't see anyone. As she returned her attention to Monique, she heard the door close. "Any idea?"

Monique either didn't hear the door or was used to such goings-on. "No idea. I asked him and he told me to mind my own business." She lowered her voice. "I've sent out my résumé to several places. I like this church, but I don't like the job. I don't like working for Wezley Butterfield. He scares me."

"He scares you?" Nikki asked. "What do you mean?"

Monique shrugged. "I don't know. I can't explain it. It's just that he's getting worse. He seems worse since he got out of rehab. *Unstable*," she mouthed.

Nikki thought on that for a moment, but, not knowing what to do with it, she smiled at Monique. "I hope you and your son enjoy the concert."

Monique watched her walk to the elevator. "This was really nice of you to do, Ms. Harper." She picked up the envelope with the tickets. "Kind of renews my faith in mankind, you know what I mean?"

Nikki hit the CALL button and smiled. "Actually, I do."

Nikki made two stops on her way back to the office, one to buy dog food and treats at the pet store, the other to make a quick walk-through in a house she was having staged for its impending showing. The *quick* walk-through wasn't.

The employees of the company she'd hired to do the staging had either been drinking on the job or had totally ignored her requests. Instead of staging the Mediterranean-style villa in Hollywood in an elegant, airy, Mediterranean style, with lots of light-colored furniture and plants, they had staged it like a medieval castle . . . or a dragon's lair. The heavy, dark furniture and swords and armor were completely out of place. She spent half an hour on the phone, then waited almost an hour for someone to come to the house and take notes as to what she had in mind for each room.

It was four by the time Nikki returned to Windsor Real Estate. She was juggling her briefcase, her handbag, and an iced chai tea when she stepped off the elevator. "Hey, Carolyn," she called.

"Ms. Harper." Carolyn stood up. "Something was delivered for you by messenger. I had to sign for it and promise I would place it directly into your hands and no one else's," she said solemnly, offering a large manila envelope. The kind that closed with a little string.

"Really?" Nikki walked to Carolyn's desk. (Carolyn never left her post. Nikki wasn't entirely certain she wasn't tethered to the desk by an invisible string, or maybe a force field kept her there.)

"You know who it's from?" Nikki set her iced tea on the edge of Carolyn's desk.

"Nope."

Slinging her handbag onto her shoulder, and placing her briefcase at her feet, Nikki accepted the envelope curiously.

"Oh, and a message. I offered to connect the guy to your voice mail, but he said it was important that you get the message today. He wants to see a commercial property you have listed." Carolyn offered a pink WHILE YOU WERE OUT slip.

Nikki unwound the string and peeked in the manila envelope: photos. Her heart gave a little trip. *Mr. M. had come through.* She closed the envelope quickly and reached for the message. "Thanks." She glanced at the note. It was from a Mr. Morrison. He wanted to see a commercial building in the Plummer Park area. At six thirty. She sighed. She really wasn't up to a showing tonight. "He didn't leave a number?" she asked Carolyn.

Carolyn had taken her seat again. "There's not one on there?"

Nikki looked at her.

"Gosh . . . I'm so sorry. I asked for it and then . . . I'm really sorry."

So now Nikki couldn't even call him back to reschedule. The message said the caller was a Mr. Morrison . . . Mr. Morrison? She couldn't remember having spoken to a Mr. Morrison about that commercial property. Or any other, for that matter, but she talked to a lot of people over the course of a week, a month, a year . . .

Nikki dropped the envelope into her briefcase, and grabbed it and her iced chai. "Thank you, Carolyn," she said.

"You're welcome," Carolyn called brightly after her.

Nikki closed the door to her office before going to her desk. She dropped her handbag on the desk; she wouldn't be here long if she was going to make the appointment in Plummer Park in late-afternoon traffic. Seated at her desk, she took a sip of her iced chai and pulled the manila envelope out of her briefcase.

The photos were eight-by-tens, in black-and-white, and as Mr. M. had warned, not particularly good. They were obviously taken for surveillance reasons, rather than for display. He must have printed them on photo-quality paper on his home computer's printer.

She studied the first one: a picture of the Bernards' side yard and Victoria's. All was quiet on the Bordeaux side, but there were a few people scattered around the visible side of the Bernards' pool. On the bottom of the picture was a time stamp: twelve fifteen A.M.

A time stamp!

Nikki began to shuffle through the photos; there were more than a dozen, one every fifteen minutes. *Please, please let there be some answer here*, Nikki prayed silently as she looked at one and then another. *Even if there were no answers, just something to go on.*

The photographs weren't as easy to interpret as she had hoped. Because they were taken from Mr. M.'s widow's walk, they were practically a bird's-eye view.

She went all the way through them. Then, again. As Astro had said and Mr. M. confirmed, the party broke up shortly after midnight. By one A.M., there was almost no one left in the backyard . . . except for someone in a chaise longue . . . and someone lying in the grass, just off the edge of the photo.

Was that Eddie in the grass? Was he already dead by the one fifteen time stamp? She squinted. All she could see was an arm and part of a sleeve, partially rolled up. She flipped through several photos, which were taken between twelve fifteen and four thirty.

She got a magnifying glass from her desk and studied the arm; it was a dark dress shirt. Eddie had been wearing a polo and hibiscus swim shorts when he died. That definitely wasn't Eddie lying in the grass. She used the magnifying glass to look at the man near the pool. *That* was Eddie in the chaise longue.

Nikki checked the time on her cell phone. She didn't have much time before she had to leave for the appointment with Mr. Morrison. She always liked to unlock a property first, and walk around to make sure there were no dead rodents in view and no squatters. Both of which she'd encountered in her adventures as a real estate broker. (Once, she'd discovered a merry maid in *flagrante delicto*.)

She looked at the pile of photos again. Then again.

Eddie wasn't in the chaise in the three o'clock photo. She flipped forward in time. Mr. M. had said there had been a bald man in the pool. She found the man in the pool, but she couldn't really make out any details. It was just a floating head, really.

Nikki's hands shook as she carefully stacked the photos in a pile and slipped them back in the envelope to look at again later. Right now, she had to get on the road or she was going to be late to her appointment. In light of the evidence in the photos, she was tempted to just skip the appointment. She could explain later to the potential client that she'd had a family emergency or something. But Nikki didn't miss meetings, not even for family emergencies.

She slid the envelope of photographs into her roomy Prada handbag, grabbed her cell phone off the desk, and dropped it, too, into the bag as she went out the door. She wondered if it was time to give Dombrowski a call. She didn't know exactly what she had in the manila envelope, but she was pretty sure she had the answer to who had killed Eddie Bernard.

Chapter 27

Nikki took North Canon to Santa Monica. The commercial building was just off Santa Monica, near Plummer Park. She found a parking place on the street right in front of the building and jumped out of her car. She wanted to turn the lights on inside, but she'd have to go to the breaker at the rear of the first floor.

She unlocked the glass door and went straight back through the building to turn on the electricity. Just as she closed the breaker panel, she heard the door out front open. "Hello!" she called. "Mr. Morrison?"

There was no answer.

Nikki slipped her Prada back up on her shoulder and headed toward the front of the building, passing from the hallway to the front room. The building was a shell that would need work, but it was in good shape and was being offered at an excellent price.

A man in a black trench coat stood just to the left of the door, his back to her.

"Mr. Morrison." She walked toward him. "It's nice to meet you. I'm Nikki Harper." She was just lifting her hand to shake his when he turned around.

"We've met."

Nikki saw his face first. It was Wezley Butterfield. Then she saw the gun.

Nikki put on the brakes six feet from him. She stared at the gun. In all her years of being a real estate broker, she'd encountered a lot of strange things, but never a client with a gun. "Mr. Butterfield?"

His hand was steady; a yellow-gold signet ring reflected the light from the overhead fixtures. "I think we're probably on a first name basis, don't you, Nikki?"

She couldn't take her gaze off the pistol. The pistol . . . the photos . . . The paint she'd picked out for her bedroom walls . . . the ring on Wezley's hand. Nikki's thoughts scattered like ripples from a handful of stones hurled into a pond. She'd almost called Dombrowski on the way over. Why the heck hadn't she called him? "I don't know what this is about, but—"

"You know what this is about," he said. His tone was calm. He didn't sound inebriated. He was stone-cold sober. "I need you to get in your car."

"I think there's been a misunderstanding, Wezley."

"No misunderstanding. You've been snooping around, asking questions because you believe your gardener was falsely accused of killing Eddie Bernard. You should have minded your own business. I need you to go get in your car," he ordered. "You and I are going for a little ride."

"Where?" she whispered, her gaze shifting from the muzzle of the pistol to his face.

"Does it matter?" He seemed almost sad.

She swallowed hard. This wasn't the first time she'd been on this end of a pistol. She didn't feel any calmer this time. Her gaze darted to the door. She wondered if she could—

"Let's go," he said. He grabbed her arm and shoved her.

"In my car?" she asked. Her bag slipped on her shoulder and she shoved it back up again.

Her phone was in her bag . . .

There was no way she'd have time to pull it out and, say, call 9-1-1. But maybe . . . She walked with a shuffling step as he pushed her ahead with his left hand. He held the pistol in his right. She could feel it poke into her ribs.

"You drive," he ordered.

"Please," Nikki begged, feeling as if she ought to be hysterical by now. But she wasn't. Her heart was pounding, but she was in control. She was thinking. Reasoning.

They were out on the sidewalk. A car went by, but its windows were up. There wasn't time to attract the driver's attention.

"Unlock it," he ordered.

She slid her right hand into her bag. "I . . . I can't find my keys." She fumbled in the bag, felt the key fob, and dropped it. Where was the damned phone?

Her fingers closed around her BlackBerry.

He shoved her again. "Get the car unlocked," he ordered under his breath. He was angry now. Which, she sensed, made him even more dangerous.

She turned her head to look into the bag for just an instant. Her thumb found the buttons. She hit one and then hit the OK button; she had no idea who she was calling. "Found them." She clicked the UN-LOCK button on the key fob and pulled her hand out of her bag.

"Don't mess with me. Where are the keys to start the car?"

It was six forty in the evening. Where the heck were the cars? she wondered wildly. What she wouldn't give for some L.A. traffic right now.

"It . . . it doesn't need a key to start it, it just needs the key to be in the vicinity," she explained.

His gaze moved to her bag. "Give that to me," he barked.

Before she could respond, he ripped it off her shoulder. She thought about trying to run, but he was so close. If he pulled the trigger, he might kill her.

He opened the passenger-side door and threw her bag on the floor. Her Prada. Thrown haphazardly on the floor. "Get in," he repeated.

She moved around the hood toward the driver's door. Still no cars. She wondered what he would do if she screamed. From the wild look in his eyes, proba-bly pull the trigger. She opened her door.

"Get in. Don't start it." He waved her toward the car, then got in the other side.

As Nikki got in behind the wheel, she wondered who she'd dialed. Maybe she'd get lucky and have dialed Jeremy or Amondo; they always answered their phones. It was more likely she'd dialed the dogs' groomer or her gynecologist. That was just the kind of luck she had.

"Put on your seat belt. You're not getting out at a red light. Drive," Wezley ordered as he slammed the door shut.

She closed her door and put on her seat belt. She never drove anywhere without her seat belt; even when being kidnapped, apparently.

"Which way?" she asked as loudly as possible, without sounding like she was trying to be loud. All she could do was pray that whoever she called had picked up and was listening now.

"Back onto Santa Monica. East."

"You want me to get back on Santa Monica," she repeated. "Should I go around the block?"

"U-turn," he said.

Nikki pulled out. "Then what?" she asked.

He had his back to the door, his body sideways so that he could hold the gun on his lap, out of view of any passersby, and still keep an eye on her. "I'll tell you."

She cut her eyes at him as she did what he said and made the turn. "There may be a misunderstanding, Wezley," she said. "About Eddie's death . . . and you."

"What did she tell you?"

"Who?"

"Eddie's mother."

"Ginny? Ginny didn't tell me anything." Her brain

was trying to run two conversations, one in her head with herself, the other with Wezley.

"Not, Ginny," he ground out. "Eddie's *mother*. Melinda."

"I'm not following."

"About me. Did she tell you Eddie promised me money and then reneged? Did she tell you how much trouble I was in? That I had to have that money?"

Nikki caught the light and turned off the side street, onto Santa Monica. "Eddie owed you money?"

"He *promised* me money. For the church. Then didn't come through. A hundred thousand dollars."

"For the Church of Earth and Beyond?" she asked. "Melinda . . . said nothing about Eddie . . . intending to give you money. Keep going? We're crossing Poinsettia," she said, trying to enunciate. *Please, please, please, let someone have picked up.*

"Stay on Santa Monica till Wilton," Wezley said. "Take Wilton to Sunset."

"East on Sunset? Are we going to your church?"

"East on Sunset. We're not going to the church."

She dared to steal another glance at him. He was sweating. Now, he looked scared. Not as scared as *she* felt, but scared. "You killed Eddie?" she said, taking a chance. Taking a big chance. But what the heck? If he was going to kill her, she at least had the right to know what had happened, didn't she?

He wiped his mouth with the back of his hand. "I didn't do it on purpose. I . . . I don't even remember doing it."

"You blacked out?"

He stared at her. "I guess. I don't remember."

"But . . . you killed him?"

"I don't remember!" He shook his head. "I don't remember any of it. But I woke up in clothes that weren't my own. Eddie's clothes. I must have . . . gotten rid of mine somehow. They must have had blood on them."

"But you don't remember killing him?" she asked, her brain still running two conversations. The answer was there . . . it was there in the pictures. She just couldn't quite see it. But something told her Wezley was wrong. She was wrong. The killer wasn't Wezley Butterfield.

"That morning, I had my suspicions I might have done something terrible," Wezley said. "I remembered arguing with Eddie. Threatening him. But I didn't mean to hurt anyone."

Nikki kept her hands steady on the steering wheel, hoping that whoever was listening was getting this all down to tell the police later, after they found her body. "The police questioned you, but they didn't arrest you."

"The detective asked a lot of questions about Eddie, about his family, and about the party, but I don't think he thought I did it. He never said I was a suspect. I thought maybe . . . I hoped I was wrong."

"What made you think maybe you were right?" she asked. "Oh, here we are. Wilton. Next, Sunset, east on Sunset," she said.

Wezley was so caught up in telling his story that he didn't notice that she was calling out the turns as she made them.

"What made you begin to realize that you *had* done it?" Nikki dared to ask.

"The e-mails." He began to tremble, but he was still holding the pistol dead on her.

"The e-mails?" she repeated.

"I started getting threatening e-mails Thursday."

That might explain why Monique hadn't been able to get into Wezley's e-mail for the last few days. He had changed his password when he started getting them to prevent his secretary or anyone else from reading them.

He looked at her face. "Someone knows I did it. He . . . he saw me. Saw *something*. He said that unless I called you off, he'd turn in the evidence."

"But you don't know who the e-mails are coming from?"

He shook his head. "Me being charged with murder? The whole rehab thing already hurt the church. People started questioning our teachings. Questioning my father's authority. The publicity of a murder trial would devastate the church. It would ruin everything my father has built. We're already in financial straits. I can't do this to thousands of people." He ran the back of his free hand over his mouth again. His signet ring caught the dying sunlight. "I could really use a drink."

I could, too, she thought. Then she glanced at him again. At his ring. And it hit her. *The photos*. Wezley didn't kill Eddie and she had the proof in her handbag. "Sunset," she called, turning onto Sunset. "Wezley . . . what if I told you you didn't kill Eddie?" she said slowly, still working through what she knew.

"I wouldn't believe you."

"Would you be willing to look at the evidence?"

"You don't understand. I can't be involved with

the police. I can't be arrested. I'm already on proba-
tion." He shook his head yet again. "I need to just dispose of you. Then it will all be over. The gardener
will be found guilty. They were *his* pruning shears.
And the church will be spared."

"But if you didn't kill Eddie, your name would be
cleared."

"You'd say anything to me at this point. I'd say anything if I were in your position."

Nikki was trying to drive as slowly as possible, but
traffic was moving pretty well on Sunset. They were
approaching the Church of Earth and Beyond.

"Wezley . . . what if I could *show you* proof that you
didn't kill Eddie?" she asked.

"But I did it."

"You didn't do it."

"He says I did it. The man in the e-mails."

"Think about it," she said, taking a different tack.
"Why would someone be sending you threatening
e-mails, saying they were going to tell the police you
did it? What would they have to gain?"

He blinked slowly. He was thinking. She could see
that he was thinking. She could also see that the
hand that held the gun was trembling.

"Why would someone do that?" she asked again.
"Did the person who sent the e-mails say what stake
they had in it? Why they cared if the guilt was pinned
on Jorge Delgado, or you?"

He shook his head.

She passed the church, trying not to think about
where he was taking her or how he intended to kill
her. Was he planning on hiding her body? Or was he

going to make it look like a random shooting? A robbery, maybe? No, no, she couldn't waste precious moments or brain power thinking about that. She had to convince Wezley that he didn't kill Eddie. Of course, the hole in the plan was what she was going to say when he asked who *did* kill him. That, she hadn't figured out yet.

"Whoever sent those e-mails, whoever threatened you, is someone close to you," she went on. "Someone who knows you suffer from blackouts and wanted to take advantage of that."

A horn blasted behind her, but she didn't look up in the rearview mirror.

Wezley was listening now.

"I can show you," she said again. "I have photos of the party at Eddie's that night, taken from across the street."

The horn sounded again, practically on her bumper. She was approaching the next intersection. The light was yellow. She couldn't speed up. She couldn't change lanes.

"These photos, they show who killed Eddie?" Wezley asked.

"N . . . not exactly. But they prove you didn't kill him." She debated whether or not to tell him the photos were in her bag. Should she risk him finding her phone, discovering that she'd dialed someone?

She decided she'd have to take that risk. "In my bag," she said, pointing to the floor.

The horn honked again and she looked up in her rearview mirror. *Couldn't this jerk see she was trying to save her own life?*

The car was a vintage metallic-gold Cadillac convertible. The driver hit the horn again.

And then she saw who was driving the Cadillac, just before his front bumper slammed into her rear bumper.

It was Elvis.

Chapter 28

The Prius lurched forward. Nikki's seat belt caught her as she fell forward and then pulled her back to hit the back of the seat.

Wezley, however, did not have his seat belt on and hit the dash. "What the hell!"

Jimmy hit her car again. Harder. Wezley flew forward, hit the dash again, and the gun fell from his hand, onto the floor.

Nikki tried to steer the car out of the lane, into a loading zone.

The third time Jimmy hit her, he picked up a little speed first. Brakes squealed. Horns honked. Under the impact, she jumped the curb, hit the LOADING ZONE sign, and bounced back off the curb.

Wezley's head hit the windshield and his body cast weird, bouncing shadows across the car, in the dying light of the day, as he fell against the seat, stunned.

And then, everything in her mind fell into place. Just like that.

Nikki knew who killed Eddie. The answer was in the photographs, just as she'd suspected. Only it was what was *not* in the photographs that gave her the answer.

She threw the car into PARK and tumbled out of the driver's seat onto the pavement.

Jimmy jumped out of the Cadillac—over the door. "Nikki!"

"I'm all right. He's got a gun!"

Cars were still honking. Jimmy had partially blocked a lane with the Caddy. None of the motorists seemed to realize that a kidnapping had just been foiled. They were trying to get home from work.

As Nikki picked herself up off the street, Jimmy ran around to the passenger side of the car. Wezley was getting out of the car, his forehead bleeding. The gun was in his hand again.

Over the hood of the car, Nikki saw Jimmy spin in midair and kick the gun from Wezley's hand in some kind of crazy judo/karate move. Jimmy then punched Wezley right in the Adam's apple.

Wezley slammed against the car. The gun fell and went skittering across the sidewalk. Jimmy scooped it up.

Wezley stumbled to his feet, gasping, and took off running down Sunset.

"You want me to go after him?" Jimmy called to her, in his Elvis voice.

"No," she panted. She came around the car and threw her arms around her brother. "You got my call! You heard me."

"I was at work when your call came in. You were

headed right for me. I just borrowed the Caddy and here I am."

She glanced at the car he'd used to ram hers, realizing, for the first time, that it had a big lime-green price tag in the window.

He held her awkwardly in one arm, the gun in the other. He flipped the safety on.

Nikki's heart was still jackhammering in her chest when she took a step back. She was okay. She was going to be okay. And so was Jorge. "E, I didn't know you knew karate."

"You didn't know The King knew karate?"

She laughed. Cars were now diverting around the Caddy's back end. No one stopped to see if they were all right. She heard no police sirens.

"I have to get to Roxbury," she said suddenly. "I know who did it. I know who killed Eddie."

Jimmy glanced at her car and frowned. "I'm afraid you're not going anywhere in this." He pointed.

Nikki turned to look at the front end of the Prius. When she jumped the curb, the wheel well had shattered and her tire had popped. The wheel was bent. She put her head in her hands, on the verge of tears for the first time in the ordeal. "I need to get to Mother's," she said.

"Ah, don't cry, little lady." He patted her shoulder awkwardly. "I can take you."

"You can do that?" She glanced at the huge, shiny gold Cadillac convertible. "In a stolen car?"

"It's not *stolen*. It's *borrowed*," he assured her.

Nikki leaned in the open passenger-side door of her Prius and grabbed her bag. The photos were still safe inside. "I'll call to have the car towed."

"What about him?" He pointed in the direction Wezley had run. "You want me to run him down? Give him another one of my karate moves?" He chopped the air with his hands.

She headed for the Cadillac. "I just want to get to Roxbury. The police can deal with him later."

Jimmy hurried to open the door for her. "Hey little girl, I'd like to take you home," he sang. Door open, he strummed an air guitar. "Come on, come on, come on."

Nikki laughed in spite of herself as she got into the car. " 'Harum Scarum,' 1965. Come on, E. Get in the car. We have a killer to catch."

Nikki made three phone calls on her way to Beverly Hills and then Jimmy popped an 8 track into the dash and they sang all the way home, sweet home, to Roxbury Drive.

It was dark when Jimmy pulled up in front of Victoria's gate, which stood open. Nikki looked at the gate, then at him. "You're not going to come in? Just say hi?"

"I don't think so," he crooned. "I should get this little lady back to the car lot." He patted the dash.

Nikki smiled sadly. "I think she'd like to see you."

He put both hands on the wheel and looked straight ahead. "Some day. But not today."

She was quiet for a second. She understood. She just wished things were different. She leaned over and gave him a kiss on the cheek. "Thanks for coming to my rescue, E," she whispered. "You may have saved my life."

"Any time, little lady." He gave her that classic Elvis lip-turned-up half smile.

Nikki grabbed her Prada and got out of the Caddy. She didn't look back as she walked up the driveway. Victoria was waiting for her at the front door. She'd dressed for the occasion: gray velour jogging suit, pearls, and tennis shoes. Her hair was done, makeup subtle but perfect.

"He didn't care to come in?" Victoria asked, watching the Cadillac and her son pull away.

"Not today," Nikki said quietly.

Victoria stared at the end of the drive for a moment, then turned to Nikki, putting her hands together. "Do we wait?"

Nikki recalled the trouble she'd gotten herself into with the Rex March case, confronting the killer on her own. But she wasn't alone this time. She had Victoria Bordeaux to back her up.

"I can't wait. Let's go." Nikki strode around the house toward the side gate.

"Should I ask why James brought you home?" Victoria said.

"Not now."

And, for once, Victoria let something go. "You have the photographs?"

"In my good old Prada." She patted the bag on her shoulder.

"Prada is always an excellent choice in handbags. They're sturdy and they hold their value."

Nikki and her mother walked through the soft grass in the side yard and went through the gate. "Does she know we're coming?" Nikki asked quietly.

"I told her I'd be over in a few minutes."

"What excuse did you give her?" The Bernards' pool cast soft light over their yard. Now, everywhere Nikki looked, she saw, in her mind's eye, the scene that had unfolded the night Eddie was murdered. The chaise longue where Eddie had breathed his final breath. The pool where *she* had washed off the evidence. The incriminating banana tree. Even the little garden wagon was parked near the roses, as if staged for the *reveal.*

"I told her I had a gift card for her hair salon. I said I received it in a swag bag and I thought she might like to have it." Victoria cut her eyes at Nikki. "She knows very well I'd never set foot in Timothee's."

Nikki walked over to one of the five tables on the terrace and set her bag down. She noticed that there was a small vase with a single rose on each table. They had not been there Friday when Nikki came into the yard in Jorge's defense. They had been here each day since; each day, fresh roses. A memorial of sorts.

Nikki opened her bag and pulled out the photos. She was spreading them out on the table when the guesthouse door opened. When Melinda stepped onto the brick walk in front of her house, the exterior spotlights came on, shining light on the table and the lounge chairs nearby.

"Oh, Victoria, you didn't have to bring that over." Melinda was wearing a jogging suit, too; pink. It didn't suit her as well as Victoria's did. "And, Nikki, what a nice surprise."

Melinda stopped a few feet short of the table and stared at the photos for a moment, then at Nikki's face. Then Victoria's. "What . . . whatever is this about?" Her voice trembled.

She knew they knew.

"These are photographs of Eddie's party," Nikki said quietly. She had thought she would feel triumphant at this moment. She'd found Eddie's real killer. Jorge would be released. But her heart felt heavy. How could a mother kill her own child?

"Would you care to have a look?" Nikki asked, gesturing to them. "The mistake I made in the beginning was looking for a crime-of-passion killer, like Jorge or Kaiser, or Rocko. Or Wezley, who conveniently had no recollection at all of that night."

"Clever, leaving options open to frame any number of people," Victoria remarked.

Nikki leaned on the table and glanced at Melinda. "What I *should* have been looking for was a premeditating murderer. Putting him in the trash; it was the first clue, but I didn't get it." She laid the photos out in chronological order: seventeen photographs, the first taken at twelve fifteen A.M., the last at four thirty A.M.

"Where did you get these?" Melinda took a step closer to the table. She'd taken the time to put on mascara and lipstick . . . to greet Victoria. At least she'd have makeup on when the police took her away.

"From Mr. M., our friendly neighborhood voyeur." Nikki looked up at the house across the street and waved. He was watching them now, too, thanks to a quick call from Victoria. Nikki's mother had her back, but Mr. M. had both their backs.

"Twelve fifteen," Nikki began. "You chased everyone off the property, which is interesting because you invited them, didn't you? The party wasn't Eddie's idea; it was yours. You invited anyone and everyone who was toxic for Eddie. His old druggy friends. People from the gym. Wezley, his rehab buddy. The e-mail invitations were sent by you, not Eddie," she guessed out loud. The look on Melinda's face told her she was right. "You even called Rocko, who he'd been arrested for punching."

"I called the pool service because there was a problem with the filter," Melinda said snobbishly.

Victoria rested her hand on her hip. "Melinda, to tell bald-faced lies is not becoming of a lady."

Nikki pointed to the first photo. "Twelve fifteen, the guests have almost departed. Just a few strays. And notice Wezley Butterfield here on the very edge of the photo. Lying on his back, passed out."

"How do you know that's Wezley Butterfield?" Melinda asked. "It's an arm."

"It's a man's arm, a man wearing a long-sleeved black shirt, the sleeves rolled up. Notice the signet ring, which Wezley Butterfield wears on his right hand."

"Goodness, look there." Victoria leaned over the table on the other side of Nikki. "I can see the ring, even without my readers."

"Twelve thirty." Nikki pointed to the next photo. "That's you, Melinda, in the same clothing we saw you wearing that evening. You're giving your son a cocktail of drugs that will make him comatose . . . if not kill him."

"I was giving him water," Melinda argued, without

looking at the photo this time. "He wasn't feeling well."

"Not as poorly as he would be feeling later," Victoria said under her breath.

"Twelve forty-five, Eddie is still in the chaise," Nikki continued, "and you're gone. Wezley hasn't moved . . . and no one has come or gone from the main house. Note the lack of shadows—from the motion detector lights—seen in the first two photos." She looked up at Melinda. "You probably got the drugs from Eddie's room. See this shadow coming from that potted banana tree?" She pointed to the photo, then indicated the tree on the terrace between the guesthouse and the chaise where Eddie died. "That shadow indicates that you've entered the guesthouse."

"This . . . this is ridiculous," Melinda protested. "Disrespectful. Victoria, are you really going to let her speak to me this way?"

Victoria continued to look at the photos. "I'm curious about all this, even if it isn't true." She looked across the table at Melinda. "Aren't you?"

"One o'clock, no lights, no shadows. All the yard lights—detecting no motion, because Wezley and Eddie are both unconscious—are out. There's just the glow from the underwater pool lamps and the moonlight. No change until two forty-five when the guesthouse motion detector light is on, again." She glanced at Melinda. "You must have been going to the gardening shed to get your little wagon." She pointed to the flat-topped wagon now parked near her roses, a wagon one could sit on to garden, or, with a little effort, use to transport a dead body.

"Three o'clock. Eddie's gone. But not under his own power." Nikki swallowed the lump in her throat. She still couldn't believe that Melinda had murdered her only son. "Notice that Wezley has not moved and that there is no indication of light coming from the main house." She pointed to Wezley's arm in the photo.

"Nothing changes until three forty-five." Nikki touched one photo after another. "Now note the *bald man* in the pool."

"What M. saw," Victoria said, obviously captivated.

"Also, the gardening wagon near the edge of the pool and a dark splotch around it where it had been rinsed off with pool water . . . containing chlorine. Probably destroying DNA evidence. Eddie was dead by then, in the trash."

Nikki took a breath. "What Mr. M. saw was you, Melinda, in the pool in your bathing cap, not a bald man. After you gave Eddie the drugs, you went into your house and put on your bathing suit and swim cap. So your hair wouldn't be discolored for the funeral." Saying the words actually made Nikki feel sick to her stomach. "You were wearing the swimsuit and cap when you killed him."

Melinda just stood there, staring at the photos. Nikki was amazed that she still remained dry-eyed.

"Four o'clock, the pool is empty and the wagon is gone," Nikki said. "But the light is on in front of the guesthouse. Note there is *still* no light from the main house. No one has gone in or out of the main house in hours. In the last photo Mr. M. provided, the guesthouse light has gone out, and Wezley is still un-

conscious in the grass, but his dress shirt is gone."
She looked up. "You had Wezley change his clothes.
He just didn't remember it. You probably told him
he had blood on him. Then, when I started snooping
around, you sent him the threatening e-mails. The
police will find them on your hard drive. Your e-mails
made him think he did it and he was going to kill me
to protect his father's church."

Victoria's gaze narrowed dangerously. "How dare
you! How dare you put my daughter's life in jeopardy!"

Melinda took a stumbling step backward. "I
didn't—"

"You did," Nikki said from between clenched
teeth, trying to keep her emotions in check. "You
planned your son's murder shortly after he returned
from rehab, unrehabilitated. Probably the night you
caught him snorting coke. You brought an entire
cast of people together to take the fall. It's the clever-
est kind of murder, premeditated, yet adapted to the
situation. Because of the fight between Eddie and
Jorge, you were able to easily frame Jorge. And you
were framing Wezley as a backup."

Melinda took another step back. "No, I didn't kill
him."

"You did. After the fight between Eddie and Jorge,
you slipped into Mother's yard and took Jorge's
pruning shears, while Jorge and Hector were in the
shed." Nikki frowned. "But you didn't kill him with
the shears, did you?"

Melinda's eyes had become glassy. She knew it was
over. "No," she whispered. "I couldn't do it."

"The coroner found unexplained blood in his chest cavity. You used something else first, before you sank the shears into his heart, causing so much damage that the original evidence was destroyed. Again, covering your tracks."

In the distance, Nikki heard a police siren, then two.

"What did you use?"

"I intended to use the shears," Melinda murmured, folding her hands neatly together. "The drugs . . . he was so out of it, I don't know that he would have felt anything. But the idea seemed so gruesome."

Melinda was silent for a moment. Nikki waited.

"I used my diamond nail file, first."

Victoria gasped.

"It's very hard . . . and pointy at the end. But then he still had the faintest pulse."

"So you finished him off with the gardening shears that have Jorge's name on them."

Melinda lowered her gaze.

"The threatening note. You left it on my car seat Wednesday morning when you came to speak with me."

"What threatening note?" Victoria looked from Nikki to Melinda. "How dare you," she said again, taking a step toward her neighbor. "It's a good thing the police are coming for you, Melinda, because your life would be in jeopardy at this moment if they weren't!"

"How could you?" Nikki asked. "How could you kill your son?"

"He wasn't going to change," Melinda said in a

small voice. "He was never going to change, or be re-habilitated. For the rest of our lives, Abe would be affected by his son's behavior."

"You did it for Abe?" Nikki said.

"Because I love Abe. Even though he doesn't love me anymore."

"You fool. You stupid fool." Victoria sounded like one of the many heroines she had portrayed on film. "Abe didn't tell you?"

The sirens were at the Bernards' gate. An unmarked car, followed by a black-and-white Beverly Hills police car, pulled into the motor court.

Melinda looked up. "Abe didn't tell me what?"

"He was still in love with you. In love with you, *again*," Nikki said. She met Melinda's gaze. Melinda was crying, at last. "He had decided to divorce Ginny and remarry you."

Lieutenant Detective Dombrowski hurried across the side lawn, two men in uniform behind him.

Nikki glanced at the detective, then back at Melinda, who had fallen to her knees. "No, no," she cried, wrapping her arms around herself. Sobbing. "My boy. My sweet, dear boy. My Eddie."

It was the first time Nikki had heard her utter his name since his death.

"Ladies," Dombrowski said, striding across the stone patio.

"The photos are on the table," Nikki told him. "They're yours. I believe Mrs. Bernard will cooperate. I'll be at Mother's when you need me."

Victoria linked her arm through Nikki's and they turned and walked toward the gate together.

"Nice job, Nicolette," Victoria murmured, patting her arm.

Nikki dropped her head against her mother's shoulder for just a second, then lifted it high.

Was there anything on earth better than a mother's praise?

Epilogue

Victoria walked onto the terrace in her pink silk robe and matching mules. "Did you see this, Nicolette?" She dropped a magazine onto the newspaper Nikki was reading at the breakfast table.

Nikki glanced at the cover of *People* magazine. She saw herself looking back. In a small inset was a recent picture of Victoria, striking, as always. "*People* magazine? I made the cover of *People?*" Nikki didn't know if she was amused or horrified.

"The headline is in rather poor taste, wouldn't you say?" Victoria took her chair at the table and pushed her empty coffee cup toward Nikki.

The headline across the top read: *Exclusive! Nikki Harper Nails Murdering Mommy.* Still staring at the glossy cover, Nikki grabbed the carafe Ina had left for them and poured her mother's coffee. "Where was this taken?" She squinted. "In front of the police station last week?"

"Apparently on one of your trips to speak with Detective Dombrowski."

Victoria sounded miffed, but Nikki didn't know why. Nikki's cell phone vibrated and she picked it up off the table. The message was from Marshall. OMG! it read. The entire message was in caps.

PEOPLE!

YOU LOOK GORGEOUS!

CALL ME!

Nikki tossed the phone down; she'd call him later. She studied the cover more closely. "I don't look bad," she admitted with a shrug.

"Thank goodness you had your hair trimmed. I told you it needed a trim." Victoria sat back in her chair, crossed her legs and sipped her black coffee. Though she was still wearing nightclothes, she'd already done her hair and her face. She looked amazing in the morning light. "At least they didn't put Melinda on the cover. Can you imagine her in that hideous jumpsuit they make you wear in prison?"

Nikki hid a smile. "You look stunning." She pointed at the small photo of Victoria in the corner. "Didn't you wear that Chanel to the Governor's ball?"

Victoria picked up her reading glasses, set out by Ina. She slid them on. "That's a nice dress. Excellent structure."

"What's it say inside?" Nikki began to thumb through the pages.

"I have no idea." Victoria gave a wave, dismissing it. "I didn't read the story."

"Wow." Nikki opened the magazine. After a minute, she said "It's mostly about you, not me. Look at these beautiful photographs." She scooted her chair closer so her mother could see. "Didn't I see this one on Mr. M.'s wall?"

Victoria leaned over, adjusting her readers. "Ah, with Frankie."

"You with *Frank Sinatra*," Nikki pointed out.

Victoria smiled, gazing at the large photo of her in a black cocktail dress arm in arm with Frank Sinatra and a small inset picture of Nikki wearing a vintage black dress that looked very similar. "You look like me," she mused. She brushed her manicured fingertips on the glossy color photo. "I wish you wouldn't do this, Nicolette."

"I didn't ask them to feature me on the cover of their magazine."

"I mean put yourself in danger." Victoria spoke softly. She looked up at Nikki with her Bordeaux blues. "I understand that you want to help others, but you could have been hurt. Or worse. Melinda was obviously not a sane woman."

"Oh, I think she was perfectly sane." Nikki sighed, not quite comfortable with the emotion she heard in her mother's voice. It seemed as if she'd spent half of her life trying to get Victoria's attention, but that spotlight, when she found it, was always too intense. "Don't tell me you wouldn't have killed me if I'd pulled some of the nonsense Eddie pulled over the years." She looked at the photos again. She was told all the time that she resembled her mother, but she never saw it. Victoria was gorgeous, and Nikki . . . while she may not have been the ugly duckling, she never thought of herself as beautiful. But looking at the two photos, she was shocked to see her mother's beauty in her own face. "Besides," she joked, "you encouraged me. You didn't want to see Jorge rot in jail, either."

"Next time we hire a private investigator," Victoria said firmly, gazing at the mother/daughter photographs.

"Next time?" Nikki shook her head. "Oh, no. I've learned my lesson. There won't be a next time."

Victoria smiled. "Darling, with Bordeaux women, there's *always* a next time."

Please turn the page for an exciting sneak peek of
Cheryl Crane's next
Nikki Harper mystery,
THE DEAD AND THE BEAUTIFUL,
coming next month from Kensington Publishing!

"I swear on my great-grandfather Geronimo's soul," Marshall Thunder, voted Sexiest Man Alive by *People* magazine, vowed. He held his hand up in some sort of Boy Scout's honor gesture.

Nikki chuckled as she approached the gaggle of women that surrounded the blockbuster movie star under one of the large white tents on the Beverly Hills lawn. He was wearing a black Louis Vuitton tux. Victoria Bordeaux's fall garden party, in her backyard on Roxbury Drive, was *not* a casual affair.

Garden party. It was a deceiving misnomer, as far as Nikki was concerned. A person ought to be able to wear shorts and a cute tank top, to a *garden party.* Instead, Marshall was wearing a tux and she was in a vintage, floor-length, Jacques Tiffeau, silver-metallic gown.

"Don't listen to a word he says." Nikki said as she caught Marshall's twinkling eye. "He's the biggest gossip I know and you can't trust his sources."

He only got better-looking with age; he was a six-foot-two Native American, with hunky muscles and a face so handsome he could make women swoon. He *did* make women swoon. And a number of men.

"Geronimo was *Apache*," Nikki continued. "Marshall is full-blooded *Iroquois*."

Instead of defending himself, or disputing the facts, Marshall just laughed and raised his crystal Baccarat champagne flute to her. "One of our gorgeous hostesses and my BFF, ladies. Does everyone know Nikki Harper?"

The young women who surrounded him, all gorgeous blondes, greeted her.

Nikki smiled *the smile*, the one ingrained in her since childhood. "Mother's so pleased you could all come," she said, through *the smile*. It wasn't fake, just . . . well rehearsed. Victoria, who had been a silver-screen star for four decades before her retirement from film, had always insisted on perfect manners from her children and her staff. Even at forty-one, Nikki felt as if she was still, sometimes, under her mother's thumb. Particularly in situations like this. She was not an A-list party kind of girl and never felt quite in her element at these kinds of gatherings, even though she'd been attending them since she was a toddler.

But a girl did what a girl had to do. For her mother. And for her livelihood. Nikki was in the business of selling multimillion-dollar mansions in Beverly Hills. And to do so successfully, she needed wealthy clients, both buyers and sellers. So here she was, mingling, smiling, and *making contacts*, while at the same time, trying to make certain all of her mother's guests were made to feel welcome.

Which reminded Nikki why she'd come in search of Marshall in the first place. "Marshall, you know Jeremy's sister, Alison?" She glanced at her side to find her companion gone.

She'd been there just a second ago . . .

Nikki turned to see Alison standing a couple of feet behind her, red-faced, obviously thrilled and embarrassed, at the same time, to even lay eyes on *the* Marshall Thunder. Nikki wondered if *speaking* to him might put Alison over the edge. Marshall had fans who became hysterical at the sight of him, mostly from the ropes at red carpet affairs. She hoped her boyfriend's sister wouldn't be one of *those* women. Nikki didn't have time to tend to fainting women; Ashton Kutcher had hollered to her across a champagne fountain that he needed her advice on a piece of property going up for sale in Malibu.

"Alison," Nikki whispered, gesturing impatiently that she should step forward. *The smile* reappeared. "This is my dear friend, Marshall. I know you've heard me talk about him."

"Is there anyone who doesn't recognize Marshall Thunder?" a honey blonde with hair extensions and serious breast enhancement, gushed. There was an echo of feminine giggles.

Alison took a hesitant step forward, brown-eyed gaze downcast. She was wearing a beige handkerchief dress that neither fit, nor was flattering. Nikki couldn't imagine anyone who could look good in the flimsy, shapeless, colorless sheath and felt badly that she hadn't offered to help Alison shop before the party. "This is Alison Sahira, Jeremy Fitzpatrick's sister," Nikki introduced, hoping that Jeremy's name might win Alison a place among the women, at least for a few minutes. Nikki had several people she needed to say hello to, and then there was Ashton.

Nikki flashed Marshall a look that said *take her. Please.*

He arched a dark eyebrow. It was a gesture *so* overused, and yet, he was so good-looking, it worked for him.

"Alison has a new business. 90210 Dog Walking. I won't say who she's working for," Nikki looked one way and then the other, as if to be certain no one was listening, "but I understand that one of her clients made quite a hit last season in a hot tub scene on *Casa Capri,*" she said in a stage whisper.

Marshall's dark eyes got big and his hand shot out to catch Alison's. "Darling, let me get you some champagne." He drew her closer. "You're working for Diara Elliot?"

Obviously a friend of Marshall's was a friend of theirs and the women gathered around Alison.

Alison glanced at Nikki uneasily, then back at Marshall. Like everyone else who worked in Beverly Hills, Alison was concerned about client confidentiality, but Nikki could tell by the look on her face that she'd give up national security secrets to Marshall if he asked. "I . . . I don't think it's a secret. I walk Mr. Melton's dog, so I guess, *technically,* I work for *him.*"

"So you see them all the time." Marshall's eyes danced. "Tell the truth. Out every night partying? Crazy fights? Cops at five in the morning?"

"No, no, nothing like that." She blinked. "A . . . actually, they're a pretty quiet couple. Just regular people. Mostly they stay in, that or have dinner at home with their friends."

"Borrring," Marshall groaned, making an exaggerated face. "So who else do you work for? Tell us something juicy!"

Nikki met Marshall's gaze over Alison's shoulder. *Thank you*, she mouthed.

He grinned and returned his attention to Alison, eager for any gossip that he could pry out of her. Marshall was a gossipmonger. He loved all of the tabloid magazines, fanzines, and nightly entertainment shows on TV, even if it was about him. But he loved firsthand gossip best.

Nikki moved on. She had no doubt Marshall would entertain Alison for a while and when he was ready to pass her on to another guest, he'd do it with such aplomb that she would feel as if she were their guest of honor, instead of the hostess's daughter's boyfriend's sister.

Nikki grabbed a French canapé as a tuxedoed waiter walked by and she popped it in her mouth. It was a delicious tidbit of toasted sourdough bread, sockeye salmon and a paper-thin slice of lemon. Scrumptious. She eyed the waiter as he made his escape and calculated when she could intercept him again. It was five thirty in the afternoon and the only thing she'd eaten that day were a few grapes she stole off a caterer's tray, midmorning.

Licking her fingertips, Nikki glanced around. She thought she'd heard someone call her name, but the pool area and grassy lawn, with its monstrous white tents, bubbling fountains and twinkling lights was so loud she could barely hear herself think. Everyone who was anyone in Hollywood was at Victoria Bordeaux's party this afternoon and it sounded as if they were all talking at once. They were so loud that the big band music coming from near the west gate could barely be heard.

"Nikki!"

She spotted her dear friend, Ellen Mar, through a wave of tuxedos and grass-length gowns. Ellen was standing with a good-looking guy Nikki vaguely recognized, but couldn't place.

Ellen was making quite a stir on Food Network. As a new chef on the cooking network, she was already one of their most popular, doing a crazy show where she made one kind of food look like another. Like . . . roasted turnips that looked like miniature lemon meringue pies, or cream puffs disguised as turkey sandwiches.

"Ellen." They kissed cheeks—for real—no air-kissing for them.

"Nikki." She was a drop-dead gorgeous biracial woman with mesmerizing blue eyes. And she was wearing a remarkable Tom Ford gown. "Do you know Ryan Melton?"

Aha, Ryan Melton. Now she recognized him. He was shorter than Nikki (six foot in her measly two-inch heels—she was a wimp when it came to heels, especially in grass) but very good-looking in a bad-boy kind of way. He reminded her of Ryan O'Neal from his *Love Story* days. He had blond hair that was a little too long; he was wearing Gucci sunglasses, and a hip, two-toned black Ralph Lauren tuxedo. "It's so nice to meet you, Ryan," she said politely, offering her hand and *the smile*.

She *did* know him, but not personally, only *of* him, from the cover of *Variety* magazine. And *People* magazine. And *Men's Health* . . . and the list went on.

Nikki dug into the cobwebs of her mind and tried to pull up what real info she had on Ryan Melton. He had been a nobody who had become somebody. He was the arm-candy husband of TV star Diara Elliot, who was playing a role on the wildly popular TV drama *Casa Capri*, Victoria's new TV drama. Hence his coveted invitation to Mother's party. He'd never have rated an invitation on his own. *Mother* didn't recognize his form of celebrity. Ryan had tried some modeling; he was too short. He'd tried some acting; he couldn't. He'd opened a restaurant; it had failed. Mostly, it seemed, he was good at being the trophy husband of a famous actress. But he *was* cute.

"Nice to meet you, Nikki." He held her hand a beat too long before releasing it. She could tell he was one of those guys who got along on his looks. There were plenty of them in L.A.

"Your mother has a gorgeous place," he went on. "We're over on Mulholland, but Diara and I have been talking about looking at a bigger place. I don't suppose your mother would consider selling? I'd love a Roxbury Drive address. Very classy."

"I'm afraid this house isn't for sale." She glanced up at the two-story Paul Williams' Georgian. Victoria wouldn't leave here until the EMTs carried her out on a stretcher. She returned her attention to her guest. "Houses go pretty quickly on Roxbury's 1000 block, but if you want to give me a call sometime, we can have a look. I'm with Windsor Real Estate."

"I know." He gave what she suspected was his version of *the smile*. Acquired much later in life than Nikki's; she could tell.

His wife of four or five years, Diara Elliot, had become a household name ten years ago, when she was a teenager and working for Disney Studios. Diara, Kameryn Lowe, Julian Munro, and Angel Gomez, called the Disney Fab Four, had been America's darlings in a sweet sitcom set in a private school . . . somewhere. Nikki had never seen the show, but she knew, from flipping through the channels, that it was still popular, even though the last original episode had aired five or six years ago.

Nikki knew all about syndication. It had paid for her boyfriend Jeremy Fitzpatrick's college and dental school and would put his children through college, and his grandchildren, as well. Jeremy had been a child star, then a teen idol, before leaving the footlights of L.A. for a normal college life on the East Coast. Only now he was back, his wife was dead of cancer and she and Jeremy . . . it was complicated, but what relationship wasn't?

Nikki made herself refocus on Ryan. He'd said something to her and she'd missed it. Her right heel was killing her. She rarely bought uncomfortable shoes, but the 1960s peep-toes she found in a vintage clothing shop on Santa Monica had been too amazing to turn down. And too cheap. Her frugality came from her mother. She smiled at Ryan.

Fortunately, he went right on talking. "I can introduce you, if you like," he said.

While trying to stand on her left foot and rub the right heel inconspicuously under her gown, Nikki glanced in the direction Ryan and Ellen were looking.

If there was a designated *beautiful people* area at the party, Ryan's wife and friends were standing in it. Or maybe it just followed them from place to place.

Ryan's wife was tall and blond. Of course she was; Hollywood was blond. And tall. And thin. The young stars, and their spouses, were all gorgeous with toned, spray-tanned bodies draped in designer gowns and tuxes. They had their heads together in an obviously serious discussion. They were probably deciding what nightclub they'd go to tonight, after the party.

"Diara," Ryan called. "Come say hi," he said to Nikki and walked away. Leaving her no other option except to follow.

"I'll catch you later," Ellen called, going in the opposite direction.

"I want you to meet Nikki Harper." Ryan pressed his hand to the small of his wife's back. Diara was pretty; she reminded Nikki of a taller version of Scarlett Johansson.

Diara slipped something into her handbag, a cute little silver Badgley Mischka that hung from the crook of her elbow. She offered her hand. "It's so nice to meet you, Nikki. Your mother talks about you on the set all the time."

Nikki wasn't entirely sure she was being genuine. Her mother hadn't had much to say, good or bad, about Diara. The twenty-six-year-old blonde was too inconsequential a person for Victoria to have an opinion on. Everyone knew the term *new money*. In Victoria's eyes, Diara and her friends were *new talent*.

"Nice to meet you." Nikki shook Diara's hand.

Ryan introduced Nikki to the other three of the Disney Fab Four, and their spouses. They all shook

hands, exchanged greetings. Her first impression
was that everyone in the group was pleasant and . . .
very young. Two other things stood out. Julian
Munro's wife, Hazel, had red hair that was almost exactly the same shade of red as Nikki's own. Victoria
called it strawberry blonde. Nikki also noticed that
Kameryn Lowe's husband, Gil, looked so much like
star Angel Gomez that they could have been brothers.

"Oh gosh, Nikki, your hair is gorgeous," Hazel
gushed. "Who's your colorist? Please don't tell me it's
Eduardo at Christophe's! I'll kill him. I just went with
this shade." She stroked her shoulder-length bob.
"He said it would look gorgeous on me. Don't tell
me it was what he had left in the bottle after your
appointment."

Nikki laughed. She liked Hazel at once; she was
polished and plucked, but she stood out in the
group. Maybe because she was the only woman in the
Disney Fab Four faction who *wasn't* a blonde.

"No need to harm Eduardo. This is my natural
color." She ran her hand over her hair, pulled back
in a simple, sleek ponytail. She'd glammed it up with
a 1920s rhinestone art deco brooch to cover the elas-
tic hair tie.

"Your *natural* color? You've got to be kidding me."
Hazel looped her arm through Betsy's. "Can you believe that's Nikki's natural color?"

Betsy was holding on to an emerald-green fox fur
Sang A handbag as if she was afraid Nikki was going
to grab it and run. Which was not likely. It was one of
the uglier designer bags Nikki had spotted that day.
And there were some *seriously* ugly, *seriously* expensive, bags wandering around. The thing in Betsy's

hand looked like a little green shih tzu hanging from a gold ring.

"Natural?" Betsy said. She kept glancing at Gil and Angel, who had their heads together again. She sounded nervous. At meeting Nikki?

That was even less likely than the possibility of Nikki stealing her fifteen-hundred-dollar fuzzy wristlet. Nikki was so unintimidating in a town of intimidation that complete strangers were always sharing intimate information with her.

"I can't believe that's your natural color," Hazel went on, looking more closely.

Nikki smiled, feeling uncomfortable under the women's scrutiny. "I *do* highlight it once in a while," she confessed. "Myself. With one of those boxes of highlighter from the drugstore."

"You do it yourself!" Hazel gasped in awe.

"Nicolette!"

Only one person on earth called Nikki by her given name.

Nikki gave the two women a wry grin. "Will you excuse me?"

"Nicolette, darling. Do you have a moment?"

Though the words were spoken kindly, it wasn't really a question. It was a command. It meant *come here now.*

Nikki walked toward Victoria, who was standing only a few feet away. She looked stunning, as always. She was wearing a gorgeous, beaded, long Chanel couture gown, in white of course. It wasn't a new gown; Nikki had seen it on her many times before. Victoria might spend ten thousand on a gown, but she got plenty of wear out of it. Petite and a natural blond, Victoria, who was somewhere in her early seventies (she's always been vague about birthdays and her birth records had been *lost* in a fire), still had that sweater girl curvaceous figure that had shot her from a soda fountain stool to stardom more than fifty years ago. Victoria wore the Chanel the way it was meant to be, with a natural grace that everyone in Hollywood wanted, but few possessed.

"Mother." Nikki smiled, feeling a flutter of tenderness for her. She and her mother didn't always see eye to eye, but secretly, they adored each other. "I met Diara and her husband. She seems quite fond of you."

Victoria looked up at Nikki. Her face sparkled with perfect makeup, a perfect smile, but Nikki could tell all was not perfect in Victoria-land.

"What's wrong?" Nikki said under her breath. She nodded to Tom Hanks, who was standing a couple of feet away, talking with a group of directors. She made a mental note to be sure to find his wife, Rita Wilson, later. She adored Rita; like Victoria, she was one classy lady. She'd always admired Tom and Rita because they were a Hollywood couple who had managed to stay together. It didn't happen often in Tinseltown.

Nikki returned her attention to Victoria.

"Beatrice Andrews," Victoria said under her breath . . . through *the smile*.

"I'm sorry?" Nikki leaned closer.

Victoria waved to someone Nikki couldn't see. She froze *the smile*, talking through her teeth. "Beatrice."

"I haven't seen her."

"That's because she *isn't here*," Victoria said pointedly. "She stood me up."

Nikki found it hard to believe anyone in this town would dare stand up Victoria Bordeaux. Although it had been ages since her last film, Victoria still had a lot of pull in Hollywood and more importantly, everyone respected her. Just dropping her name could open doors and everyone was looking for an open door in their business, even stars who had been around forever, like Beatrice Andrews.

But theirs was another complicated relationship. Victoria and Beatrice had a past. Nikki had never gotten the whole story. She'd gotten *none* of the story from her mother. What she knew, she'd picked up over the years. It had happened in the seventies. Victoria and Beatrice, who had been good friends, had done a movie together. Beatrice had been engaged to wealthy financier, Alexander Mason. The movie wrapped and Victoria and Alexander went to Mexico for the weekend . . . and married. Husband number four. The marriage wasn't long-lived. Beatrice's hatred for Victoria, however, was.

"Maybe she had another engagement," Nikki told her mother. "Or maybe she's sick."

Victoria rolled her eyes. "I don't suppose we could hope for a case of the bubonic plague?"

Nikki laughed. "Mother. You said you didn't have a problem with Beatrice. You said you were fine working with her on this show." *Casa Capri* was set in the Napa Valley against the backdrop of the wine industry. A modern-day *Falcoln Crest*. Her mother's character was the new matriarch come to town to do battle against an established matriarch, Beatrice's character. Network television was buzzing with excitement in anticipation of Victoria's permanent role.

"That was before I started working with her. She's just awful, Nicolette. Let's call a spade a spade. The woman can't act. She never could. She'll drag down the ratings and we'll be cancelled and that will be the legacy I leave." Victoria pursed her perfectly lined and lipsticked lips. "Cancelled on a TV network."

Nikki nibbled on her lower lip. "You sorry you took the job?" Nikki had advised against taking it. Her mother was too old for the rigors of network TV. She didn't need the work and she certainly didn't need the fame. Nikki didn't know why she'd take the role in the first place. "It's not too late to—"

"I'm certainly not sorry!" Victoria's stunning blue eyes, the "Bordeaux blues" they were called, flashed with annoyance. "Did you know *that woman* is threatening to walk off the set and halt production if I'm not replaced, at once? The nerve!"

"Mother, she's not going to walk off the set."

"Of course she won't." Victoria glided away, smiling. "If I kill her first, it won't be necessary for her to walk off the set, will it?"